AF490216

the seaside sisterhood

SEASIDE SISTERHOOD
BOOK 1

JESSIE GUSSMAN

contents

acknowledgments

Cover Art by Carpe Librum Book Design
Editing by Heather Hayden
Narration by Jay Dyess
Author Services by CE Author Assistant

Listen to the unabridged audio for FREE performed by Jay Dyess on the Say with Jay channel on YouTube. Get early access to all of Jay's recordings and listen to Jessie's books before they're available to the general public, plus get daily Bible readings by Jay and bonus scenes by becoming a Say with Jay channel member.

one

"DID you text your mother and tell her that we were coming?"

Quincy shifted in the passenger seat as her husband turned into the lawyer's office, where they were going to close on the house that they had owned since they were married more than twenty years ago.

"I forgot," her husband said, and didn't say anything else.

Quincy waited. Derek knew that she and his mother didn't have the greatest relationship. If there needed to be communication between the two of them, he always did it. It wasn't that she hated her mother-in-law, Beulah. It was just that... Beulah never seemed to like her very much, and Derek was happy to handle the few times a year they needed to discuss anything with her. After all, Beulah had retired and moved with her husband to the Outer Banks about the time Quincy and Derek got married and settled in West Virginia.

When Derek didn't say anything, putting the car in park and flipping the sunvisor up, Quincy couldn't help herself. She spoke again.

"Don't you think you should?"

He knew as well as she did that they were heading to the Outer Banks as soon as they closed on the property. After staying at a hotel tonight, they would get there sometime tomorrow, and Quincy didn't want to be an inconvenience. Even though Beulah seemed to welcome the fact that Quincy and Derek were coming down to live, to help her with her cleaning business and to help take care of her husband, Derek's father, Sonny, who was struggling with Parkinson's disease.

Derek didn't say anything as he picked up his phone, read a text, and then sent off a reply. She was used to it, him doing business on his phone, but they really needed to get moving.

"Don't you think you should?" she finally said.

He didn't even glance up. "I'll do it after we're done here."

She jerked her head, which he didn't see because his eyes were glued to his phone. Sticking her own phone in her purse, she took her seatbelt off and opened her door. The warm spring air held the scent of flowers and cut grass as she climbed out of the car. They were five minutes early, so there was no rush. But Derek liked to be early.

She did too, but he was better at following through than she was.

She waited at the front of the car for what felt like several long moments until Derek got out and joined her there.

He didn't exactly join her, since he didn't wait for her, but instead strode into the building while she trailed after.

Hopefully, this move to the Outer Banks would fix whatever had happened in their marriage. She didn't think it was her. But maybe she had changed since the twins had graduated from high school and had gotten jobs and become productive members of society.

In her opinion, Derek had gotten more reserved, less interested in home life, and more consumed with his work. She had tried to do things like date nights, special dinners, and church activities together, to give them something to do, but Derek had resisted.

Maybe it was her. She had gained an extra twenty, okay thirty, pounds since she'd hit menopause. And it didn't seem like any type of diet or exercise would help the pounds come off. She weighed a good fifty pounds more than she had when she got married, and she supposed Derek might resent the fact that the woman that he was currently married to didn't look the same as the girl he proposed to all those years ago. But to be fair, he had less hair and was a lot less fun. She liked to think that they both changed and matured. Wasn't that a normal thing?

Derek, still a gentleman, held the door open for her as a cold rush of air conditioning blew out when she stepped in.

She should've brought her sweater, but it had been such a nice day, and they had everything all packed up. Most of their things had gone either to donations or to her friend Rose, who held a yard sale every weekend of the summer. They had a few things in storage, and the rest were packed in the back of their car. Beulah already had a furnished house, and they were moving in with her. They didn't need all of their things.

It had definitely been harder for her to let go of the memories that had accumulated after twenty plus years of marriage; Derek hadn't seemed to care.

The lady sitting behind the desk stopped typing and looked up with a smile. "Mr. and Mrs. Morgan?" she asked with a brow raised. She was young, her skin unwrinkled, not sagging, no sun spots. Her hair full-bodied and beautiful, her eyes perfectly made up.

"That's correct," Derek said, taking the lead as he usually did. Quincy appreciated that about him. Some women had husbands who seemed to want to follow them, rather than the other way around. She couldn't imagine being married to someone who wouldn't take charge.

"Excellent. Your realtor, Candy Green, is already waiting for you," she said. "If you can just give me your driver's licenses, I'll make copies, and then we can go join her."

Quincy dug in her purse for her driver's license. She did bring it, didn't she? She hated when she did these kinds of things. Why couldn't she keep her purse organized? Why did everything seem like it got thrown in there in a big pile, and she ended up digging and panicking?

Derek already had his driver's license handed over, and the receptionist had already made a copy before Quincy found hers.

"I thought you forgot it. That would be just like you."

Quincy wanted to laugh and look into her husband's eyes and just share a quiet, private joke about her inability to stay organized, but the irritation in his voice was unmistakable. It wasn't something that he was in the mood to laugh about, obviously. Maybe moving had bothered him more than he let on. It just manifested differently in him. Instead of him being able to say, "This bothers me, I'm sad," he got grumpy and quiet and irritated.

She didn't know, and she didn't know what to do to fix it either. He was the man she was married to, and when she said those vows, she meant them for life. For better or for worse, whether her husband was kind to her and shared jokes with her, or whether he was irritated and short and buried himself in business rather than face the emotions of leaving the only home they'd ever known.

"Thank you," the receptionist said as she handed Quincy's driver's license back. "That's such a good picture," the receptionist said.

Quincy's eyes widened, but she remembered to say thank you. Did the receptionist mean that the picture looked nothing like her?

Or maybe the receptionist liked her longer hair, since two years after that photo had been taken, she had cut it all off. It had been thinning out anyway thanks to the hormonal changes of menopause, and she was tired of it plugging up the shower drain.

"If you two would follow me," the receptionist said, coming around the corner of her desk and walking with brisk, businesslike strides to the large, heavy doors that led into the bowels of the building, where Candy awaited them.

At least she would be a familiar face in all of this. Candy had been the real estate agent for the last year as they worked to sell their home. She'd given them helpful hints and tips, and when they had a few minor repairs to make, she'd given them the names of trusted contractors that she knew and used all the time. She gave them tips on how to stage their home to sell it quicker, and had worked with them as they dropped the price three separate times.

It had been an emotional roller coaster, but Candy was very good at what she did, and Quincy loved her.

She seemed to be one of the few people that could make Derek smile these days, and for that, Quincy was also grateful.

"If you two could just wait in here, the lawyer will be in shortly." The receptionist held the door open while they stepped into a large, clinical room, dominated by a table with at least fifteen chairs around it, the wood heavy and dark. Expensive.

Candy, looking cute and sweet and very small sitting in one of the chairs on the opposite end of the table, smiled as they walked in and stood.

"I'm so glad to see you," she said sweetly. Oh, to be young again, innocent and cute the way Candy was.

"It's good to see you too. This place seems so formidable." Quincy gave an exaggerated shudder and held her hand out.

But Candy wasn't looking at her. Her eyes were on Derek.

Quincy didn't blame her. Derek was the commander of the two of them, and the one that needed to be appeased in all circumstances. Quincy would go along to get along, but Derek would demand his way. It was best to keep him happy, and Candy, like a good salesperson, had figured that out.

Quincy felt a little bit odd standing there with her hand out, waiting for Candy and Derek to finish shaking.

It was irritating the way they seemed to hold onto each other, like they couldn't let go.

Derek was saying something about the weather, their hands still joined, and Candy looked like she was hanging onto his every word.

Quincy stared at their joined hands.

Derek hadn't touched her, not even her hand, in... Quincy couldn't remember how long. When he got in bed at night, he was very careful to stay on his own side. They never passed in the bathroom, and even at the supper table he watched the news while they ate. It was a habit he had fallen into after the twins had graduated from high school and moved out, and she had called him on it. He had said that the house seemed so quiet since the kids were gone, and she honestly couldn't fault him for that. It seemed quiet to her too. She had had to find things to do to keep herself occupied so the quietness of the house didn't bother her. Still, when her husband came home from work and when they were eating supper together, it seemed like the time to talk, not have a screen flashing in front of their faces. But if that was the way he coped, she couldn't fault him. But it went from the way he coped to the way they did things over the last couple of years.

Finally, Candy turned from Derek and took Quincy's proffered hand.

Was it just Quincy's imagination, or was she not quite as effusively nice as she had been with Derek?

Quincy tried to shrug that off. She always felt like people gave Derek far more deference than they gave her, but that was because he almost commanded it. He just had that presence about him. The presence that told people that they needed to pay attention, because here was somebody important.

She didn't know how he managed to do that without even saying a word, but sometimes it made her proud. Other times, like now, it was irritating.

"Are you all ready for your trip to the Outer Banks?" Candy asked as they settled themselves in their chairs. She was looking at Quincy.

"I think we are," Quincy said, making sure to include her husband in that, since Candy seemed to be talking solely to her.

"It should be beautiful this time of year," Candy said.

"I'm sure it is."

She loved the ocean, but she never really dreamed about living beside it. Still, it would be a change of scenery, and perhaps good for their marriage. She certainly wasn't going to tell this young girl that, though. No matter how good she was at her job, she was the age of

Quincy and Derek's children. In fact, Quincy had mentioned to Derek about setting Candy up with Randall, their son.

Derek had seemed shocked by the very idea, and in hindsight, Quincy wished that she had pursued that option. After all, she would miss Candy in an "I liked working with her and had almost become friends with her" kind of way.

"I think I have all of my papers in order, and we could actually sign the things that I need you to before the lawyer gets here."

"Let's do that. I'd like to get this done as fast as we can," Derek said. Quincy glanced at him. She didn't realize he was in a big hurry. He hadn't acted like that or insinuated that in any way on their way here.

"All right, that sounds good," Candy said, shifting through her papers, which were perfectly organized, a complete foil to the disorganization in Quincy's purse.

She was able to get them through all of the papers before the lawyer walked in.

He was a gruff, older gentleman, the kind of man who seemed like he did everything by the book. Probably why he had become a lawyer.

He had all the papers in order, and soon everything was signed and they were all shaking hands.

"I'll have my assistant file these at the courthouse before three o'clock this afternoon, and then everything should be finalized." The lawyer nodded. "Nice doing business with you. Can you see yourselves out?"

They nodded, shaking the lawyer's hand as he held the door open for them, and they walked toward the door through which they had entered.

Somehow Quincy ended up in front, with Candy and Derek following behind.

Shouldn't she be walking beside her husband? she thought as she opened the large door, automatically stepping back and allowing the two of them to walk through first.

Whatever they were saying was being said in tones too low for her to hear, and Derek barely looked at her as they walked through.

He was allowing her to open the door for him? That was weird.

They must be in an extremely interesting conversation, although she couldn't imagine what that would be. What in the world would Derek have to talk to Candy about? Not just because of their difference in age, but Candy was sweet and chirpy and a real go-getter in business, true, but young enough to be Derek's daughter. Maybe she was a little bit like Quincy had been when she was that age. Sweet and innocent and full of life and optimism.

She sighed. Menopause had a way of knocking a person down and making them feel old and beat up and ready to throw in the towel.

The receptionist smiled and nodded as they walked through, but Candy and Derek were in such deep conversation that they didn't even seem to notice.

Once they got out in the parking lot, Candy and Derek still continued their conversation, with Derek seeming to forget that they had parked right next to the door and instead continuing to walk down the walk to the only other car that was in the front area of the lot. A bright red convertible.

It suited Candy perfectly.

"You need to tell her now," Candy said, and she no longer sounded sweet or nice. She had stopped on the walk and had both hands on her hips, her bracelet jangling and her hair blowing softly in the wind, framing her sweet, heart-shaped face as she glared up at Derek like a teenager upset with her father.

"Fine. I'll tell her."

Quincy couldn't figure out what in the world they were talking about. What woman would Candy want Derek to talk to? Their business with Candy was done. He should be saying goodbye to her, not promising to talk to someone. And why was she so upset?

Derek swallowed and then lifted his chin and turned slowly toward her.

two

QUINCY HAD STOPPED by their car, and Derek was twenty feet further down the walk.

He made no move to close the distance, even though he was looking at her like there was something he wanted to say.

"Derek, we have a long way to go. We need to get moving if we're going to drop these last things off and get to the hotel so we can get a good start in the morning. Your mother should be expecting us, if you texted her like you said you were going to."

She didn't want to air any of that dirty laundry out in front of Candy, but Derek was looking at her in a way that made fear crawl like a jar of spiders had tipped over in her stomach.

He swallowed again and then looked at his hand, waving it around, with his mouth open, but no words coming out.

It was a tell, one she knew well from being married to the man for twenty plus years. He was nervous about something, and upset.

So Candy wasn't the only one upset. But why wasn't Derek walking back toward her?

Something wasn't adding up, and for some reason, something that had happened two weeks ago ran through her mind, one of those quick flashes where a whole lot of thought seemed to happen in just a second or two. Candy had come over to their house to talk to them about the closing, to let them know what was going to be happening and that type of thing. Things that Quincy thought could have been taken care of over the phone, but for some reason, Derek and Candy insisted that she needed to come. Oddly, it had been a Wednesday night, when Quincy normally went to church. Derek had always gone with her when the kids were there, but once they had moved out, he had gone more sporadically, until he finally quit, although it had been such a gradual shift that Quincy hadn't really noticed until he hadn't been to church in months.

Still, it was odd that he would schedule something for Wednesday night when he knew that she was busy. And in fact, they hadn't told her about it.

Her husband was a busy man, and he had made all the arrangements with the realtor. She had been busy with other things, wrapping up everything that they had done with their lives in the last twenty odd years. She'd only found out about it because she had decided not to go to church that night. There was a guest speaker there, one she'd heard before and hadn't particularly enjoyed. She knew that was a silly reason not to go to church, but she supposed she just wanted to spend a little extra time in the home that they would soon be leaving.

When her husband had seen her home after the time that he knew she should be gone, he had seemed surprised and questioned her about it, and then shortly after that, the doorbell had rung, and Candy had appeared.

Quincy hadn't gotten upset at the time, since she had forgotten more than once to inform her husband of something that was happening. She wouldn't want him to get upset at her for an honest mistake like that. That's what she told herself, and she accepted their explanation that they had simply forgotten to tell her.

She didn't know why that ran through her mind just then, standing on the sidewalk facing Candy and Derek as Derek waved his hand in the air and his mouth opened and closed with no words coming out.

But it was at that moment that the thought that had been in the back of her head all along surfaced.

They hadn't forgotten to tell her. They had deliberately not told her.

"I'm not going to the Outer Banks with you."

Derek's words hung in the air. He sounded almost angry. She hadn't done anything to upset him. She didn't know why he would be angry at her.

Candy still stood with her hands on her hips, a mulish look on her face, as she raised a brow at Derek, as though wanting him to continue.

Derek lifted his chin a little more, glanced at Candy, and then centered his gaze back on Quincy.

"We're not going to the Outer Banks?" Quincy said, not really comprehending, although the new realization that they had deliberately not told her still echoed around in her head. There was a conclusion she needed to draw from that, but she was resisting. She couldn't quite grasp it, because her brain didn't seem to want to.

"No. I'm not going to the Outer Banks. You can still go if you want to."

"Where are we going to go? We just sold our house." She was confused. She felt unsteady. Her husband didn't look right, and while she stared at him, out of her peripheral vision, she could see Candy still standing there. Still waiting, only now her arms were crossed over her chest.

"I don't care where you go. Candy and I are in love with each other, and I'm moving in with her."

Quincy stared at her husband. The man she had spent the last twenty or so years with. The man she had dated for two years, and who had begged her to marry him. Begged, when she had been less than interested.

But his constant badgering had worn her down, and she had

agreed, although she had wanted to use her nursing degree to travel, see the country, help at different hospitals throughout the nation as a temporary nurse, and get paid an outrageous amount of money to basically live her dream life.

Instead, she got married, then had given up her job when the twins were born.

Now her husband didn't want her anymore? Where was the man who couldn't wait to get married? Who had asked her every day for months if she was ready to marry him? Who had promised to spend the rest of his life with her, for better or for worse, in front of God?

Was that all his word meant to him? Was that all a vow that he stood before God and promised was worth? Just a few words, "I'm not going with you"?

She wanted to laugh, she wanted to cry, she wanted to scream, she wanted to attack him and scratch his eyeballs out. Even Candy didn't escape her wrath. She'd like to smack that smart little child in the nose.

Plus, even now, even with all of this rolling through her, and her not being able to quite come to grips with the idea that her husband was leaving her, she didn't understand why Candy couldn't see that if Derek would do it to her, Quincy, he would do it to Candy too. If a man's word wasn't good, it wasn't good.

"So you don't want me anymore?" She hated how that came out. Insecure, sad, wobbly. Like she needed him to want her in order for her to have confidence and walk through life with her head up.

"It's just like you to put it in the worst light possible," Derek said, his voice holding disgust.

She blinked. "What other light is there to put it in?"

She was not the bad guy in this situation. She was the victim, although she hated that status. She didn't want to be the victim. The victim didn't have any power. The power was with the people who weren't victims.

She wanted to take a hold of her life, to steer it in the direction that she wanted it to go, but she wanted to do it with her husband.

"I'm not in love with you anymore. And you're not in love with me. Don't try to tell me that you are. We've been heading this direction for a while. And you're just denying reality if you don't think that that's true."

Her husband threw those words at her, and each sentence felt like a smack on the face.

"That's not true." He'd already told her that if she denied it, she was denying reality, but that didn't mean that he was right and she was wrong. Because he was wrong. It wasn't true. She didn't know, as he claimed, that the relationship was over. Far from it.

She had thought this new direction would be just the thing to recharge the relationship and bring them closer together.

"You've been cheating on me?" she finally asked, and she couldn't help it, the pain came out. What was wrong with her? Sure, she wasn't a cute twenty-year-old anymore, but she was the woman that he had married. And he wasn't a cute twenty-year-old anymore either, to be honest.

"I don't have to stand here and listen to this. You'll hear from my lawyer. We can split everything equally. There's no need to get complicated about it. Now that we sold the house, all there is is money. You get half and I get half."

She narrowed her eyes. "No." Why was that not right? It just didn't sound right. On the surface it did, half and half, but...

"I told you she wasn't going to take it well. You should've sat down and had an adult conversation about it, instead of confronting her as you're leaving. I don't know why you didn't listen to me." Candy stamped her foot and folded her hands across her chest. She no longer looked like a cute little girl. She looked like an angry teenager.

"I told you to let me handle her. I can do it. I don't need you telling me what to do," he paused, and then he said, "honey."

That endearment, that one word, it turned Quincy's stomach. It made her feel like she was going to throw up. To hear her husband, her man, the man who had pledged his life to her, calling someone else honey... It straightened out her feelings in a hurry. Instead of wanting to laugh, now she had the most overwhelming urge to cry, and she knew she wasn't going to be able to stop her tears.

He was in the process of throwing her away like so much trash. Just simply told her that he wasn't going to go with her, and that he was going to divorce her and that she would hear from his lawyer.

She wasn't going to give him the satisfaction of breaking down in front of him. Of letting him know that he had just leveled her life.

"You don't get half. I stayed home and raised our children, took care of our home, and invested my life in my family, expecting to share half of your pension when you retired. I have nothing from those years, other than what you earned. What I enabled you to earn because I was home taking care of you. I'm not going to just walk away from that. You'll be hearing from *my* lawyer."

She had no idea whether any of that was true or not, but she made her grand exit, turning on her toe and stomping to the car. And then she realized...he had the key.

"I suppose you're gonna keep the car?" she said, turning a quarter of a turn so she faced the sidewalk and didn't look in his direction.

"I don't want your stupid car. It's about time I spent a little of *my* money and lived a little. A convertible is much more my style."

And that's when she realized that Candy didn't buy the convertible. Quincy's husband did.

There was a sound at her feet, and she realized he'd thrown the key at her. It had dropped beside her, and then skidded under the car.

She gritted her teeth. There was nothing for her to do but get down on her hands and knees and reach under the car.

Thankfully, Derek and Candy were obviously not watching her, because she heard the rumble of a motor catching behind her, and then the little growl as it idled, before the growl became a bit of a roar as they backed out, and then... They drove by her, the tires screeching just a little, but she didn't look. Because she touched the key with the tip of her finger. If she could only get underneath the car just a little bit more, she could grab a hold of it.

Her stomach felt like it was filled with sand. Her husband was leaving her.

No. Her husband had left.

What was she going to do?

Where was she going to go?

She almost had the key, but as she went to grab it, she accidentally pushed it further under the car.

She wanted to lay down on the concrete and cry. Already tears were seeping out from underneath her eyes.

Lord? Really? You couldn't just make it easy for me to get the key, after my husband did this to me? You could just pick the key up and put it in my hand. Why are you torturing me?

But of course, there was no answer.

And then something that she'd heard not long ago came to mind.

Instead of asking God "why" when she was in a tough situation, why didn't she ask Him, "How can I use this to bring glory to You?"

She knew that was the job of anyone still on earth, to have a relationship with the Lord, and to bring glory to God. Because that was what people were created to do.

She resisted the impulse, asking instead, *God, how can You find glory in this? I'm just embarrassed. I went all in on my marriage, and my husband left me for a kid. Where's the glory in that?*

There was no answer to that either.

She managed to get her legs out from under her, lie down on her stomach, and push herself underneath her car far enough that she was just able to grab the key. Hefting herself up off the concrete, she was just in time to see the old lawyer stopped on the sidewalk, staring at her.

"Are you okay?" he asked, and while his voice seemed impersonal and his demeanor gruff, beyond that he actually seemed rather caring at this point.

"My husband just told me that he was leaving me for the realtor. And we sold our house ten minutes ago, and I have nowhere to go."

"What were you going to do? Where were you going to go?"

"His mother has a place on the Outer Banks. But I can't go live with her. She doesn't even like me."

He nodded slowly.

Why was she even talking to him? He didn't know her, other than the impersonal relationship they had, as he did the paperwork for their house.

But... he seemed kind, and maybe she was just desperate to latch onto anyone who would show her the slightest bit of kindness after the agony of what her husband had just done to her.

He had left her. It still didn't seem real. There was a part of her that said if she could just talk to him, reason with him, he'd see the light and realize the stupidity of what he'd done.

It was probably a good thing he'd thrown the key on the ground. If she hadn't been so busy trying to get it, she probably would have made a fool of herself begging him to take her back.

"Why don't you go ahead and go. The ocean has a way of helping a person heal."

The lawyer paused, looking down, and seemed like he was going to start walking away.

"Do you need anything?" he finally asked as he looked up at her.

His gaze was direct, and he didn't seem embarrassed that the tears were now flowing freely down her face.

"I think I'm okay now. Thank you."

He nodded, but didn't go anywhere, as though loath to leave her standing there crying.

"I just need to get in my car," she said, holding up the fob in her hand.

He nodded again.

"She might not want me there. She's never liked me."

"She's older now. Maybe she needs help."

She didn't say anything to that. That was actually the reason they were going. Because Beulah did need help. Sonny, with his Parkinson's, had been getting steadily worse, and Beulah was having a hard time balancing her cleaning business with taking care of her husband as well. Things were starting to gear up for tourist season, and she and Derek had said multiple times how nice it was that their house sold so they would be down there for the busiest season of the year.

While Derek had not told Beulah that they were arriving tomorrow, she was expecting them and anticipating their arrival.

"You really think I should go?" she asked, knowing that he knew nothing about her family situation and really couldn't give her good advice.

"Sometimes getting out of your environment, going somewhere else, is helpful. And like I said, the ocean is healing. Something about standing there and realizing how small you are, and how big God is, it puts things in perspective."

She nodded, thinking that she wouldn't have pegged that man for a Christian. But he seemed to be. At least he was talking about God, not mother nature or some other thing that society made up to try to downplay or eliminate the role of God in anything.

"Thanks," she said, and he nodded again, waiting for her to unlock the car and get in before he strolled away.

A nice, older gentleman who seemed to have old-school manners. The kind of manners that were becoming extinct in modern society.

But she didn't believe in coincidences. God didn't make mistakes, but put everything together on purpose. So the lawyer came out at that exact time, because God knew she needed someone to encourage her to continue on doing what they had planned, not give up.

All right, Lord, if You want me to go to the Outer Banks and see if Beulah will still take me, then... that's what I'll do.

She decided not to text Beulah, though, because if Beulah was going to tell her no, she didn't know what she was going to do. But

Beulah would hardly deny her a place to stay the night if she showed up on her doorstep just before bedtime.

She had never made such a long drive by herself in her life before. It was a full eight to ten hours to get to the Outer Banks from where she was in West Virginia.

Normally her husband did all the driving, and she read the map, and then eventually the GPS, and found good places to stop to eat and to stop for gas and sometimes even to stop just to look around and enjoy.

Each had their job. But now, everything would be on her shoulders.

Could she drive ten hours?

She supposed she wouldn't know until she tried. With that thought, she pushed the button to start the car, looked in the rearview mirror, and then put it in gear.

three

QUINCY PARKED her car in the hotel parking lot. In all their married years, she had never gone in and reserved rooms. She made the reservation online, and Derek went in, talked to the receptionist, did whatever a person did in the lobby, while she waited in the car, usually with the kids, but eventually the kids were old enough to go in if they wanted to. Still, there was no point in dragging all of their things in if they were just going to enter through a different door, so she always waited in the car.

Regardless, she'd never done it before in her life. Never even seen anyone do it.

She sat in the parking lot, staring at the big, intimidating walls of the hotel. It wasn't anything special, just one that looked like it didn't have bedbugs and had a gym, because Derek would want to use it in the morning before they left.

At the thought of her husband, her eyes pricked with tears again.

Could she hold it together long enough to go in and get a room?

She wanted to cry just from the thought of having to do it herself. Of all of a sudden being alone. It was so wrong! How could he leave after she had given him more than twenty years of her life?

Why couldn't he have decided to not get married to her in the first place? Then she wouldn't have wasted half her life on him.

Had she cycled through the stages of grief and reached anger?

She wasn't sure. She felt like she was spinning in the stages, because part of her was furious with him, while part of her felt like she could barely hold it together, and if she tried to walk, she would end up in a puddle on the floor.

And then, impossibly, part of her felt lost. What did she do without Derek? He was her other half. The other piece of herself. He knew how she liked her toast, what temperature she preferred their bedroom at night, which Christmas decorations she loved the best, and what she was going to order when they went to their favorite restaurant. They had a favorite restaurant.

He knew her almost as well as she knew herself. And she knew him the same way.

Except... obviously she didn't.

Part of her wondered/hoped if maybe he would change his mind. Was he really in love with Candy? She was a child. How could she ever understand Derek? She had no idea what it was like to have a baby, raise children, struggle to make the mortgage payment when the dishwasher, hot water heater, and roof needed to be replaced all in one month.

At the thought of that, she almost cried again. They'd been through so much together. How could he just throw her away?

And that thought brought a new and even more terrifying thought. What was wrong with her?

She swallowed. Was she too fat? Too ugly? He always said her feet stunk. Was that the problem?

He had bad morning breath and armpit odor that even deodorant couldn't mask. But she loved him anyway. Or maybe not just in spite of those things, but she loved those things as well, even if it was annoying in the summer when all he had to do was walk through a room and she could tell that he was perspiring.

She leaned her head back on the headrest, closing her eyes,

trying not to cry. She had to go in. She had to get this room. She had nowhere else to go.

Taking a deep breath, she yanked the door open, grabbed her purse and the key fob, and walked in.

It wasn't as hard as what she thought it would be, and she finished up the transaction and waited for the receptionist to write the room number on the card holder.

She hadn't known the license plate number of her car, and he'd asked that. She wondered what Derek had done. Did he really have their license plate memorized? He never texted her and asked her to get it for him.

She did know the make and model and was able to give that, or at least a good guess, since the receptionist did not double check.

"Your room number is 306. Take those elevators right there, around the corner to the left. This is the closest door, although you can also use the side door if there's no parking out front."

The receptionist handed her the key and sounded like she'd given that spiel a million times, which she probably had. Different room numbers, different people, but same general idea.

Being the receptionist at a hotel would not be hard. It would be a job she could do.

She could go back to nursing, she supposed. Although she really didn't want to. It had been such a long time since she had graduated with her degree that things had probably changed so much she would have a hard time keeping up with the technology and would feel like she didn't belong, even if she could get someone to hire her. That would be hard.

"Are you okay?" the receptionist asked, and Quincy realized she was still standing there, looking at the key.

"Yeah. I'm fine. Thank you."

Fine. She was fine. Like her world hadn't come crashing down, and she didn't feel like she was going to implode, like her chest was on fire and she couldn't put it out.

How could Derek have done this to her?

And yet did she still love him?

She wasn't sure whether she still loved him or not, as far as the mushy gushy feelings went. She believed that love was actions. And she had shown him as much as she could with her actions that she had loved him.

Would she take him back?

That was a hard question. If he came back, begging for her to take him, would she?

She wanted her life back. She didn't want to have to make a new life. She didn't want to have to do it by herself. If they were going to make a new life, she wanted it to be with him!

She didn't want to have to rebuild everything.

She gritted her teeth together as she pulled out the overnight bag she had packed that morning, back when her life was normal and this hadn't happened.

Maybe it was a bad dream. Maybe she would wake up and find out that none of it was true. Oh, wouldn't that be nice? She wouldn't have to deal with the idea of being fifty-one years old and on her own with no house, no job and no idea of who she was separate from the man she'd built everything with, who now wanted nothing to do with her.

She managed to get herself up to her room, although she had gotten off on the second floor when the elevator stopped there to pick up someone else, thinking it was hers. Then she had to wait for it to apparently go down and up and down again before it stopped to pick her up again.

She felt like an idiot, but those were the kinds of things that Derek took care of, and she didn't have to think about. He knew what floor they were on. She just followed him off the elevator when he went. He knew where their room was. He handled the key. She didn't have to worry about losing it, because Derek had it. If she wanted to go somewhere, she just asked him what he'd done with it, and then set it back down wherever he put it. He did all of those things. And now... it was on her.

The weight of responsibility, of doing all the things that she had been doing, plus all of the things that Derek had been doing, felt heavy and impossible. How was she going to live?

He was the one who took care of all the things that she had no idea about.

Back when they had all of those expenses in one month, she hadn't made a single phone call about the roof or to order a new appliance, or to even figure out that the hot water heater actually needed to be replaced and didn't just need... something else. Whatever hot water heaters sometimes needed. She didn't know anything.

Then again, if Candy couldn't cook, Derek would starve to death, because she wasn't even sure he could boil water or knew how to turn the stove on.

He was spoiled that way. She had cooked every single mouthful of food that he had ever eaten, unless he'd gotten it at a restaurant, or a few times they visited his mother.

She made sure both of their children knew how to cook before they left the house. After all, she had had some very real fear that her husband would starve to death when she was in the hospital with the twins.

She finally made it to her room, fumbled with the key—again, Derek always did it. All she had to do was carry her coat and purse and follow him.

Now she was carrying her coat and her purse and the luggage and the key and the key fob to the car and the weight of all the things that she was now going to have to do by herself, plus the even heavier weight of the rejection. That probably stung the hardest.

She managed to get the door unlocked, got everything in hand, made it through, throwing things down on the first shelf she came to, and then going back and flipping all the locks she possibly could on the door. With Derek in the room, she never gave a thought to her safety, but now... now it was all on her.

Feeling more alone than she had ever felt in her life before, she wrapped her arms around herself and walked over to the window, pulling the outer curtain back and looking through the gauzy inner curtain. The sun shone on the parking lot, blurred through the filmy material, as her eyes filled with tears.

Was he really leaving her? She wanted to call him, to ask if he was serious. If he truly thought about this and really wanted Candy more than he wanted her, his wife, the woman that he'd spent the last twenty plus years with.

She couldn't stop the big, wrenching sobs that started at what felt like her very soul and came out, making noises she didn't recognize from herself at all.

She didn't feel like taking a shower, but she didn't know how thin the walls were, and there was a small thought in her head that someone might call the police thinking that there was a real problem going on in her room. So she walked to the bathroom, turned the water on, and just dropped her clothes on the floor. She stepped in the shower.

A long time later, she lay on her bed, staring at the ceiling. Not the slightest bit sleepy. The shower hadn't done anything to help. Maybe it had drowned out her sobs, but it hadn't fixed anything. She was scared to death. Sure, she could call her kids. Stacey or Randall, either one would be happy to hear from her and welcome her in, but both of them were living in one-bedroom apartments, working to save enough money for a down payment on a house. Neither one of them had wanted to continue to live with their parents. Both of them had wanted to try to make their own way in the world. She almost smiled when she remembered that they had rented apartments in the same apartment complex, because while they wanted to make their own way in the world, they hadn't wanted to be too separated from each other.

That had been years ago, and they still came around, and Quincy would say that they had a close relationship with her, but... they were independent adults. Living on their own. If her kids could do it, surely she could too?

At the very least, she couldn't ask her children, who were living on their own, for help to help her live on her own.

Plus, she didn't want to be the one to break the news that their father had cheated on her and dumped her like yesterday's trash and was now dating some floozy that was approximately their age.

Candy was a nice person, and she didn't want to think meanly about her, except she had known that Derek was married, and she had cheated with him anyway, knowing that she was breaking up a family.

Quincy held Derek responsible, completely and totally, but Candy was not exactly lily white either.

She rolled over, punching her pillow, although it didn't land with a satisfying whack, but rather glanced off the edge of it, and her knuckles hit the back of the headboard, and it hurt more than helped.

Just that little pain started her tears flowing again.

Really, Lord? Like I'm not already hurting enough, You couldn't give me the satisfaction of landing a punch on my pillow? I had to hit the headboard?

It wasn't God's fault. None of this was. It was her. She was too fat, too old, too wrinkly, her hair was thin, she hadn't shaved her legs enough, there was that one time where she let her armpit hair grow for two weeks. That was probably it. That was why he left her.

That was the question that ran through her mind the most. She rolled over, staring again at the ceiling, not the slightest bit tired. Why? Why? Why?

She didn't understand. Why did he leave? Why wasn't he happy? Why didn't he tell her that he wasn't happy? What could she have done to change things? Was there anything? Why didn't he give her a chance? Why didn't he talk to her about this?

Was he so overcome with lust for a child that he didn't think that he might be ripping up what they had spent decades building?

She had trouble breathing, pulling in breath. Her chest felt empty, like there was nothing in there.

How was she going to continue on?

After another hour and a half of tossing and turning and not feeling the slightest bit tired, she sat up, turned the light on, and then wondered what in the world she thought she was going to do. Turning the light on didn't help her feel less scared and alone.

And, behold, I am with thee, and will keep thee in all places whither thou goest.

The verse that she'd memorized a long time ago ran through her head.

"I know You're here, God, but You declared that I should be one with my husband, and I've lived that for the last twenty-three years. And now he's ripped it apart. I did what You wanted me to. He's the one who didn't. Why am I the one suffering?"

She got up, throwing the covers back and padding over to the table where she'd left her purse. Her Bible was in it, and she pulled it out, grabbing her glasses as well, and walking back over to the bed.

The glasses were a new addition in the last couple of years. Up until that point she had had perfect vision, and had just assumed that she always would. It had been a shock when she had started needing glasses to read.

Maybe that was why he didn't want her. She was breaking down, while Candy was in the prime of her youth.

But that didn't make sense, since Derek was breaking down too. He needed glasses a year before she did.

Lord, I need something from You. I don't even know what. I feel like I'm going to die. No, I just feel like there's no point in living anymore.

She was not suicidal. That was not a solution to her problems. It certainly wasn't something that she would do, especially considering the pain and agony it would put her children through.

But... the future looked empty, and very hard. She wasn't expecting to have to live out the years after menopause by herself.

She thought she was going to have a partner, someone to share them with. A new life.

She opened her Bible to Isaiah, one of her favorite books. Maybe subconsciously she was looking for one of the verses of comfort, or where God promised to hold her hand, to walk through the waters with her, but instead, her Bible fell open to Isaiah 43:19, and she read it aloud.

"Behold, I will do a new thing; now it shall spring forth; shall ye not know it? I will even make a way in the wilderness, and rivers in the desert."

Quincy sat there, feeling a little bit of calm flow over her.

It didn't take the pain away. It didn't make her heart feel like it hadn't been broken into a million pieces. It didn't make the future suddenly click into place where everything looked rosy. But it was a tiny little whisper of hope, a soft, gentle reminder that God was there, God was working, and what she saw as the worst thing that had ever happened to her, a waste of twenty-five years, a devastation and a rejection, could be the start of something new and beautiful, if she would just turn her eyes to Jesus and allow Him to guide her - make a way - through this season.

I want my husband to come back, Lord. I want this to be a bad dream. But I know the second isn't true, and the first is highly unlikely. And I know that You have something beautiful for me, not just to make me happy, because I guess for a little while I forgot that my purpose here isn't to be happy, or even to be loved by my husband, even though I feel like it's what I deserve. My purpose here is to bring glory to You, and if there's some way that You can get glory out of my broken heart and devastated life, Lord, show me how. Because I don't see it.

She still didn't feel that much better, but the calmness that stole over her allowed her to feel tired and sleepy for the first time since she'd tried to lie down after her shower.

She closed her Bible, thinking about those new streams, the rivers in the desert. She felt like a desert, and she didn't feel like there were any rivers around, but God could do it. God could do it.

four

QUINCY WOKE IN THE MORNING, her eyes grainy and sore, and... after one look in the mirror, she knew she would scare small children with the way they were puffy and red. She just wanted to hide in the dark, alone.

Thankfully, the sun didn't get the memo, or maybe it decided to come out, or maybe God commanded it to come out anyway, because it was bright and beautiful outside. A gorgeous spring day, and if the temperature lived up to the promise of what she could see outside her window, it was the perfect day to arrive in Whispering Hope Harbor.

She still wasn't done cycling through her mind, trying to figure out what she did wrong, but the little thread of calmness that Isaiah 43:19 had given her the night before still wound around, in and out of the anxiety and devastation she felt from the rejection of her husband.

She grabbed her phone, hoping against hope that there was a message from him, and hating herself that even after what he'd done to her, she was practically begging him in her mind to message her, let her know that he'd changed his mind, that he didn't want to explode everything that they had built together. But there was only a message from Stacey, one of the twins, congratulating them on selling the house and telling her to let her know when they arrived in Whispering Hope Harbor.

Obviously, Stacey didn't know what Derek had done, and Quincy did not have the mental bandwidth to discuss it now. So she just sent back a message saying

> I'll let you know! Have a great day!

And then a

She sent a

> Good morning

text to Randall, who sent a checkmark back.

He was much less chatty than Stacey, which made sense.

Before she set her phone down, she pulled up the photo app, and on a whim, started scrolling through, seeing scenes of their life, the house all packed up and ready to go.

And then, in one of the pictures of the packed-up house, she saw Derek and Candy standing together, leaning close and talking.

How had she missed that before?

In several other pictures, she caught the two of them together in the background, one in which their feet were together, another where it almost looked like they were holding pinky fingers, and yet another where Candy looked longingly across the room, where Quincy remembered Derek to be standing while she took that particular photo.

She'd missed those signs? How had she been so blind?

Because she trusted her husband, that's why. Of course she

trusted him. She would never even think of cheating. She never even looked at other men.

And yet, Derek had dealt her a blow, and... of course it would be silly for her to expect him to text her this morning to find out how she was. He didn't care about her anymore, remember?

She had never checked out of a hotel before, but she knew Derek had usually done something with the key cards, so she got all of her things together and walked down to the reception area.

There were several people talking to the clerk, and her eyes snagged on a bowl that held other key cards and a sign that said, "Drop your cards here."

Her room was all paid for, and she didn't have anything else to say to the receptionist, so she assumed that meant her.

She dropped the cards, waved at the receptionist, who smiled at her, and then, as their eyes met, the receptionist—different from last night—moved her brows down in concern.

Her eyes. They were red and swollen. She always got like that when she cried. She hated it, because she looked terrible. Maybe that's why Derek had left her.

No. She had to stop thinking like that. She had to remember that if Derek had character and integrity, he wouldn't have cheated. It had nothing to do with her, and everything to do with the lack of morals and values on Derek's part.

Feeling resolute on the outside, but shaky and uncertain on the inside, she walked out of the hotel, took a deep breath of the warm spring air, and tried not to wonder whether or not she could drive ten hours by herself.

five

TWO HOURS INTO HER JOURNEY, the majestic outline of the Appalachian Mountains had given way to flat hills, and Quincy couldn't stop the rolling tape in her head. All the things she thought she had done wrong, all the things that pointed to this end, all the things she knew she could've done better.

To get her mind off of that, she tried to think of someone she could call. Even after the events of the last twenty-four hours, Derek was the first person who popped into her head. It was like she had to remind herself that he no longer wanted her.

Still, it was tempting to call him and ask if he was sure, very sure about that decision. But if he wanted her, he would've called, texted, messaged her somehow. It wasn't like he couldn't get a hold of her. He even had the hotel room that she had reserved last night. She hadn't considered that he might've shown up, and he never did. Of course.

To keep herself from calling her husband, to either yell at him or beg him to take her back, she thought of her best friend from church, Jody.

They weren't super close, but she was the best friend she had, so she dialed her number.

"Hello?" Her familiar voice came on the phone.

"Hey, Jody. How are you?"

"I'm just fine. I wasn't expecting to hear from you. Is something wrong?"

"No. Nothing's wrong." Quincy stopped abruptly. She'd said that automatically, without even thinking. Of course something was wrong. Her husband had left. But she supposed the house wasn't on fire, or she wasn't in an accident, or some kind of major emergency like that. That was the kind of thing that she would've thought that she might have to say was wrong, not the words that were about to come out of her mouth.

"Actually, there is something. I'm not in danger or anything like that."

"Oh good, I'm relieved to hear that," Jody said, sounding curious.

"Did I get you at a bad time?" There, her natural concern for others took over. Rather than thinking about herself, she was concerned that she might be inconveniencing Jody.

"No. I just got finished with a project that I'm doing for work, and I had a few minutes to talk anyway."

"Oh good."

Quincy tapped the steering wheel with her finger. She wasn't sure if she could get the words out without losing her ability to function. It would be dangerous to do that while she was driving.

Glancing down at her speedometer and seeing that she was going five miles an hour under the speed limit, she pressed a little on the accelerator as she said, "I—" and then lapsed into silence.

"Did you close on your house? Was that today?"

"Yesterday. And yes, we did."

"Then you must be at the Outer Banks now!" Jody said, sounding excited for her. And she would be excited for herself. After all, living along the beach was a dream come true, and to be able to live full-time at the Outer Banks was crazy amazing. Except... it wasn't turning out the way she thought.

"Well, it's not quite the way it seems," Quincy said. "I'm not there yet."

"Oh, did Derek go before you? Are you driving there yourself?"

"Yes. I'm driving myself. And no, Derek didn't go before me."

"And he's coming after you? Is he driving a U-Haul or something? I'm sorry, I didn't even consider that you guys might need help packing up your house. I should've offered."

"No. It's not a big deal. We've been doing that over the last few months after we finalized our plans."

"Oh. Then you've been working on it for the last few months. I suppose when you stretch it out like that, it's not a big deal."

"Yeah. It took our house longer to sell than what we expected, but..." Why was she talking about these banal things when that wasn't what she wanted to talk about at all?

"So... what was it that you called about?"

Jody didn't seem to know how to ask her question. Everything so far in their conversation sounded like it was just peachy keen.

"Derek left me. He left me for the realtor."

"Oh my goodness," Jody said, her words coming out shocked and slow.

Then the line was quiet, as though Jody didn't know what to say.

"I didn't know who else to call. I'm sorry."

"Do your kids know?"

"I would say no, because Stacey would've texted me right away."

"I would think so, if her father had told her. But apparently he didn't." There was a delicate pause. "Weren't you going to live with your mother-in-law at the Outer Banks?"

"Yes."

"Does she know?"

That was a great question. Yesterday, when Quincy had asked if Derek had told his mother when to expect them, he said he would text her later. Had he texted her? Had he told her?

"I didn't tell her. I don't know if Derek did or not."

"I hope the coward didn't," Jody said, and Quincy loved her for it.

Sure, it wasn't very nice to call someone else a coward, but Quincy needed that right now. Needed someone else to confirm what she was feeling—that her husband was a total, complete jerk. That he was a coward, and worse than a coward, he was a snake and a cheater and a liar and a destroyer of people's lives, someone with no character and no integrity. Yeah, coward didn't even begin to scratch the surface of what Derek was.

Still, it made her feel better.

"Thank you," she whispered.

"Thank me? For what?" Jody asked.

"For calling him a coward. I've spent the last twenty-four hours wondering what was wrong with me. Why he left me. I'm not perfect, and all of my faults seem to be magnified right now, but..."

"There's nothing wrong with you. Of course, you're a sinner just like I am. But there's nothing wrong with you. Nothing that should make your husband cheat and leave... I assume he's cheating?"

"Yeah. With our realtor."

"Oh, that's so gross!"

"She's Stacey's age." Jody knew her daughter, who had gone to church and still did.

"Oh, that's so icky. Why do men do those kinds of things?"

She didn't want to bash on all of the male gender, although... right now she hated every man she'd ever met, and millions she hadn't. Okay, maybe she did want to bash the entire male gender. But it wasn't right.

"Yeah. I'm not sure why I called you. I just... I'm driving by myself, and I'm not even sure my mother-in-law's going to let me stay. She's not been the most warm and welcoming person in my life."

"Yeah, I only remember seeing them in church maybe once. They didn't seem to visit that often, and... I remember you guys taking a trip to the Outer Banks last summer. Maybe it was when you were deciding whether or not you were going to move there?"

"Yeah. Derek wanted to make sure that the accommodations

were up to his standards." At the time, Quincy thought it was sweet that he was concerned about her, because that was the way he phrased it, but in hindsight, she was the one who really didn't care. He was the one who had major concerns about his level of comfort.

"It's normal you needed somebody to talk to. That's what happens whenever you get slapped in the face by life."

"Yeah. I guess I wanted you to let me know that I wasn't crazy for thinking that there was something wrong with my husband, not me. Although... you're right. I'm a sinner, and it's so easy to look back and think of things that I could've done better. I just didn't. I thought everything was okay the way it was."

"And it should've been. It doesn't matter how terrible of a wife you are, he doesn't get to cheat and he doesn't get to leave and break his vows. That's wrong."

"Thank you."

"Of course. I'm just telling you the truth."

"Good. I feel a little delicate right now, but I don't want to be lied to."

"I'm not going to lie to you."

Maybe Jody was a better friend than what she thought. She appreciated a friend who wasn't going to give her a bunch of platitudes that weren't true, but at the same time, Jody was right. It didn't matter how terrible things got between Derek and her, the idea of cheating or leaving was absolutely off the table for her. She would never even have thought of such a thing.

"I don't know what I'm gonna do if Beulah doesn't allow me to stay. I... I've lost everything."

"You haven't lost everything. You're still healthy, aren't you?"

She didn't really want to be told about the good things still in her life, and for some reason that irritated her. But it was true. Wouldn't this be so much more terrible if she were dealing with cancer or some other terrible health issue?

"That's a great point. Thanks."

"Of course. And—"

"But I don't have a home. If Beulah says I can't stay without Derek, what am I gonna do?"

"You'll come right back here, and the church will take care of you. Pastor will of course do something."

"Of course," she said, although her tone lacked conviction. Would they actually do something for her? She couldn't think of anyone else who had gone through something like this where the church had come in and given them a place to stay. They certainly prayed for them.

"I can add you to the prayer list," Jody offered, as though reading her mind.

"No. Please don't. I don't want Stacey or Randall to find out that way."

"All right. You can call me when you're sure that they know, and that everyone else that you need to know knows. But I'll definitely be praying for you. I can't imagine what I would do if Bernard left me."

Was there a little bit of condescending superiority in her tone? Like she was better because she still had a husband?

No. It was just Quincy's imagination. It was her insecurity, now that her husband had left, that there was something wrong with her, something inferior about her now that she didn't have a husband, or couldn't keep her husband.

It sounded terrible when she put it like that.

"Thanks for talking," she finally said. She didn't really know what else to say. She didn't call to bash her husband, although it did feel really good to have Jody call him a coward. And she didn't want to bash men in general either, although she had no use for that half of the population. How many women did she know whose husbands couldn't stay true? They just cheated like it didn't mean anything and destroyed their marriages like they weren't worth a hill of beans, as her mother would've said.

The scenery had gotten flat, and while she knew she still had several hours until she arrived at her destination, it was heartening to see things change and know that she was on her way.

"I wasn't sure whether I could drive an entire ten hours myself, but I'm more than halfway there, and I think I'm gonna make it."

"Of course you're going to make it. You're one of the most put-together people I know. When you put your mind to something, you get it done. Whether it's a project at church, serving your husband with love, or driving for ten hours."

Jody's confidence gave her confidence, as they chatted a bit more before they said goodbye and hung up.

She hadn't figured anything out about her future, although it was nice to think that there would be a safety net in her church if Beulah rejected her.

What was she going to say to Beulah?

Hello, did your son tell you that he cheated on me and left?

That hardly seemed like a neutral way to begin a conversation. And whose side would she be on? After all, Derek was her son. She should be on his side, except his side was dead wrong. Would Beulah even take her anyway? Would she reject Quincy the same way Derek had?

How could she start the conversation to make it seem like she didn't hate her husband?

Whoa. Wait a minute. She had to make it *seem* that way? Did she have hate in her heart toward him?

Lord, I know it's a sin to hate people. You said it was the same as murder, but... does it count when your husband cheats on you and leaves you and blows your life up in your face? Are you allowed to hate then?

She knew the answer to that. It was always no. But God didn't expect her not to have emotions and feelings. He created her, and He gave those things to her, and He knew how she would react to the events of the past day or so. After all, Jesus showed human emotion when Lazarus died. He also showed human emotion before He was crucified, fear so great that He sweat great drops of blood. She'd never been that afraid. She looked down at her arm just to check to make sure that she wasn't that scared now. The pit of her stomach kind of felt that way.

No blood. So she wasn't as afraid as Jesus was.

That was strangely comforting.

Maybe she was just grasping at anything to comfort her now.

She thought back to her wedding day. She had been so young and stupid.

No. That was very negative. She was young and naïve and hopeful. Would she still have married Derek if she had known what was coming down the road? What decisions would she do differently if she could do it again?

Would she do anything differently?

Choosing not to marry Derek would mean that she wouldn't have Stacey and Randall. But if she hadn't married him, she wouldn't know what she was missing. The idea of life without her children was almost unthinkable. But... maybe she would've married someone else, maybe they would've had more children rather than just the twins, since Derek had wanted to quit at that. She had to admit he was right about it being overwhelming at first. But they'd gotten the hang of it. By the time the kids went to kindergarten, she felt like she had everything under control and could've had more children, but Derek said absolutely not and told her to get a dog instead.

She'd never gotten the dog, although now she kind of wished she would have. But then the dog might be homeless now, too.

Definitely after the twins had left home, she and Derek had drifted apart. Or maybe it had started before that. She was in charge of all the things the kids did, although Derek was a good dad and showed up to recitals and presentations, and sometimes he even helped with homework in the evening, although a lot of times he worked on his business, and she was the one who answered the questions and tried to figure out new math.

She hadn't been taught phonics in school either, and that was the way her children learned to read. She had to teach herself that as well. Derek hadn't concerned himself about it.

She hadn't fussed at him. He was busy with other things. She was happy to take care of the children. It gave her a purpose.

But maybe she should have insisted that he be more involved. Maybe the great gulf that seemed to be between them now wouldn't have developed if she had reached out to him more. But she thought she was doing him a favor by covering for him and giving him the freedom to grow his business.

six

SHE STOPPED TWICE MORE for gas, more to stretch her legs than because she needed it, and by the time she finally saw the ocean, big and bold and blue on the horizon, with the coal tipples and the huge docking areas for ships, her legs were sore and her back hurt, but she was confident she could make it.

It was just the bay, but the water still had a calming, soothing effect on her, and she soaked it in.

Then she got to the bridge that disappeared under the water, and her hands started to shake while her heart pounded.

She'd never driven through this part of the road before, and the idea of all of that water surrounding her made her claustrophobic. She couldn't get out if she wanted to. She was stuck down here, and if anything happened, she was as good as dead.

By the time the road returned to sunlight, her hands were slick with sweat, and she could barely breathe. It felt like a panic attack. Probably was. Why was she even thinking about those kinds of things? When Derek drove, it wasn't something she even worried about. She actually liked the bridges and the tunnels and enjoyed them. But they would be just as stuck if anything happened whether he was driving or whether she was.

Why had she allowed it to affect her like that?

Maybe it was the idea that now she was on her own. It was all up to her.

No. God was still with her, even though it truly felt like she couldn't feel Him at all.

Lord, where are You? Help me to put my hand in Yours, because just taking one more step feels impossible.

Then she looked out over the flat expanse of island as she came over the bridge and onto the Outer Banks. She would go down through Kill Devil Hills and Nags Head, and eventually come out on the windswept beaches of the southern Outer Banks. Pea Island, she thought the one island was called. She couldn't remember the rest of their names, but she did remember that there weren't a whole lot of houses between there and Ocracoke.

Whispering Hope Harbor was a good thirty miles down, but not quite to Ocracoke. And she didn't need a ferry to get there. It was one of the only small towns between Kill Devil Hills and the ferry to Ocracoke.

There was a church, a grocery store, a diner, and several dozen houses. Most of them with permanent residents.

One thing there wasn't was any real estate for sale. And the stuff that was for rent was way too expensive for her. If Beulah would not allow her to stay, Quincy would have no choice but to turn around and come back.

The idea was disheartening, but she couldn't allow herself to dwell on the negative. She had to think positively. God was going to work this out. She just had to follow Him. There would be a place for her, whether it was on the Outer Banks or somewhere else. And this was going to work out for God's glory and her good. He promised. She just couldn't see how.

seven

AS THE SUN SET, Quincy crossed the bridge into Whispering Hope Harbor. The sky looked like cotton candy, as delicate pink clouds floated gently in a powder blue sky.

It was a glorious sunset, with the entire sky showing off the colors of God's creation.

Used to living in the mountains as she was, she didn't always get to see a huge sky and the sunset, since the trees and houses blocked it.

How different this was going to be.

She had a window cracked, and the fresh sea air seeped in, filling her lungs and maybe giving her a little extra courage as Beulah's weathered cottage came into view. Her mother-in-law sat on the porch, slowly rocking in one of the white rocking chairs, freshly planted flowers in the planters on the banisters.

She did not look happy. But then again, Quincy couldn't remember too many times when Beulah did look happy. She was a bit of an austere woman. Her silver hair worn in a practical bob, her face weathered but still handsome, and those sharp blue eyes that missed nothing. She was a sturdy woman, built that way from years of work. And that was one thing that Quincy could definitely give her. She was a hard worker.

She had started her cleaning business, Beulah's Best, fifty years prior, around the time Derek had been born, when Sonny's fishing boat had been damaged and he'd been out of work. She needed to earn money to pay the bills, and she had. Eventually, her cleaning business had done so much better than the fishing that Sonny had sold the boat and helped her. Now, with his Parkinson's and dementia, she was the one who needed help.

The town of Whispering Hope Harbor sat on a wider part of the island, off the main road, just out of sight of the main road. If Quincy remembered correctly, one could still hear traffic going by. Although the only traffic was on its way to Ocracoke, or back, and there wasn't a whole lot. Even in the summer. Although things were much busier then.

She pulled slowly into the extra parking place beside the house, said a small prayer, asking for courage and favor with Beulah, and then pulled the latch and got out.

What was the worst that could happen? Beulah would tell her to leave, and she would get in her car, drive back to Nags Head, find a hotel for the night, and figure out what to do in the morning. It would not be the end of the world. *That* had happened yesterday when her husband walked out.

She almost laughed at the thought. That was not going to be the end of the world, although... it still felt like it. He hadn't called all day. She had checked her phone multiple times, hoping that he'd text or at least ask about her. How could he go from being married to her and seeing her every day, to not caring whether or not she made the ten-hour drive to Whispering Hope Harbor and whether or not she was okay?

She walked to the front of the house and gave Beulah a smile as she paused at the bottom of the steps. Should she walk up? It would be that much further she would have to go if Beulah sent her packing. But she didn't want to stand at the bottom of the steps and look up to have this conversation while Beulah looked down on her.

And there was the confused look on her face, as she was clearly expecting Derek.

"Good evening," Quincy said. "It's beautiful here. That sky. Those colors. God is amazing."

Beulah looked at the sky in surprise, as though she hadn't even noticed the sunset. Wasn't that what she was out here watching?

If Quincy lived here, that's where she would've been, or walking on the sound side of the island, which was more peaceful than the ocean side with the waves crashing all the time, although there was a majesty in that that inspired her and energized her and gave her... joy.

"I guess it is nice," Beulah said, confirming the fact that she hadn't been paying attention to it. "I was expecting you guys several hours ago." She leaned over and looked behind Quincy as though Derek was set to pop out any moment. "Where's my son?"

"Well, that's probably why I'm later than you expected. I drove myself. And I stopped a lot more than we would have if Derek had been driving."

"Where's my son?" Beulah asked again, and her comment wasn't welcoming. There was a hint of suspicion, as though Quincy had left him back in West Virginia, buried under the front porch or something.

"You haven't talked to him?"

"I sent him a text yesterday, asking him when you guys would be here, and he never answered me."

Her tone was accusing, as though it was Quincy's fault that Derek hadn't answered.

"I found out yesterday after we closed on the house that he was leaving me for the realtor, Candy."

This was Beulah's son. She loved him. Quincy did not want to speak badly of him, but there was no way she could dress that up as anything other than the truth.

"I was shocked. I did not see it coming. I'm sorry that I wasn't able to warn you, or to make other arrangements. We just closed on the house and... this was where we were planning on going, so... I've been doing what we planned."

"I see. Where is Derek staying?"

"I don't know. I haven't heard from him since he stood on the sidewalk outside of the lawyer's office and told me that he was moving in with Candy. I assume her apartment? But I don't know."

Her words were soft, and she tried to keep the hurt out of them. Her whole heart and chest felt like they were on fire, and the pain from yesterday was bright and fresh and hard and made her sick to her stomach. It reminded her that she hadn't eaten anything all day. She just hadn't been hungry. The hotel had offered a breakfast, and she'd taken a yogurt and forced herself to take a spoonful, but afraid she was going to throw up, she'd thrown the rest in the trash and walked out.

"You guys hadn't been fighting?"

"No. I thought we were getting along just fine. We talked about the house, talked about normal things. I guess looking back I can see that we weren't as close as maybe we had been ten years ago, but it was a gradual thing to me. And even so, I didn't feel like I was particularly estranged from him. So no. No fighting, nothing along those lines. Nothing to warn me at all. I was... taken completely by surprise."

"I'm surprised too. You guys have been married for twenty-five years?"

"Almost," Quincy nodded. Her whole future depended on the good graces of this woman. This woman who was supposed to be her mother-in-law, but who felt more like a stranger. Although she did admire her for what she had done with her business, how she had raised her children, and now, taking care of her husband.

"So what are you going to do now?" Beulah asked, like she hadn't been planning on giving Quincy and Derek a room and having them stay and help her.

Quincy tried not to blink or act surprised. She also tried to project confidence, but not arrogance.

"I thought I would stay with you. You need help with Sonny, you need help in your cleaning business. I told you I would help, and I mean to keep my word." Then, even though she didn't want to, she added one more sentence. "But if you don't want me to stay, I understand."

After all, if Randall cheated on his wife and left her, would she want her daughter-in-law to move in with her and keep Randall from visiting? She loved her son, even if he made a horrible, terrible, world-shattering mistake like that. But... would she cut her daughter-in-law off? She hoped not. But she couldn't say for sure. If she had to choose between her daughter-in-law who had done nothing wrong, and keeping a relationship with her son who had come out of her body and who she had raised from the time he drew his first breath, she wasn't sure she could choose the one who was innocent.

Before Beulah could answer, the screen door rattled, and Sonny shuffled out onto the porch.

He had aged greatly in the year since Quincy had seen him, walking with a cane, his gray hair wispy in the wind, his eyes slightly dim, and his face with several days of stubble on it.

He looked old and frail, and nothing like the vibrant and funny man she remembered from earlier in her marriage.

This was something she wanted to talk to Derek about immediately. If he were here, they would retire to their room and discuss how his father had changed and gotten older, and she would've felt bad for Derek, and he would've said that he was so glad that they decided to come and help and that he got to spend time with him before he passed.

"Don't worry about it if he doesn't recognize you. He's less and less in reality these days." Beulah spoke out of the side of her mouth as Sonny stepped out, allowed the door to close behind him, and used his cane to take several more steps onto the porch until he stood beside the chair Beulah had been sitting in.

"Hello, Sonny," Quincy said, not expecting the man to even look at her, let alone recognize her. He looked nothing like what she remembered.

"Quincy. I thought you'd never get here. Beulah kept saying that you'd be here to give her a hand. She needs it, now that I can't help as much as I used to."

His voice was just an echo of its former self, but he recognized her!

She had seen Beulah's eyes open wide with surprise, and then a little bit of hope. Like... maybe he would get better instead of worse. But everyone knew that dementia didn't get better.

"Yes. I'm here to help your wife if she needs me. With whatever she needs." She smiled and nodded at Sonny, who put a hand out and grabbed a hold of her forearm. It wasn't a handshake, it wasn't a hug, but it was a touch of another human, a connection, and it made her want to cry. Someone cared.

"Well, go get your things. You know where the spare room is, and we were just going to have sandwiches for supper. So nothing fancy."

"Are you sure?" She forced herself to ask, although she wanted to turn around and run to the car. There was a part of her that wanted to get in it, and leave. But where was she going to go? What was she going to do? She wanted to curl in a ball and dissolve in a puddle of pain. But she couldn't. She had to keep living somehow.

She glanced at Beulah, lifting her brows in question.

Beulah nodded a shallow, almost imperceptible nod.

It was enough. She was allowed to stay. The relief was instant.

"Thank you. You're right. We stayed in the spare room when we came last year. I'll get my stuff settled, and then I'll give you a hand with supper."

"If you drove all the way from West Virginia, you're tired. Don't worry about helping tonight. Tomorrow is enough time to get settled and jump in and give us a hand." Sonny spoke, and while Beulah wasn't exactly nodding along, she gave a quick jerk of her head as though she were in agreement.

"I'm not very hungry." Quincy figured she might as well be honest. She probably wasn't going to eat any supper.

"Breakfast is at six sharp. If you miss supper, that's the next meal." Beulah's voice didn't have much compassion in it. But Quincy honestly wasn't expecting much from that quarter. She was cognizant enough to know that there might be a choice to make between Quincy and Derek, and she wasn't sure who Beulah would choose.

Interesting that Sonny hadn't noticed that his son wasn't there. Or hadn't thought to ask about it.

"I'd like to help you," Sonny said, but he made no move to walk forward, and Quincy shook her head.

"Don't worry about it. I don't have much anyway. We didn't figure there was much point in bringing a whole lot of stuff with us."

Why was she saying "us" and "we"?

But she knew. When she decided to pack light, it was because she and Derek had talked about it and decided together to pack light. To leave and sell and give away most of their things. After all, they weren't exactly at the age where they needed to start downsizing, but there was no point in doing a lot of extra work to take things with them that they would eventually have to unload. It had been hard to leave some of the sentimental things behind, but that was life.

She had no idea when she was packing up that she would be leaving her husband behind.

The sky had darkened, the sun completely gone, and a soft breeze lifted her hair as she walked to the car. The first hurdle was over. Beulah had allowed her to stay. For how long, Quincy wasn't sure, but she knew that, despite her broken heart and the pain she still felt so deeply she could hardly breathe, this was her purpose in life right now, and with everything she had, she was supposed to help these two people who had raised the man she had married and whom she had loved for more than two decades.

eight

QUINCY LOOKED around the small room that would be her home for the foreseeable future. She had unpacked her clothes, put them in the dresser drawers, put a couple of the keepsakes she brought along with pictures of her children on top of the dresser. The pictures she brought had Derek in them too. She hadn't considered unpacking and trying to find different pictures, or going to the storage unit where they had put all the things they weren't taking, and trying to find pictures that only had her children in them, not her husband.

She'd brought a family picture. Derek and she were sitting in front, with the twins behind them, Randall's hand on Derek's shoulder and Stacey's hand on hers.

It was her favorite picture they'd ever taken, taken when the twins were seniors in high school.

Maybe it wasn't her favorite picture. There were so many family portraits they had done over the years, when the kids were little, elementary school age, junior high, when both of them had braces and acne and begged her not to display the pictures on the wall.

She loved those pictures though. The ones that showed that her family was growing and wasn't perfect, but was trying.

Except... they weren't trying anymore, apparently.

Taking the picture, she set it face down on the dresser. However this worked out, she hoped that she could stop feeling pain every time she looked at Derek. Stop feeling this feeling of disbelief.

Her Bible was on the nightstand, and as she pulled the covers back and settled down in bed, she got it and set it on her lap, running her hand over the worn cover, the familiar feel, the knowledge that everything God wanted for her was contained within its pages. Opening it was like visiting with an old friend, which was how Jesus felt to her. An old friend, except here she was going through the most difficult time of her life, and one thing Jesus never experienced was divorce.

But He knew about loss. He knew about suffering. He knew about family. Betrayal.

Her phone buzzed, and despite herself, she got excited. Her heart started hammering, and hope blossomed in her chest.

Maybe this was Derek texting her to let her know that he'd changed his mind. That he wasn't leaving their family, that he wanted to try to patch things up and put things back together.

She wasn't so naïve as to believe that it was all going to be peaches and cream once that happened, but she would take him back. She wanted her family, her dreams, her hopes, the plans they had for their life. She wanted her best friend back. Derek wasn't perfect, far from it, but he was her best friend.

With trembling fingers, she picked up her phone and turned it over.

It was from Derek!

She swiped the phone on as she tried to contain her excitement. Maybe he'd changed his mind. Maybe he was at least concerned about her, and was asking how she was, if she'd made it safely, saying they needed to get a plan together, or even better, that he was on his way down and would be there this evening!

Where would he sleep?

She shoved that thought out of her head. If he was coming, they would figure it out. She could forgive. Sure, it would be hard to forget, and hard to trust again, but she would do it. She really, really wanted her family to stay together.

It took a moment for her eyes to focus on the text.

Her heart sank, and her throat closed, and it felt like she sank deeper into the mattress as she read.

Our divorce doesn't have to be complicated. I'd like it to be as simple and straightforward and quick as we can make it. I have the basics drawn up, and I'm willing to meet you somewhere near here to go over them tomorrow or the next day.

Quincy blinked. That was it? Divorce? Papers? No "Did you make it okay? That was a long ride, and I normally drive." No "How's Mom?" or "Dad?" Or... he didn't ask about the kids. Didn't mention whether he'd told them or not. Didn't even mention that he hadn't told his parents. Didn't ask if she did.

There were so many questions that ran through her mind. If he was intent on going through this, there were so many things they were going to have to figure out, people they were going to have to tell, who was breaking the news to everyone?

She took a breath. She knew she should answer him. Ask all of those questions, try to get something worked out, but she wrote back with the only thing that she could think of to say.

I don't want a divorce.

nine

QUINCY BLINKED her blurry eyes and looked at the clock. 5:30 AM. It was finally time to get up. She wasn't sure if she'd slept at all after she had sent her text message to her husband, with all the feelings swirling in her chest, rejection, grief, anger, fear and loss, like this person who had been her best friend didn't even care if she was okay. All he cared about was the divorce and splitting everything equally.

He had come back with

> We can do this the easy way or the hard way. I prefer the easy way. Tell me when you can meet to go over the papers.

She hadn't responded. She wasn't driving back. She thought about the terror she felt in the tunnel coming to the Outer Banks, and thought about going back through that same tunnel, under the water, dealing with the panic, and decided that even if she did want to meet him, she just didn't have that in her right now. She had too many other things she had to deal with. She was scared to death. She'd have a major panic attack in the middle of the tunnel, cause an accident, and kill a bunch of people, including herself.

She wasn't going to drive back. Not to look at papers, and not unless there was some kind of major emergency that would necessitate her having to figure out how to deal with her panic. But for now, one thing at a time. She had to deal with the emotions and feelings this major rejection from her husband brought, and the idea of being divorced and splitting up her family and her future not being what she thought it was going to be. That was enough for anyone to deal with at a time.

Plus, she had her mother-in-law that she had to figure out. Beulah hadn't been unkind the day before, but she hadn't been overly welcoming either, especially when she found out her son wasn't with Quincy.

Beulah had mentioned that breakfast would be at six o'clock.

By the time Quincy had gotten up, brushed her teeth, and gotten dressed, it was 5:52. She hoped to make herself useful, and perhaps that could begin by helping with breakfast.

But she smelled bacon frying as she walked out of her room and heard murmurs from the kitchen.

The cottage wasn't overly large, with just three small bedrooms, a great room that doubled as a living room and dining room with an open kitchen, and a bar dividing the kitchen from the rest of the house. The second floor held two bedrooms and a bathroom between them. Quincy's bedroom was on the right, and the one on the left was closed. She hadn't opened the door to see if it was actually a bedroom, or if Beulah was using it for storage or something else.

Not that it mattered, unless Derek came and needed a place to sleep.

Of course, the couch looked comfortable, and Quincy would sleep there before she would share a room with her husband until they had things straightened out.

That's okay, isn't it, Lord?

She swallowed. She knew the Bible taught forgiveness, but... was a person allowed to deal with the pain they felt before they forgave?

Or did they have to forgive immediately?

Maybe that was a question she wouldn't have to deal with, since Derek hadn't exactly asked for forgiveness.

"Good morning," she said, hoping she sounded cheerful, but knowing she looked terrible.

Sonny looked up from where he sat at the table, a newspaper open in front of him.

"Good morning," he said, looking a little confused, like he didn't recognize her this morning.

"Morning," Beulah said briskly, as she cracked several eggs into a bowl.

"Can I help with something?" Quincy asked, as she came and stood on the other side of the bar, her hands on the counter, ready to do anything Beulah asked.

"I didn't get the garbage taken out this morning, and the garbage guy will be here shortly. Just set it by the mailbox."

She nodded, happy to have a job.

"Is this the only garbage that needs to be emptied?"

"I didn't even check the bathrooms," Beulah said, sounding a little distracted.

"I can do it. Do you keep the bags anywhere specific?"

Beulah told her where they were, and she emptied the one in the kitchen, tied it, and set it outside the door, before sticking a bag back in and then going to the bathroom.

She recalled that the garbage cans upstairs in both her bedroom and the bathroom had been completely empty, so she didn't worry about them.

The one in the bathroom was only three-quarters full, but she decided to empty it anyway. She remembered Beulah being very frugal, but she didn't think that frugality meant that a person swam in trash just to save a trash bag, so she emptied that one as well, and then carried them both to the curb by the mailbox.

Just in time too, as the truck pulled up before she was able to turn around and start walking back.

She picked the bags back up and walked to the back where a tough-looking guy hung on, dropping down as the truck slowed.

"Morning," she said cheerfully.

"Good morning. It's beautiful today."

She didn't feel beautiful inside, but just lifting her face to the wind, smelling the salt air, and knowing that she was by the ocean, lifted her spirits more than she would've thought. Had Beulah known that she needed to step outside and let the fresh air and sunshine do their work?

She hardly thought Beulah was that perceptive, but maybe she wasn't giving the woman enough credit.

"It sure is. I can't think of anything else I'd rather do than live here by the ocean and get to ride down the road with the wind in my face. I'll be surfing later today." The guy grinned and winked as he took the garbage from her, thanking her.

She nodded and smiled. There was someone who loved their job, loved their life, and seemed happy.

She didn't even look to see if he had a ring. He seemed older than she was anyway, although he'd mentioned surfing, and she thought that sport belonged to the young.

Not that she thought of herself as old, just too old to surf.

She waved a hand before she turned and started walking back to the house.

The walk and the air had done her good, and she felt a little better as she stepped inside.

She walked to the sink and squirted some soap on her hands, rubbing them together as she asked, "Thank you for giving me that job. A little walk outside was the perfect way to start the day. Is there anything else I can do? "

Beulah had been walking to the refrigerator, but she stopped with her hand on the handle.

"That's true. Going outside really does help. Makes me feel better when I'm a little down."

Quincy paused, her thoughts jerking to a stop. Beulah got down?

She just seemed like the kind of person who put her head down and worked and did whatever was in front of her. She didn't remember Derek ever saying that his mom got depressed at all.

But she supposed that maybe life did seem a little hard, especially with Sonny not being well, and dementia wasn't something that a person got over. The future looked bleak.

"Maybe I'll get up earlier tomorrow so I can take an actual walk. But I'll try to remember that garbage day is Thursday and make sure I get it out there."

"All right," Beulah said, and she seemed almost happy. Maybe she was happy to have one of her jobs taken off her shoulders. Or happy to have a little bit of help.

She set a cup on the table and then motioned to a place on the opposite side of Sonny.

"You can sit down. All I need to do is put the eggs on the table then we're ready."

Quincy nodded, sitting where Beulah had told her to, and bowing her head as Beulah sat down and said grace.

The few times she'd eaten with Beulah and Sonny before, Sonny had been the one to say it, and she wondered at the change. Was he so far gone that he didn't know how to pray anymore?

She didn't ask about it, but helped pass the plates and dishes around until everyone was served.

They ate in silence until Beulah said, "I need to check on the business today, but my normal caretaker, Jackie, can't come. So I guess I won't be able to."

Quincy paused with a forkful of egg halfway to her mouth. She had no appetite, but she thought it would be rude if she didn't eat, and so she was forcing bites down, even though they tasted like nothing and felt like sawdust and she'd already drunk three-quarters of a glass of water just trying to get the stuff to go down her throat.

"I'm not sure what that entails, but if you think I can handle it, I'd be happy to stay so you can go."

She thought maybe it was a hint, but the way Beulah's head

jerked up, her gray hair swinging softly by her ears, it probably wasn't.

"Do you think you could do that?"

"I think so. I had trained to be a nurse years ago, although it's been years since I worked in that capacity."

"That's right. I'd forgotten. Well, I can show you what Jackie usually does. It's not hard. It's just... you have to be here, and you can't leave. I don't even go shopping unless someone can watch him anymore."

"All right."

Did Derek know how far his dad had sunk?

The thought came before she could stop it. Derek wanted a divorce. He didn't want to stay together. She shouldn't care what he thought. But she did. She couldn't just turn off her caring and not give a flip anymore.

Unlike him, apparently.

No. She didn't want to get bitter. She didn't want to allow those unkind thoughts and feelings to sneak in. She didn't want to be that person.

But it was going to be hard, she knew. After all, once she figured out for sure that Derek wasn't coming back, she was bound to be angry at him. Angry for everything that he had done, and more angry than what she was now.

"After we're done here with breakfast, I can show you what needs to be done with Sonny."

"All right. I can do the dishes too. I didn't bring a whole lot to keep myself occupied, because I thought I was going to be helping you, so I need things to do."

She wasn't going to beg; that was as close as she was going to come. She pretty much needed to stay busy, or she was going to go insane thinking about her husband.

"There's more than enough to keep everyone busy. Things have fallen behind at the business, with me being unable to do anything unless I have someone to care for Sonny, I have let a lot of things go."

"All right. That's why I'm here. To do whatever I can to help you. So just give me jobs."

She wasn't thinking about money. But she probably needed to. They had planned to invest the money from the sale of the house, and then live on the interest. And Beulah had said that they could both work in her business. They figured that they wouldn't need a whole lot of money. They were downsizing, not buying new stuff.

She wasn't going to worry about that right now either. Derek wanted to get everything figured out, but... she just didn't think she was going to be able to sign papers and end it that easily. When she had made her vows, she had meant for better or for worse.

But there was nothing in the vows to say what she should do if her husband no longer wanted her.

Sonny didn't say much during the meal, seeming to have trouble following any conversation that they had. He had a look of almost perpetual confusion on his face.

She'd seen various dementia patients, knew they went in and out of lucidity, and also knew that each one handled it slightly differently. Some people got angry and frustrated, some got quiet, and some just seemed gently confused. Sonny seemed to fall into that last category, thankfully. She wasn't sure if she could handle an angry Sonny.

His care routine didn't seem to be that hard, and after Beulah finished explaining everything to her, Quincy said, "I think I can handle it. And I have your number in case I can't. How far away are you going to be?"

"I clean houses all up and down the Outer Banks. I actually have two really big accounts that are up in Kill Devil Hills. It's quite a drive, but they pay really well. Unfortunately, they take the entire day to clean, and it's been hard to keep help."

"Normally they turn around in a day, don't they?"

"Yes. People can check out at ten and check in at four. So you have six hours to clean. It's nice because you don't have to worry about starting too early in the morning, but... when I don't have help, that's an awful lot of cleaning to try to get done in six hours."

"Do you get penalized if you don't get it done in time?"

"Not unless I'm really late. Every once in a while, I can't get it done and people will complain, but the homeowners know that finding help is hard, and finding good help is even harder. I make sure I'm good help."

"That's smart. Job security."

"Yes. Those houses are Friday and Saturday and Sunday. The other days, I clean smaller houses here."

"Right."

"I can show you about it at some point. But I need to get going now."

"All right. Thank you. Have a good day," Quincy said, wishing that the distance between Beulah and her didn't seem so far. Beulah hadn't mentioned a word about Derek, hadn't asked about him, hadn't asked how she was, or anything.

She supposed maybe she was scared, or respectful and didn't want to broach a subject she knew would be painful. Maybe she felt like she had too much stuff on her plate, with Sonny and the business that seemed to be overwhelming her, the way Quincy felt like she had too much on her plate dealing with the emotional fallout from her husband rejecting her and leaving her and cheating on her, to the point where she didn't think that she could drive back through the tunnel to look at his papers.

Maybe they all needed grace. She needed to give grace to Beulah, who was doing the best she could. Just as she needed Derek to give grace to her and not push her to look at the papers when she didn't even know if she could make the drive back.

She couldn't look to Derek and expect grace though. She knew that just because of the way he had treated her the last day and a half. If he didn't care whether or not she could make a ten-hour drive to the shore, he certainly wasn't going to care about giving her a little space to get used to the idea before she looked at the divorce papers.

She didn't even know how it worked. If she looked at the papers and signed them, would they be divorced?

She wasn't sure.

"Who are you again?" Sonny said, as she went back to the table and finished clearing off the rest of the dishes.

"I'm your daughter-in-law. Derek's wife. Quincy."

"Quincy. Have I seen you before?" Sonny asked, squinting at her like he couldn't see her very well.

"We've met a few times, yes. But it's okay. You don't have to remember me."

"Good. Because I don't. I think I'd remember a cute little thing like you."

She wasn't cute, nor little, but she smiled anyway.

"You probably would have," she said. A lot of times she felt like it was just best to agree with a dementia patient, if they weren't doing anything that was going to harm them. If he decided that he was going to be walking out of his house and heading off down the road somewhere, she was probably going to have to put up a fight, but correcting him about minor details seemed silly.

Sonny nodded his head, and then tilted it to the side, his bushy eyebrows swaying gently as his head moved.

"You have kind eyes. Just like my mom's."

Quincy blinked. When was the last time someone had given her a compliment? She felt like she was surrounded by cold, impartial people who didn't really care about her, and she wanted to put her arms around the old gentleman and kiss his cheek.

But her hands were full of dirty dishes as she straightened from the table, ready to carry them to the sink.

"Thank you. That was very kind of you. I'm sure your mom was a very nice lady."

"She was. She kept us in line, that's for sure, but she was a good woman. A moral woman. Hard to find those kind nowadays."

"It sure is," Quincy thought. Only she added in her head that it was hard to find a moral man.

61

ten

TAKING care of Sonny was not that hard, and she had too much time to think. So that evening, when Beulah came home, she offered to go grocery shopping.

She didn't have a ton of money in her account, but she did have some. The money for the house had been going into their account that was linked to their investments, while the checking account that they had used for household expenses was at a different bank.

She wasn't quite sure how they had ended up with accounts like that, but regardless, she wasn't worried about spending the money they had planned to invest. She didn't even know where they were going with that. Although, she had been overcome with some really dark thoughts in the late afternoon and had checked all the accounts to make sure that Derek hadn't drained them all.

He hadn't touched anything, other than gas and several restaurant bills.

Apparently, Candy wasn't much of a cook.

No. She wasn't going to think little catty thoughts like that. She pushed back on the idea and was able to pull herself out of the funk before she spiraled down into man-bashing depression.

Still, she was grateful that Beulah made her a quick list of groceries and told her to take her time, that they wouldn't start making supper for another hour at least because Beulah wanted to lie down for a bit.

Sonny snored in a chair, and Quincy figured that it would be fine for her to take her time. Maybe walk around the town a bit and meet some people.

She tucked the grocery list in her pocket and walked out the front door, the air feeling rejuvenating, just as it had before.

The Whispering Hope Diner was just a block and a half down the street, and a half a block before she got to the grocery store.

The smell of coffee and the sight of a waitress smiling and laughing drew her inside.

She had an hour, and grabbing the groceries wouldn't take that long. She could sit here for thirty minutes, drink a coffee, and... maybe make a friend.

A cheerful bell jingled over her head as she opened the door and stepped inside.

"Howdy, sweet lady!" The waitress, a cheerful-looking woman with well-defined laugh lines, who looked to be in her mid-fifties, greeted Quincy as she walked in.

"You can sit anywhere you want, and I'll be with you in a minute." She grinned, exposing dimples, as she nodded and then bustled off to take the order of a couple sitting at a booth by the window. Her gray hair was pulled back, probably to keep it out of folks' food, but the ponytail swished, and it looked like her hair might fall to her waist if it were down. It was streaked with gray, but looked thick and full and pretty.

She was slender, but not teenage thin, and had a stride that ate up the ground.

There was an energy around her, an aura that spoke of friendliness and kindness, and, Quincy felt like she was the kind of person that she could tell her whole life story to, and who would actually care.

There was just a warmth and caring about her that a person felt as they stepped into her presence.

Quincy shook her head. Maybe she was just so desperate for someone to be kind to her that she was projecting things on people that weren't there.

It was quite possible, although she hoped her first impression was true, and the woman would turn out to be a friend.

She settled herself at the bar and pulled her phone out.

No new messages.

At least Derek wasn't harassing her to go sign the papers. But he wasn't sending any messages showing that he cared about her either.

Did she need to get over him? Did she need to let him go?

Part of her wanted to just drop him, move on with her life, and forget there was such a thing as a Derek, getting everything she could out of her marriage, every single penny she was owed.

Another part of her wanted to hold on, hope that he came to his senses, hope that what they had together, and the wife that she had been to him, would somehow come to the surface and jerk him out of this haze that he must be in when he saw Candy.

"Hey there, I'm Shiloh, and I'll be your waitress. Can I get you something?"

"It's nice to meet you, Shiloh. I'd like a coffee, black, please."

"Coming right up. You new in town, or just passing through?" she asked as she turned and grabbed the coffee pot and then a cup from under the counter, flipping it over and setting it down right side up before she carefully poured the hot, steaming coffee into it.

It smelled like heaven. Beulah hadn't made coffee that morning, and she'd had a low-grade headache all day because she hadn't gotten her caffeine fix.

"I'm new in town. I moved in with Sonny and Beulah. I watched Sonny today, but I think I'm going to be helping Beulah with her business." She paused for a moment, but she knew, this being a small town, anyone who knew anyone would eventually find out this next part, although she really didn't want to say it. "I'm her daughter-in-law."

"Oh. Her daughter-in-law. She's mentioned you a few times when they've been in. You're married to her son, Derek, right?"

"That's right. He... left me."

Somehow it hadn't gotten easier to say those words. But she also thought it was okay to tell Shiloh, even though she hadn't told her children yet. She needed to figure that out. Someone was going to need to tell them before they found out from someone else.

"Oh. I'm so sorry." Shiloh shook her head. "But you're living with his parents now?" Her voice held a little bit of uncertainty and a bit of disbelief.

"Yeah. We had been in the process of selling our house, and we had planned to come help his mother, who is taking care of Sonny, who has dementia."

"Yeah, that's too bad. He was such a sweet old man, always a gentleman, always willing to help with anything. A handyman, and he told great stories too. Still does, but he doesn't always know who he's talking to."

"Yeah. That's exactly how I knew him too." It was funny—he was the sweet, kind side of the relationship, and Beulah was the harder, less happy, more moody side. They fit together perfectly, with Sonny always gently teasing Beulah out of her bad moods.

"So anyway, Derek told me after we closed on our house that he wouldn't be coming with me. Apparently he fell for the realtor."

"You're kidding me?" Shiloh said, shaking her head, her brows drawn, and immediately Quincy felt like Shiloh was totally on her side. "That's terrible. She's probably a twenty-year-old kid too."

"Yes. She's almost the same age as our twins. In fact, our twins might be a little older."

"What's wrong with men? Why do they do these kinds of stupid things? Why can't they value longevity and a good foundation and a family that they spend a lifetime building?"

"Good question. I've been asking myself the same things, and a hundred million more."

"I totally get it. Your world's just been turned upside down. It certainly makes sense that you'd be asking yourself a lot of different questions. Is he being a jerk?" Shiloh asked, having set the coffee cup down and seeming like she had all day to sit and chat. It was funny, because Quincy wouldn't have said that she needed a good talk, but maybe it was just that Shiloh was so easy to talk to.

"Not really. I suppose not. He could be a lot worse."

"I think there's always a worse."

"Yeah. But he hasn't been awful. Except... he already has papers drawn up on how we can split our assets, and he wanted me to drive back and look at them and let him know when I could meet him back where we lived, which was ten hours away. I just got here. I've never driven that far myself, and... it was really hard when he didn't text and ask me if I got there okay. I mean, it was like he didn't care about me at all. He ditched me, and all of a sudden it was like he never knew me. Like we're not even friends. And he was my best friend."

"That's awful. You must feel so betrayed."

"I do. I feel betrayed and adrift, like I'm hoping so hard that this is a bad dream, but it doesn't seem like it is. I think it's my reality."

"Yeah, I'm not a dream. I'm flesh and blood. Lots of flesh. I don't know how much blood," Shiloh said, standing up and slapping her hips, which were ample, but not fat by any stretch of the word.

"I've got more flesh than I used to have too. I wondered if that's the problem. I'm not attractive to him anymore? I'm too fat?"

"Don't say that. I mean, men are what they are, we can't change that, but regardless of how you look, he made vows, and if he can't keep them, that's his problem. Not yours. If he didn't like the way you looked, he could've talked to you about it, although..." Shiloh gave a humorous laugh. "That probably wouldn't have gone over very well. I know I wouldn't have wanted to hear my husband talk to me about how I didn't look very good or how I could improve how I looked. I could've told him to go take a shower once in a while."

Quincy couldn't help it. She snorted.

"That was one thing I never had to worry about. He was definitely clean, almost meticulously so. Although he expected me to be that way too. Which was annoying at times, but I tried to do that, because that's what married couples do. They give and take for each other, right?"

"That's right. And if someone doesn't look exactly the way you think they should, you might encourage them to get healthy, but you don't leave them for a twenty-year-old."

eleven

BEULAH PICKED the bowl of boiled potatoes up off the table. This was not what she had planned when her son and daughter-in-law had said they were going to come live with her.

"I can get that. You worked all day, and I don't mind," Quincy said. She seemed so eager to help. It was hard for Beulah to deny her, and often she didn't. But she didn't want her to get too comfortable. After all, if Derek was going to divorce her, it would be awkward to have Quincy living here when Derek visited.

"Thank you," she said.

It was the third day that Jackie hadn't been able to make it.

"I'll be sitting out on the porch." She paused, and then glanced at Sonny. He had given her a hard time the night before because she hadn't been kind to Quincy. Not that she hadn't been kind. She hadn't been welcoming. Hospitable. He had mentioned the verse in the Bible about entertaining angels unaware.

Figures he'd be lucid when she really didn't want him to be.

Beulah was very aware of what the Bible said. But her loyalty had to lie with her son.

Didn't it? As a mother, she absolutely believed that, but as a

Christian... Quincy was the one who had been wronged. And Derek was the one in the wrong.

"All right. Maybe once I have the dishes done, I'll come out and sit down for a little bit. If that's okay?"

She nodded. "It would be nice. There's ice cream in the freezer if you'd like some."

"I saw that in there, but I hated to ask."

"Anything that's here is yours. Help yourself."

She couldn't begrudge Quincy anything. She'd done everything she could to try to help around the house. She'd mentioned getting started helping with the cleaning business, but... Beulah was reluctant.

"You're going to sit with me for a little bit, sweetie?" Sonny asked, as they walked to the front door together.

"Isn't that what we usually do in the evening?" she asked, trying to sound young and sweet again. They had always enjoyed their evenings, holding hands on the porch and watching the world wind down into nightfall. On warm summer nights, they could often hear the waves crashing on the ocean side of the island.

And if they were feeling really energetic, they might walk hand in hand on the beach, although walking on the sound side of the island was her favorite. The sunsets were gorgeous, and the water calm and almost glasslike in the evenings when the wind died down.

Sonny was having a good evening and had been lucid throughout supper.

Now, he held the door open for her with a gallant half bow as she walked through. She tapped his arm with her fingers and laughed. "You're such a flirt," she said.

He grinned at her, and she had a little glimpse of the love and laughter they used to share together.

It had been a hard life, and they had never been rich, but they'd made enough to get by on and raise their son. Plus, they got to live by the ocean, and who wouldn't love that?

"You were nicer to her tonight," Sonny said, as though he had been lucid all day. But this morning, he hadn't known who she was, and had seemed confused about who he was too. She knew, and had seen, that his times of dementia were growing longer and more frequent, while his times of knowing where he was were shorter and happened less often.

"I took what you said to heart."

He sat down on the swing, and she sat down beside him. He put his arm around her, and she shifted so that their legs touched and she was cradled under his arm. It was a familiar position, one they'd shared often over the decades they'd been married. "I always listen to you."

He snorted. "Except when you don't want to."

She thought she'd been a good, submissive wife. She tried hard to do what the Bible said and ignore what society told her to do. It was always anti-Bible, as though society had somehow figured out a better way. She'd subscribed to that notion for a while, but she had finally figured out that if she wanted to go to God when things got hard, she shouldn't ignore what He had told her to do. And since the last time she had spoken a world into existence was never, she figured that she probably ought to try to live her life God's way. That's when she'd gotten serious about obeying and submitting to her husband, even though it grated.

"You laugh, but you know I tried. It's not easy."

His hand came down on her arm, and he pulled her close, giving her a side hug and touching her temple with his lips.

"You've been a good wife."

Their marriage time was drawing to an end. The doctor had said that Sonny could live for quite a few years after the dementia completely took over his mind. So maybe she'd be married, but in name only. He would either need to be cared for full-time at a facility, or they would have to hire someone. She didn't have the money to hire anyone, and she didn't want to send him away where she would only be able to visit him when she could get away from the island. In the summer, that would be almost never.

There were drawbacks to living where she did.

Maybe she should throw in the towel. Move somewhere where she could be within walking distance of a good, long-term care facility. One that wasn't too expensive. The one in Nags Head was more than she could afford, and she definitely couldn't afford to live right beside it. Prices up there were outrageous.

Prices down here weren't much better.

"You have. And you did try to be nice to her today."

"I just... our loyalty has to be with Derek. He's our son."

"If Derek cheated on her, and then decided to leave her for another woman, he's in the wrong. All day long. And Quincy's been with Derek almost as long as Derek was with us."

But Quincy didn't come out of her body the way Derek did. She hadn't raised Quincy from a baby, nursed Quincy from the time she drew her first breath. Sent her off to kindergarten, helped her with her homework, stayed up and listened to her cough at night, wondering whether she should be taken to an emergency facility or not.

But Sonny was right. Quincy had been in the family longer than she hadn't been.

"Why don't you get her started in the cleaning business? You know you can use the help. Especially since I haven't been going lately." Sonny paused. "Why haven't I been helping you?" He tilted his head to the side and turned those beautiful baby blues on her. She'd been unable to resist them when they were young and carefree, and even now, looking into them, she felt a stirring of that old, familiar, "I'd do anything for you" feeling.

"Because you need care here at home." It was hard to deal with his shifts in and out of reality. He didn't remember anything of not knowing things when he was lucid, and when he wasn't lucid, he didn't remember anything of reality. And when he was slipping in and out, those times were really confusing.

"I want to help. You know I do. Ever since I sold my fishing boat, I've been your right-hand man."

"It's more like I've been your right-hand woman. We worked well together over the years."

That was true. They did have a little nest egg put back, but not nearly enough to pay for a long-term care facility for any amount of time.

"Let Quincy help."

She nodded, and then looked out across the scrub brush and marsh to the beach below, and out across the glassy, still surface of the sound. The sky was cotton candy colored and reflected in the water. Her absolute favorite time of day. The only thing that would make it better would be to have a big, full moon hanging low in the sky.

She didn't want to let Quincy help, for some odd reason. True, if Derek came back, it would be awkward, but it was more than that. She thought it was the idea that she might soon have to give it all up, and it could go to Quincy. She wasn't ready for that, didn't want to face that, and didn't want to even think about it. With Quincy working, she would be forced to.

But not only that, she didn't want to get too buddy-buddy with Quincy. What if she left? After all, if Derek insisted on going through with the divorce—which he hadn't said a word to either her or Sonny about, separating, being with someone else, or getting divorced. They hadn't heard from their son in over a week. But if he did, if he insisted on going through with it, Quincy would no longer be a part of their family. Would Derek still come if Quincy was around?

There were too many questions, with no answers. She hadn't thought she'd ever have to navigate something like this. Derek and Quincy had seemed as solid as a couple could be.

"You know that whatever happened with her and Derek, it's not Quincy's fault."

"I know."

They fell into silence, the creaking of the porch swing the only sound between the two of them as the wind rustled through the scrub brush and darkness slowly deepened over the little stretch of land they lived on between the sound and the ocean. Sometimes at night, especially this time, she felt so little and lost. Such a tiny speck in such a large and almost barren land.

Then she thought of her neighbors in Whispering Hope, and was heartened. There wasn't a whole lot that all of them could do together to stem any major problems, but it was the idea of not being alone.

Maybe that's what Quincy needs right now.

She wasn't sure where the thought came from, but it struck her. Quincy probably felt really alone. She'd lost her husband of more than twenty years, and she had moved away from any friends or church family that she had and was staying with the only family she really knew.

And yet, Beulah had been less than welcoming.

"I think everything's done inside," Quincy said as the door opened and she stepped out on the porch.

Beulah tried not to show how startled she was.

"Who are you, and what are you doing in our house?" Sonny asked, his voice gruff, offended.

That was how fast it switched from one side to the other. One moment he was a loving husband who was giving her gentle, godly advice the way he'd done throughout their whole marriage, and the next second, he was a stranger, angry and belligerent and not recognizing anyone.

"And who are you?" he asked, looking at Beulah like he'd never seen her before in his life. "We must know each other, since you're all snuggled up to me. Unless you're a loose woman?"

"No. You might not remember right now, but we're married. And have been for quite some time."

She saw the pity cross Quincy's face, and it bothered her. She didn't want people to pity her, but if their situation were reversed, she would pity Quincy.

She supposed if Quincy talked about having her husband leave, she would pity her then too. At least Sonny had never left her. At least not physically. Mentally, he was slowly putting more distance between them every day.

It wasn't the same though, and she knew it. Except... she was closer to the end of her life than Quincy, and this was the beginning of the end for her. Quincy, on the other hand, could find love again.

"Since you're here, you might as well sit down," Sonny said, after Quincy had frozen at his question.

She gave a little smile, and then glanced at Beulah as though for confirmation that it would be okay to do so.

Beulah nodded. Usually Sonny wasn't angry or mean. Just confused.

"It's so pretty out here," Quincy said as she sat in the rocking chair on the other side of the porch.

"It's a great place to think. To relax after working hard all day. I don't think I would enjoy it nearly as much if I weren't so tired and busy. There's just something about resting after hard work that makes a person feel good."

"I agree. A little relief from the burdens of the day before you go in and try to sleep."

She took a trembling breath. She was going to try to reach out to her daughter-in-law, even though they'd never had a great relationship, and she wasn't sure where they stood now.

"Are you sleeping okay?"

twelve

QUINCY TRIED NOT to blink in shock. Her mother-in-law was asking about her? She'd been here for three days, and her mother-in-law had not broached the subject at all.

"I guess. Better than I was anyway. I'm not crying all night, which is an improvement over the first night anyway." She tried to make her voice light, like she was joking, but she wasn't, not even a little bit. It was true that she wasn't crying, but... she definitely wasn't back to normal. Not even close.

"Have you heard from him?"

"No. Not since the first day I was here when he told me that he wanted me to come back to look at the papers that he had drawn up and sign them. I didn't tell him I would, because I have no intention of driving back."

"He wanted you to drive back?" Beulah asked, sounding shocked. Like she was wondering what kind of son she had raised.

"Yeah. He did. And I had just driven here. It's ten hours."

"Yeah, that's quite a drive. Have you ever made it by yourself before?"

"No. It was my first time, and I wasn't sure I could do it. I was afraid of the ten hours behind the wheel, which wasn't terrible. But what really got me was the tunnel under the water. I almost had a panic attack, and I am not eager to go back through." She paused for a moment, wondering whether she should share with her mother-in-law, and then figuring that her mother-in-law had started the conversation and seemed to be reaching out, she could respond in kind. "I'm scared that I'm going to have a panic attack in the middle of it and cause a big accident. I think I need to stop talking about it and stop thinking about that, because I'm pretty sure that I'm not going to be able to do it if I keep focusing on all the bad things that could happen."

"I've always heard that that's a bad idea. We're supposed to imagine positive outcomes."

"That feels like lying to myself. But I guess I've been doing it a lot lately, because I keep expecting Derek to call or text or show up, telling me that he wants me back, that he made a big mistake, and that he can't imagine life without me, or at least that he doesn't want to break up our family."

"Would you take him back?" she asked. Her voice sounded hopeful.

"I think so." She tapped her finger on the arm of the rocking chair. "I suppose it's something that evolves in my head. I go from being really angry at him, to being really hurt that he would cheat on me, to just wanting it to be over with. To be able to start my life again before I get any older. But... if he came back, I know it would be hard, but yeah. For the sake of our twins, for you guys, because I don't want my life to be totally trashed and the last two decades to be worthless, yes. I'd want to put our family back together."

That was all true. But she wasn't sure she would be able to do it if Derek weren't repentant and sorry and willing to change. She didn't want to have a relationship where she was constantly afraid that her husband was going to cheat on her again. But should she be the one to call the shots?

"I've been thinking about what the Bible says, and I'm not entirely sure what the right thing to do is."

"Meaning?" her mother-in-law said gently. It was a completely different tone than Beulah had ever used on her before. It made her feel like she cared about her. Was that true? She hoped so, because it felt like there were very few people in her life that cared right now, with Shiloh at the diner being one. She hadn't been back to the diner, though.

"Meaning, I'm not sure what God wants me to do. Whether God wants me to just sign whatever papers Derek puts in front of me. Should I? Or should I fight for our marriage? Should I fight for our family? Should I fight for the vows that we made, hoping that he'll come to his senses and come back? Because if I sign those papers, I'm moving on. I'm not going to sit around and hope that Derek comes back, and if he does... I don't think I would take him. I would say, you made your choice. I just... I don't know what to do."

"Shouldn't you do what you want to do?" she asked. "Do you know what that is?"

Quincy's head dropped, and she looked at her lap for a moment. And then, in a small voice, she said, "I don't think, as a Christian, that I'm supposed to ask myself what I want. I'm supposed to ask, what does God want? And then, to the best of my ability, I'm supposed to do that. I figured that much out over the last three days anyway. But my problem is, God seems to be silent. He doesn't seem to be telling me what to do. I've been begging Him to show me, to let me know, but... I don't know. That's the other part of the reason why I haven't agreed to Derek's suggestion that I go sign papers." And then a question occurred to her. "Has he been in contact with you?"

"No. He hasn't said anything to either one of us. And I didn't message him. I guess he probably knows that we know, if he knows that you're here?"

"He never asked if I got here safely, never asked if I was still coming. I suppose he knows that I stayed in the hotel that we booked the night we signed the papers, but I never told him what I was doing after that." She lifted a shoulder. "He doesn't seem to care."

Beulah looked absolutely aghast.

"I'm sorry. Sometimes I wonder what kind of child I raised. That he could be so terrible."

"Don't be too hard on yourself. Sometimes kids don't turn out despite the best their parents can do. I don't know your son, but you seem like a really nice person. And you don't want to live with that guilt." Sonny patted Beulah's knee.

A surge of pity, similar to the one that she'd felt just a little earlier, went through Quincy at the sight. Beulah was dealing with her own problems in her marriage. Not Quincy-shaped problems, but problems nonetheless, and just as large. And now, she had issues with her son too. That must be just as hard to deal with.

"I'm sorry I brought all this on you. You'd still be living in oblivion if I had decided to do something else."

"Sometimes it's better to face problems head-on. And the fact of the matter is, I truly do need help with the cleaning service. Jackie is supposed to be coming tomorrow. Would you like to go with me to clean?"

"I would love to."

"I can show you the schedule and stuff tonight. It's in a little bit of disarray. I'm not used to having to do my job and Sonny's job as well."

"Sonny? Who's that?" Sonny asked.

"He's someone that I work with. He used to help me a lot, and he doesn't help so much anymore," Beulah said gently. Like she wasn't surprised that Sonny asked that question about himself. Although it had shocked Quincy.

"He shouldn't leave you high and dry like that. Give me his number. I'll give him a call for you."

"Thank you. I appreciate your help," Beulah said easily. "But this is my favorite time of night. Can we sit here and enjoy it for a little bit?"

"I've got a cute girl under my arm. I'll sit here as long as you want, sweetie."

Beulah smiled and snuggled deeper into Sonny's embrace.

Quincy looked away. She had wanted to grow old with Derek. She had thought someday they would be sitting on the porch, each of them helping each other in their old age, but that wasn't the way her life was going to be. She wasn't going to have a fiftieth wedding anniversary. She wasn't even going to have a thirtieth. She wasn't going to have an intact family. She was going to become a statistic. One of the fifty percent of Christians whose marriages did not last.

It hardly seemed fair, because she wanted her marriage to last. She wasn't the one who had left it, and she would still try to repair it if she could. But Derek had determined that she would be a statistic, and she didn't have any more say in it.

They sat out for a little while, and then Beulah allowed her to help put Sonny to bed.

Once they had him in bed with the lights turned down, Beulah took her back out to the great room.

"I don't know if you've looked in the spare room upstairs, but that's where I have my desk set up and supplies stored. It's a pain in the butt walking them upstairs, but it's the only place I have to store them."

"I see. I didn't look in."

"All right. Then if you're still okay with it, I'll take you upstairs and show you."

"Yes. I'm up for it."

They walked through the kitchen and moved up the stairs together.

She followed Beulah as she opened the door and walked into the spare room.

She wasn't kidding about storing things. There were big boxes of paper towels and toilet paper and what looked to be a spare sweeper, and mop and bucket. In the far corner, in front of the window, there was a small desk with a computer sitting in front of it, a basket full of receipts, and some file folders on top, with a filing cabinet underneath.

"I've been trying to do everything online, but sometimes you get paper receipts, and you have to scan them and put them in. I've been looking at a few apps I can put on my phone, but I haven't spent the money on them."

"I totally understand. With a small business, you have to be careful of what you spend your money on."

"Yes. And computer programs seem especially priced for larger businesses, or bigger investments."

"I see."

Beulah took her over, made a few clicks on the computer, and pulled up the schedule.

"There is an app you can download for your phone. But this shows the schedule of when we need to clean houses. When people book them, we see it and need to adjust accordingly. Once you download the app, you get notifications on your phone when things are booked, so you know when you need to go clean."

She sighed. And Quincy got the feeling that she was exhausted.

"This needs to be updated too. I... try to keep track of things. Once we know that a house needs to be cleaned, I schedule the two girls that help me part-time and the one that helps me full-time. Two of them live up in Nags Head, and one lives down in Ocracoke."

"Now there's me. Although... I'll definitely need you to train me on what exactly I need to look for."

"I have a list. Different things that we need to make sure are checked off the list before we call a house clean. We have to be careful with our timing, although we already talked about that."

"I understand. The house is open at a certain time. People expect to get in."

"Yes. So there are times where you really need to move it in order to get done within the allotted amount of time."

"All right."

She ran a hand through her hair and straightened from the desk.

"This is my problem. By the time I have time to work on this in the evening, I feel so frazzled and exhausted that it's hard for me to concentrate, to look at the screen for more than a few minutes, let alone concentrate on trying to figure out a better schedule."

"If you'd like me to try to do it, I can. I didn't use this program, but I did something similar for our church. Just as a volunteer. I wasn't the secretary or anything. But I scheduled the cleaning crews, as well as the junior church and Sunday school teachers. It wasn't as complicated as all of this, but I might be able to figure something out."

"If you could do that, I would be greatly appreciative."

She wished Beulah would've said something a few days ago, because being home with Sonny had given her nothing but time to think about Derek and his betrayal and how bleak the rest of her life looked. She would've loved to have had this to focus on, to get her mind off of all the things she thought about but shouldn't be.

"Maybe tomorrow after we get home from cleaning, if you take a nap, I can come up here and look at it." She laughed a little. "Maybe I'll be so exhausted I'll need a nap too. I'm not used to working all day at manual labor."

"It does take a certain amount of time to get used to. But I found that as I get older, I get tired faster. I suppose that's normal, but it's hard to accept."

"I'm sure it is."

They straightened, and Beulah switched off the computer.

"I'm sorry I was less than welcoming when you came. I... I'm still not sure what I need to do, but I'm praying for you, and for Derek, and hopefully the Lord will work things out."

"Oh, I know He will. I just don't know if He'll do it in the way that I want, and I don't know if I have the strength to do it in the way that He wants."

thirteen

"SO WHAT ARE you going to do?"

Quincy sat across from Shiloh at the corner table in the diner, tapping a finger on her water glass while looking out the window, but not seeing the glassy stillness of the sound.

"I don't know. I don't know what I'm supposed to do." She sighed. "I wish God would just tell me. You know? Make it easy. Just let me know what I'm supposed to do, and I'll do it."

They sat there in silence for a little while. The diner was practically empty on a Tuesday afternoon. She had been helping Beulah for the last four days solid, working from the time she got up in the morning until she dropped into bed at night. Beulah said that Friday, Saturday, and Sunday were their busy, hard days. And then Monday they had a spring cleaning to do at one of their normal rentals, which made that a difficult day as well. So Beulah had insisted that she take Tuesday afternoon off.

Somehow, she ended up at the diner.

"He didn't even offer to meet you halfway?"

"No. He sent two more texts, each one more threatening than the last, like he can somehow force me to come by being mean to me." She closed her eyes and leaned her head back. "I don't want to defy him. I'm not doing it on purpose. I just... I didn't want this, didn't want him to leave, don't want a divorce. I don't want to drive back through the tunnel. Plus, it's a ten-hour drive! And I can't just leave. I'm helping his mother, for goodness' sake. Who he never even told that he was leaving me and shacking up with some chick that's half my age." She pressed her lips together, knowing that she sounded bitter. "Not that I'm upset about that or anything." She rolled her eyes and laughed along with Shiloh.

"No. Not bitter at all."

"It was obvious, wasn't it?"

"It was. And that's probably coloring your decision-making too."

"I know it is. That's why I wish God would just tell me. Because I want to tell Derek to go suck an egg."

They laughed again at her juvenile expression.

"I don't know what the answer is. I know sometimes I struggle to hear God. I've been praying for you, that you'll do the right thing. But I guess... I guess if he wants a divorce, you can either hold onto your marriage and fight for it, or you could just give him what he wants."

Her southern accent somehow was soothing, as Quincy sat across from her, wishing that there was some nugget of wisdom that she could clutch to her chest that would make everything okay.

"I want to fight for my marriage. I don't want to be divorced, but it seems... it seems silly for me to refuse to sign whatever papers he wants. I mean, if he wants to leave, I don't think it's up to me to stop him. It's up to him to stop himself. Otherwise, I just look... bitter and angry." She huffed a breath. "I think we've already established the fact that I *am* bitter and angry, but I don't have to allow that to be the way I act, right?"

"Yeah. I'd love to see you fight for your marriage. I'd love to see it work, but I don't think you're going to endear yourself to your husband by refusing to sign the papers and being a block to what he wants." She paused. "I don't know if it's possible to do this civilly or not."

"Derek and I always had a civil relationship. I mean, I thought we did anyway."

The loud clang of a barely working motor filled the silence that had settled between them.

It was the third time Quincy had seen that beat-down old truck. It looked like it was barely held together, and in fact, as it drove by the diner, clanging down the road, the back bumper was indeed held together by duct tape.

"The dude who drives that looks like he's homeless. Does he need help?" Quincy asked, maybe a little grateful to have something else to focus on other than herself and her problems. Shiloh was only too happy to sit and listen, and she gave biblical advice, which Quincy appreciated, although she seemed just as stumped as Quincy did about what she should do.

"Sometimes looks are deceiving," Shiloh said with a shrug of her shoulders.

"You telling me that dude is a billionaire?" Quincy asked with a little laugh, grateful for a light topic.

"No. I'm not saying that at all." Shiloh sat with a little smile on her face. "I'm pretty sure he was going to see if he could hire Beulah to clean up his rundown, barely habitable beach cottage. Using 'cottage' in the absolute loosest term of the word possible."

"You've got to be kidding me," Quincy said, throwing her head back and putting both hands on either side of her forehead. "Because you know who she's going to send to do it."

"That's what you wanted when you came here, wasn't it? To help?"

The truck had disappeared out of sight as Quincy's phone buzzed. "I bet you that's either Beulah telling me I have a job tomorrow, or my husband telling me he hired a hitman to come take me out so that he can have his divorce."

"Wow. Doomsday all the way around. Maybe it's a notice from someone saying that they're going to give you a million dollars."

"Then there'll be two millionaires in Whispering Hope Harbor," Quincy said, grinning at her friend as she picked up her phone.

It was Beulah.

> I just booked a job a few minutes ago.
> Remind me to tell you about it when you get home.

"Well, I don't know if it's the seaside ramshackle cottage of the closet millionaire resident of Whispering Hope Harbor, or if it's something else. But she does have a job for me."

"That's better than having your husband hire a hitman."

"I'm just not sure I even care. Come take me out. Go ahead." Honestly, she really didn't care. It wasn't that she wanted to die. She definitely wasn't suicidal. She just didn't care. What was the point in the struggle? What was the point in fighting? She didn't want to fight anymore. She didn't care what happened.

"That's not necessarily a good place to be," Shiloh said gently.

"I know. But it's a better place to be than crying into my pillow at night, begging God to have my husband come back, realize the error of his ways, that he's madly in love with me, and that the other woman doesn't hold a candle to what he had with me. That hasn't happened, and I'm sick of wishing for it. I don't want to not be enough anymore. You know? It's easier to not care."

"We're not necessarily going for easier. That's not what life is about."

"I know."

The bell rang over the door as a couple walked into the diner.

Quincy glanced at her watch.

"I better go," she said, sliding out from the booth along with Shiloh.

"Thanks for coming to see me. Makes the afternoon go a little faster when you have a friend to share it with."

"Thanks for talking to me. I still don't know what I need to do, but it's good to know that I'm not stumped over something that's easy if it's stumping you too."

"I think you'll figure it out. You'll do the right thing," Shiloh said, leaning in and giving her a full-on hug, which Quincy returned. It felt good to have someone care about her. It felt good to have the human touch too.

"I'll see you sometime. Apparently I'm working tomorrow, but maybe I'll be around on Thursday."

"Stop in anytime. We're open early, so you can stop in and get a coffee before work."

"All right. I'll keep it in mind." They waved, as Quincy nodded at the couple who had settled at a table by the door, and then made her way out.

As she was walking down the sidewalk toward Sonny and Beulah's house, her phone dinged again.

Maybe it was another job. Or maybe it was her husband and his hitman.

She chuckled a little as she pulled her phone out. Derek wasn't that bad. She probably couldn't joke about it if she was truly afraid that he might do that. Although, he was used to getting his way. Maybe she should just go ahead and give it to him. It wasn't that she didn't want him anymore. She did. She wanted to be married. She wanted her family. But... she didn't want to fight with him. And while she would stand for her marriage, she kind of felt like standing for her marriage against the wishes of her husband wasn't quite what being a submissive wife was all about. But... was she supposed to be submissive? Or was she supposed to stay married?

She couldn't really get either one to sit right.

She pulled the text up. It was from her husband.

> I'm sick of playing games. We need to get these papers signed. Stop being so petty and bitter, and give me a time when you can make it to sign them. Sometime in the next week.

It was not a nice text. Not even close. It raised the hackles on the back of Quincy's neck. She wanted to tell him he could shove the papers where the sun didn't shine, but it was kind of like telling him to go suck an egg—juvenile, and not her best moment as a Christian.

Lord, I want to hate this man. I want to hate him for what he's done to me, for the pain he's caused me, and the rejection that he has put me through, after promising to love me until death do us part. Okay, I could go on and on about that, but I'll try not to.

She could just picture God rolling His eyes at her.

Lord, help me to be kind, help me to show love, and help me to reflect Jesus in everything I say and do. Give me the words to know how to answer him.

She had barely quit praying when her phone started to ring.

It didn't take a rocket scientist to figure out who it was. Sure enough, Derek was calling. She had reached Beulah's house, and her feet slowed as she walked around to the back porch and sat down on one of the empty rocking chairs.

"Hello?" she said, wondering why she was so nervous, out of breath with her heart thundering. It was just her husband, the same man she'd been married to for the last twenty-three years.

"Quincy, why are you ignoring me? You're being such a child. A petulant child. I'm surprised you even answered the phone."

"Ask her about the papers. Don't get off track."

There was a muffled, unrecognizable voice in the background, which Quincy assumed was Candy.

"I need these papers signed. The sooner the better. When can you come back?"

"How do you know I left?"

She didn't mean to be difficult, but he kept assuming that she was somewhere when he really had no idea.

"You're not at our house, so you're either with one of the kids, or you rented a place somewhere. It's not that hard to figure out, Quincy. It's not like you're a complicated person."

So he really didn't know where she was? She could hardly believe that.

Maybe she didn't want to tell him. Maybe she didn't want him to know where she was. Maybe he didn't realize he was asking her to drive ten hours. She tried to take a deep breath on that thought and have it soothe her anger and irritation at how her husband had been treating her.

"I'm not unwilling to sign the papers. I just don't necessarily want to drive the whole way to you. Could we meet somewhere?"

"Seriously? You're gonna quibble over a few miles?"

She chewed on the inside of her lip. She would give him what he wanted. She wasn't going to fight. Sure, she would like to keep her marriage together, but it was obvious that he was determined to end it. Her only question now was how much was she going to fight for? What was hers?

"What do the papers say?" she asked, stalling for time.

There was some murmuring in the background, like Candy was telling him what to say, and then he might have said a few words in argument to her, but Quincy couldn't make any of it out. Like maybe Derek had put his hand over the phone.

"We need a separation agreement in place so that we can be divorced in six months. Without a separation agreement, we have to wait a year."

She had a year. Would her husband come to his senses in that amount of time? She tried to think if it was worth it to try to fight him to wait, and finally decided again that she wasn't going to fight.

"All right. So you want me to sign the papers so that we have a separation agreement in place so that we can be divorced in six months?" She stumbled over the word divorce. It wasn't something she ever wanted to be, not a word she ever wanted to say.

"That's right."

"So what is the agreement?"

"I made it as fair as I could. I was the one who worked

throughout our entire marriage, so I'm the one who should get the most, but you're taken care of as well."

"Whoa. Wait. I worked at home, and yeah, I didn't bring in money, but you had meals, you had childcare, you had a house cleaner, you had someone to go to every single school function that your children had so you didn't have to, someone to wash your clothes and iron your shirts and—"

"I've heard enough. I came up with a deal that I think is fair. If you don't like it, come up with your own deal."

"Right. I will. And then I'll let you know when I'm ready to meet." She took a breath. "Is that all you wanted?"

"You can't let her go! She needs to come sign these papers. The baby is gonna be born before we can even get married."

Quincy coughed. It felt like she was choking on her heart, which seemed to have jumped into her mouth somehow.

That was definitely Candy in the background, and she was....pregnant.

"Congratulations." She managed to say, although her voice didn't quite sound like hers. It sounded like it belonged to someone way far away, and she wasn't even sure that she was still in her body. She felt like she was hovering somewhere above it. The whole "I don't care anymore" thing seemed to have evaporated, since she really did care. And it hurt. A lot.

She had wanted to have more children, but Derek hadn't. So they didn't even try. And that was all there was to it.

"Are you sure this is what you want? Are you truly sure you don't want me anymore, and you want to be with her?"

She shouldn't have said anything. She felt pathetic, like she was begging him to come back to her. But God didn't condone pride, and she could hardly save her marriage if she wasn't telling him what she wanted.

"She's so pathetic."

She heard that clearly, and it just added to her embarrassment.

"I wouldn't have done this if I wasn't sure. You don't know what being married to you was like. It was hell. And I'm finally out of it."

"Hell? I don't understand. I did everything you wanted me to do."

"I'm not gonna talk about this. There's nothing more to say."

She pushed the words that wanted to come out back down her throat. Her chest already felt like it was too big and needed to expand somewhere, but was painfully suppressed. Swallowing all of the things she wanted to say made it feel worse, but she knew that eventually she would be happy that she didn't spew everything that was in her mind. She would just sound as pathetic as what they said she was.

"I told you, I'll come up with my own separation agreement, and I'll be in touch about meeting somewhere to sign it. If you don't have anything else to say, I'm going to go."

"You have a week. I've waited long enough."

That was all he said before he swiped off, and she looked at her phone. It was no longer connected.

She allowed her hand to slowly fall down into her lap.

So Derek was going to have a baby with his girlfriend. His girlfriend was eager to get married apparently.

She couldn't see them getting back together after this. He'd made his choice.

"Good evening. Did you have a nice, relaxing afternoon?" Beulah said, as she came out onto the porch, the smell of something savory and delicious following her out.

"I guess." She could hardly confide in Beulah. It was her son that they were talking about, and she didn't want Beulah to hate her son. She didn't necessarily even want Beulah to know what her son was doing, because she would surely not approve, although maybe it would just remind her that there were sides, and she needed to take one, and she should be on the side of her biological child.

"You don't sound very happy," Beulah said, as she sat down on the swing with a visible sigh of relief.

"I thought you weren't working today?" Quincy said, seeing that Beulah looked like she was exhausted.

"I wasn't going to, but then when the call came in for a job tomorrow, I figured you could do it, and I could take off tomorrow and give Jackie the day off. Spend a little time with Sonny."

"Oh. I'm sorry. You could've said something to me and I would've helped you, or at least come home and made supper."

"Don't worry about it. You worked hard. I know it's a little bit harder to get into the swing of things. Once you've gotten yourself toughened up a little, it'll be easier for you to work a little more."

"I'm sure you're probably right. That was very considerate of you. Thank you."

Nothing that she could have done would have erased the call that she'd had with her husband. And she supposed eventually she needed to have that call, to find out that Candy was pregnant and that Derek had zero desire to be married to her, that apparently she was a terrible wife.

A terrible wife.

And she'd worked so hard to be a good one.

Could she talk to Beulah about it? She wanted to ask if Beulah thought she was a good wife, but the question was pointless. Beulah didn't spend enough time with them for her to be able to say whether or not Quincy could've done anything better.

"All right. I just came out to take a load off for a couple of minutes and because I saw you walking around the side of the house. It looked like you were on the phone." That seemed to be an open-ended statement, like Beulah was giving Quincy time to confide in her if she wanted to.

Quincy looked at the older woman, thinking about how they didn't really seem to understand each other all of those years that she had been married to Derek. But Beulah seemed like a really nice lady, a hard worker for sure. And she'd taken Quincy in, even though she knew that it could cause problems with her relationship with her son.

"I was on the phone. I was talking to Derek. I wasn't trying to keep anything from you, but I know that you're in a delicate position, because he's your son. I guess I feel that what he's doing is wrong. Because I would like to stay married, and... he doesn't want that." She looked down, the words coming out a little slowly. She ran her finger along the edge of the rocking chair. "I wouldn't mind talking to you about it, but again, I know you love your son, and I don't want to make him look like less in your eyes."

Beulah was quiet for a few beats as she swung gently on the porch swing. She sighed. "That's very considerate of you. And you're right, I haven't been very happy with my son. Not only because of what he's done, but he hasn't told me yet. I don't know what I'm going to say to him when I finally do talk to him. After all, does he think he can just leave his wife and pick up a new one, and I'm not gonna notice? And then, there is the fact that you're here. What am I going to do? But if you need someone to talk to, I'm here."

"Thank you. I do appreciate that, but I don't want to drag you into it. You need to love him, no matter what. And I don't want to be the reason that there's anything between the two of you."

"I can respect that," Beulah said, standing up from the swing and coming over and putting her hand on Quincy's shoulder. "Supper is ready, whenever you are."

"Thanks. I'll be in," she said. She wasn't the slightest bit hungry, and didn't know if she could eat anything, but she hated to not sit down at the table and try because Beulah had made the effort to make something, and it seemed rude to not appreciate that. After all, she knew how that felt, since she'd cooked for a family for years, and more than once had had one of them complain that they didn't like what she made.

She never took it personally, but it was a little disheartening to go through all the work of cooking for people only to have them say that they didn't want any.

When had she been a bad wife? When had she done whatever it

was that she'd done that was so terrible that Derek didn't want her anymore?

She had been telling herself that it wasn't her, that it was his lack of character, but he had said on the phone tonight that there was something she didn't know. She didn't know what it was like to live with her. That implied that there was something wrong with her. So maybe it was her fault after all?

That question didn't sit very well with her, but she needed to go inside, and she had to stop thinking about it. She couldn't solve any of those problems now, and she couldn't fix anything either, so she might as well try to point her face to the wind and follow God wherever He led her. Currently, it was as a cleaning lady working for her mother-in-law in Whispering Hope Harbor.

fourteen

THE NEXT DAY dawned warm and clear. Quincy had been getting up early, but it was so nice out that she decided to take a quick walk along the beach. She left a note on the table, just in case Beulah got up and wondered where she went, and then after glancing at her watch and figuring out exactly how much time she had, she stepped off the porch and followed the path down to the sound side of the island.

She'd never realized that the sunrise spread all over the sky. She typically thought the sun rose in the east and set in the west and that's where the sky changed colors, but the whole area over the sound turned delicate shades of pink, and then blue, and then orange, and then deepened and darkened and danced across the still, glassy water, reflecting back and magnifying the beauty.

She was so busy watching the sunrise that it shocked her to realize that a house had come into view on her right.

It was a cute cottage, well cared for, with tulips blooming in planter boxes on the porch railing.

A slender woman, beautiful and classy even from that distance, stood holding a steaming mug, staring at the ever-changing sky.

She didn't think the woman had noticed her, because she had

taken only a few more steps before the woman glanced her way, seemed surprised, and abruptly turned and walked into the house.

That was odd. Most people in Whispering Hope Harbor were friendly and went out of their way to greet a person.

She made a mental note to ask Shiloh about her. If there was news in the community, Shiloh typically knew it.

She had to admit, she was curious about the woman. Who was she? Why was she living in such a private, sheltered place? Was she married?

She just seemed intriguing, and her bearing and posture seemed to scream wealth and money, or class or something.

By the time she got back, she had put the woman out of her mind, and she felt renewed down to her soul.

Sonny was confused and didn't know either her or Beulah at breakfast. Beulah seemed stressed and worried.

"I can come help you with the project today," Beulah said as they cleared off the table.

"No. You said yesterday that you were going to take today off, and I think you need it."

"That walk on the beach did you good," Beulah said, holding the scrambled eggs that Sonny had barely touched, as she looked at her daughter-in-law.

Quincy knew it did. She hadn't figured anything out, hadn't even tried, but somehow just enjoying the beauty that God had put on display, and it seemed like just for her, had given her a calm peace that she hadn't felt in a long time.

She felt ready to tackle the world, or a terrible, difficult cleaning project.

"You call me if you need me. I've got a feeling this project might be more than we bargained for. And remember, you have all the authority you need to negotiate terms."

"Thank you. I looked at some of the pricing that you had done yesterday on the computer, and I think I have a pretty good idea of what we offer and what I should say."

"All right. I trust you. This is going to be your project, and I'll stay out of it unless you need me."

"Thank you. I appreciate your trust."

"I'll take care of these things. You go on."

Quincy nodded, smiling at Sonny, who scowled at her as she walked by, running up the stairs to put her cleaning smock on and grab some equipment to throw into her car. It wasn't that far, but it was too much to carry in one trip, so she needed to drive. Too bad, because it would've been a nice walk.

She followed the GPS, and it took her outside of town, not very far, and turned toward the ocean side of the island.

That was where the more expensive real estate was, and she expected to see a massively large, thirty-room mansion, like many of the vacation homes were.

So when she topped the rise and the house came into view, she did a double check on the address.

It was definitely where she was supposed to be, but it wasn't a multimillion-dollar mansion. It was a rundown, what looked like very barely habitable, shack.

Once, thirty years ago, it might've been a handsome cottage, although it was never a mansion.

Still, it had amazing ocean views, and it was the only house within sight on the beach, so it had fantastic privacy as well.

Despite all that, she wasn't sure if she'd seen a more rundown house in the entire time she'd been at the Outer Banks.

Several of the wooden shingles were blown off of the roof, the shutters hung haphazardly, the wood was weather-beaten, and several boards were missing. The porch hung at an odd angle, and Quincy wasn't sure what door to use, since she wasn't completely sure the porch would hold her weight.

The back door was lower, although no less wobbly looking, and it was the place where she finally figured she'd try, as she got out of the car, checked the address one more time, then shoved her phone in her pocket and decided to walk to the door and knock before she carried any of her equipment.

As she came around the corner of the house, she saw the old truck that she had noticed multiple times in town, chugging slowly down the road, blowing blue smoke and dripping rust, leaving a trail of oil like Hansel and Gretel's breadcrumbs.

The man driving it always had a ball cap pulled down low over his face, but the one time she'd caught a glimpse of him, he seemed tall, with broad shoulders, salt and pepper in his beard, and shadowed eyes under the cap.

Digging deep to find enough courage to step up and knock on the door, she tried to remember the peace that she had felt during her walk, the way her problems hadn't melted away but had seemed less intrusive.

After she was done today, she had planned to contact a lawyer, after all. She still needed to face her problems head-on. But she felt more equipped to do that. Although she still didn't have any direction as to which way she should go. She supposed she didn't really have a choice if her husband insisted on a divorce. She couldn't and wouldn't force him to come back, and she didn't want to fight. Although she also didn't want to just roll over and give him everything she'd built with him. But what was fair?

She pushed those thoughts aside and focused on trying to look professional as she rapped smartly on the door.

She stood there, staring at the chipping paint, which at one point might have been blue but just looked like a dingy gray now.

No one came after what felt like a really long time, so she rapped again.

"What do you want?"

She spun to her right, seeing a man coming around from the front of the house, the side that faced the ocean.

"I am with Beulah's Best Cleaning Service. We scheduled a consultation and cleaning for today?"

Beulah had told her that she had told the man she spoke with on the phone that they would have to examine the house and give a quote before they could clean. He had insisted that he wanted it cleaned immediately, so Quincy had been instructed to walk through the house, give a quote for cleaning, and then, if the man was satisfied with her job, he was going to hire them to clean on a weekly basis. Perhaps biweekly.

Comprehension dawned on the man's face, which had dust from perhaps sanding drywall on it. There was also white dust in hair that normally would be dark, she thought. But his eyes were blue, deep and bright and bold. The hints of intelligence in those eyes, and perhaps even a sense of humor, contrasted with the rundown look of the place, and the man's dust-covered overalls, with a hole in one knee, and the threadbare T-shirt he wore that stretched over broad shoulders. The man looked like he worked for a living.

"I'm sorry. I'd forgotten that you were coming."

"If the homeowner doesn't want me, I don't have to stay."

"No. You're scheduled to come. I just got involved in the work that I was doing and forgot that I was supposed to meet you and show you what needs to be done."

It wasn't clear to her whether he was the homeowner or not. She guessed maybe he was a contractor, as she was, but perhaps someone who knew the homeowner well.

It didn't matter to her. She had a job to do, and as long as they paid her for it, she could deal with anyone.

"There's going to be a lot of renovating going on here over the summer, and we're looking for someone to clean up on a regular basis, so we don't get drowned in our own mess and trash."

"I guess you've called the right company then," she said, stepping over what looked like broken blinds on her way to the back door.

The man stepped to the door before her and had to give it a good yank before he was able to get it open. It creaked and sagged on its hinges.

"This is one of the things that needs to be replaced," he said, indicating the door.

"I'm not sure I would be able to get it open," she said, a little worried. "If I'd been here by myself, I might not have been able to get in."

"I'll be around when you're here, so if that proves to be a problem, you can just let me know and I'll help you."

She walked into the house, glancing around at the open area. It looked like the views from the windows would be amazing, but it was in genuine disarray—mid-renovation, covered in dust, with what looked like a makeshift kitchen, plastic sheeting stuck to the walls and covering most of the windows.

"I guess I didn't introduce myself. I'm Enoch."

She stopped and turned slightly toward him. He closed the door and held out his hand.

"I'm Quincy, from Beulah's Best."

"Good to meet you, Quincy. All right, as you can see, there are renovations going on, and I highly doubt we'll be done before Labor Day." He took a deep breath and looked around the room as though he were lost in all of the clutter. "We'd like to have someone here two days a week. To tidy up the kitchen, do any dishes, sweep, and, if possible, you can scrub the floor as well. There's also a laundry room back here. You do not have to carry laundry through the house, it's like an obstacle course, but all the dirty laundry will be here in baskets, and I'd like to have it washed, dried and folded before you go."

She nodded, having taken her phone out, taken a few pictures, and made notes. She continued to follow him as he showed her the plants he wanted watered, and explained what he'd want done on a weekly basis, and then, as the house became more finished, he would add to that.

It sounded good to her, and she told him so as they met back at the front door after a quick, ten-minute tour.

"This sounds very doable. I'm guessing I would need at least five hours two times a week. Depending on how much laundry there is."

"I don't think there would be more than two loads a week. Possibly three."

"Would Monday and Thursday work for you?" she asked, trying not to hold her breath. Friday through Sunday were the busy days. Tuesday or Wednesday would work better than Thursday, but she figured he wasn't going to want her to come clean on consecutive days.

"Those days would work fine."

"That's great. We're usually busy over the weekends, and I couldn't pencil you in then."

"Will you be the one coming?"

There was something in his voice that made her turn to look at him, really look. She had assumed he was a slightly unkempt contractor, and since she'd been married for twenty years, she wasn't in the habit of checking men out, or gauging whether or not she or they were interested.

Maybe it was the fact that her husband had blatantly rejected her, and she was wondering what was wrong with her, or maybe it was just the idea that she'd been considering not standing in the way of Derek's divorce. Or maybe... she was pretty sure if it wasn't for that, she wouldn't have noticed and taken a second look, but she found herself turning and meeting his eyes, trying for a couple of seconds to read the expression on his face.

Maybe she was out of practice, or maybe there was nothing there to read.

"Yes. It will be me." Beulah had already given her the authority to bid the job and schedule it, since she would be the one doing it. "Why?"

The man shrugged his shoulders and wrapped a hand around his neck, rubbing absentmindedly. "I want someone trustworthy. I may have expensive equipment lying around, and that type of thing. I don't want to constantly be wondering whether or not someone's going to walk off with stuff. Not to mention, they could see it all lying here and come back and take it later."

"No. That will not happen. It will just be me, and I've managed to make it this far in life without ever stealing anything. I have zero plans on beginning a life of crime at my age. I think it's rather late for do-overs." Boy, was it ever. But there were some things she just didn't have a choice about. Like getting divorced. Starting a life of crime would be more change than she could handle.

"I don't know about that." He looked around the house. "This house is probably older than you are, and it's getting a do-over."

"Houses and people are like apples and oranges." She paused for a moment, and then said, "No. It's like apples and monkeys."

His eyes crinkled, and one side of his mouth quirked up. "You know what I'm saying. It's never too late. I'm starting a new career."

She blinked. "You're getting out of the construction business?"

His eyes held her steadily for a moment. "Do I look like I'm too old to start something new?" he asked. Without allowing her to answer, he continued. "I bet I'm older than you are." He held up a hand. "Don't tell me. I'm not trying to get personal information out of you. I'm just saying, I'm doing it, and I don't think I'm too old."

He had a self-deprecating way about him that was so different from Derek's arrogance that it felt refreshing. She found herself wanting to stand and chat.

"I wasn't going to tell you how old I was, so don't worry about it."

He just grinned.

"And yeah. I guess you're right. People start new careers all the time. I didn't mean to imply that they couldn't."

She had been talking about her personal life, but that seemed rather inappropriate to go into with a stranger. Plus, she might be seeing him for a while this summer as he worked on this renovation, but he would be done and then he would be moving on and leaving her here with Beulah and the cleaning business and the shambles that her life was in. It felt like this house. Trashed.

"Are you a local?" he asked, and by that question, he gave away the information that he was not.

"My husband's parents live here. He grew up here, and I'm living with them, helping in Beulah's cleaning business."

She didn't mean to give away all that information. She should've just said no. She wasn't used to guarding what she said.

"So you're married?"

She nodded. There was no way she was going to talk about that. She might not be for very long, but this man did not need to know it. It wouldn't make a difference to him whether she was married or not.

"I can see why you'd want to move here. It's pretty. I assume you're starting over somehow because of what you said before. Why would you say you're too old?"

Why would she indeed? She felt like she was too old to start a relationship. She already had children. Whoever she would be with would probably have children. They would have to try to figure out how to make that work. It wouldn't feel the same. Two people trying to blend two families together. She liked the family that she had. She didn't want to try to blend someone else into it. And since when was she thinking about blending families? She was trying to figure out whether or not she should allow Derek to have his uncontested divorce. That was so very far away from trying to blend a family together.

"This looks like it's going to be a beautiful place once you're finished."

He grunted, and she thought it might've been a laugh.

"Seriously. I know it's a mess right now, but look at that view," she said, nodding out the window at the ocean that stretched out until it met the horizon beyond. "I can just picture sitting in here in the living room, maybe beach décor, some turquoise, comfortable chairs, high enough that you can look out the windows easily. Who wouldn't enjoy working in such a place?"

She didn't know why she was going on about it, other than to change the subject, and maybe the house kind of reminded her a little bit of herself. Was there some potential underneath what felt like the wreckage of her life? Could she eventually be more than just a disaster, completely wrecked by the rejection of a man who was supposed to love her and had pledged his life to her?

"Well, thank you. I think you're right. I can kind of see the thing in my head, but until it actually comes together, I don't know whether I'm dreaming or dealing with reality."

"I would think that once you get good at your job, you'll know whether what's in your head is accomplishable in reality." She hoped she was encouraging him in his new profession.

"I guess you're probably right."

"All right, who should I call to give the quote to?"

"You can just give it to me if you have it. Or I can give you my number if you need to work it out."

"This looks pretty simple and straightforward." She gave him a quote based on what Beulah and she had talked about, told him the number of hours that she could plan on working and the days, and he agreed that that would be fine.

"All right then, since today is Wednesday, I can start tomorrow if you'd like."

"I would like," he said, another twinkle in his eye. But he didn't linger.

"I'll give you the code for the door, in case it's locked, and then you can let yourself in and out. I'll probably be around, but if I'm not, since you are not a thief and don't plan on becoming one, I'll just let you take care of it yourself."

She acknowledged his reference to her earlier words with a slight incline of her head. "That sounds fine."

He held his hand out, and she shook it.

As she was driving away, she realized that Enoch had never given his last name, and she hadn't asked for it. As she pulled up to her next job, a vacation rental near the marina at Whispering Hope Harbor, she wondered why she even cared. It didn't matter what his last name was, or anything else about him for that matter.

She pushed it out of her head, pulled up the notes for the vacation rental on her phone, and got out of her car.

This was just a typical turnover, and she stripped the beds, loading up both washing machines before she started in the kitchen. She had been working steadily for two hours when she noticed movement down by the pool. Glancing out the window of the bedroom she had been cleaning, she saw a woman dressed in khaki shorts and a collared shirt with a logo on it. Her short hair was sunbleached and she seemed to be about the same age as Quincy.

The woman must be there to clean and service the pool. She was a little surprised, although she didn't know why, other than the woman was older than she would have expected and she typically thought of that as being a man's job.

Gathering up the floaties and pool noodles that had been left in the bedroom, she figured she would take them down and go out and introduce herself. Chances were, they would be seeing each other quite often over the summer.

Walking out, she set the things she carried neatly in the designated box, then strode out underneath the deck overhang into the sunlight.

The woman must've caught movement out of the corner of her eye because her head jerked around, her eyes wide.

"You startled me. I wasn't expecting to see anyone else here."

"I'm the cleaning lady," she said, feeling a little weird introducing herself like that. But only because she hadn't gotten used to it. This was her job now.

"I'm the pool lady," the woman said with a straight-up smile. "My name's Sharon." She walked over with her hand out, dragging a hose or something along behind her, a floatie drifting lazily in the pool, like it didn't have a care in the world.

Quincy found herself being almost jealous of it as she shook the lady's hand.

"I'm Quincy, working for Beulah's Best."

"I see. I've heard about Beulah's daughter-in-law, and the situation you're in."

Quincy's eyes widened.

"How do you know I was her daughter-in-law?"

"It's a small town. News travels fast." Sharon lifted a shoulder. "You'll probably have to get used to it if you're going to stay for any length of time."

"I guess I'm just surprised, that's all," she said. And then she realized that Sharon had mentioned her situation. "So you know my husband cheated on me?"

"It happens. Unfortunately. Men are rats. But what do we do?" She lifted a shoulder again, giving Quincy a measured look, before she turned back to look at the pool. "Can't live with 'em, can't live without 'em, and you can't shoot 'em."

Quincy smiled at the familiar saying. She couldn't say that it hadn't gone through her head a few times in the last week or so.

"Sounds like you've had some experience."

"Not really," she said, with what Quincy was beginning to believe was her typical no-nonsense approach. "My husband died seven years ago. As far as I know, he didn't cheat on me. But he did leave me rather destitute, and also, somehow, my son blamed me for all of it. I started Coastal Clear Pools just to survive."

"And your son?" Quincy asked gently, feeling like that was where the emotion was for Sharon.

"Haven't talked to him. I've got grandkids I've never met. I know that from social media. I guess he blocked me, but I have friends," she said, with a smile that didn't really contain any humor.

"That's sad," Quincy said, thinking about it, and she couldn't help but wonder if she would be more upset if one of her children wasn't talking to her than she was in having her husband leave her. She honestly thought she probably would be. Although, it wasn't the fact that Derek wasn't talking to her, or didn't want her anymore, necessarily. It was just the idea that she was so blindsided by it all. She'd trusted him, and all the other things.

"Have you tried to reconcile?" Quincy asked, and then held a hand out. "I'm not pushing, just asking. That sounds terrible. I can't imagine what I would do if one of my children decided that they were mad at me for some weird thing and stopped talking to me."

"Yeah. It's exceptionally painful. And yes. I've tried reaching out, but he told me he didn't want to have anything to do with me. I honestly think it's less what I did, because I didn't do anything, and more that seeing me reminds him that he doesn't have a dad anymore, and it hurts. So it's just easier to block me out." Sharon lifted a shoulder and twisted the hose in her hand.

"That's awful. You'd think that a death would make people closer and bring them together."

"I think it can do either, depending on how we look at it and how we handle it." She raised her brows and sighed. "I just know I've done everything I can, and the ball is in his court. I periodically reach out, and have been rebuffed every time. It's... hard. But life goes on."

"It does."

"For me and you," Sharon said, a nod to Quincy's hurt and pain. Although it was nice to find someone who treated her normally when she felt like she was a walking tragedy.

"Thanks. It's nice to have solidarity in sisterhood."

"Us working women need to stick together. This town is full of people who will tell you how to live. You might as well have a few people in your court who won't."

"I don't mind advice. I don't always take it. Sometimes it just doesn't make sense for my situation. But I don't mind people trying to show me what worked for them, and let me borrow a little of their wisdom, since sometimes it seems like I have precious little of my own."

"I hear you. Me too," Sharon said with a short laugh.

Her khaki shorts and navy blue polo with the Coastal Clear Pools logo on the pocket suited her no-nonsense personality. Her gray-streaked hair, cut short in an impractical cut, framed her face and perhaps made her seem younger than what she was.

"I don't have any grandchildren yet." Quincy hadn't even thought about grandchildren. "Neither one of my children are married."

"My son got married before my husband died, and those are the pictures that are on my mantle and bedstand. That's how I remember my family."

"I'm so sorry about the loss of your husband."

"Yeah. You have a big change like that, and it shifts everything. I know he didn't mean to die, but it inspired my 'men are rats' comment. Still, it's like I said, life goes on, and you have to pick up the pieces and just keep going. Because nothing stops and waits for you."

"Speaking of, I better get back to work. But it was really nice meeting you. I hope we'll see each other again."

"I'm sure we will." Sharon said. "My house is just a few houses up from your in-laws. We'll have to get together sometime before things break loose and get insanely busy over the summer."

"Yeah. And then plan on taking some time this fall to enjoy the slower pace as well."

"You've got it. You endure the summer and enjoy the rest of the year." She waved, and then turned her attention back to the pool.

Quincy walked back in the house, feeling like she just might have made a friend.

fifteen

QUINCY GRIPPED the wheel tighter and tried to take deep, calming breaths. She was almost to the tunnel, and part of her wanted to stop and turn around.

But in church the week before the pastor had talked about how it took two to fight. That contention was often because one person wanted their way and wasn't willing to give it up.

Even though Quincy felt like she had the high road—she wanted to stay married, she wanted to work things out—it was still her causing the contention. Sure, her husband had left, and that was wrong, but if he wasn't willing to change, it had to be her.

She knew that a lot of people would disagree with her, would say that he was just as wrong as she was, but she couldn't control him. She couldn't change what he was deciding to do. The only thing she could do was to change herself. And she was not going to be prideful and demand her own way. As much as she would love to have a reconciliation, to put their family back together, to be parents to their children, she just wasn't going to stand in his way if he wanted to leave. She wasn't going to fight about it.

Maybe she was making the wrong decision, but it had felt suddenly clear and calm last week in church, and plain as day that she needed to do what her husband asked of her. Until they were divorced, technically, he was still her husband, and she was commanded in the Bible to obey.

That wasn't a popular thing either, but she wasn't interested in what was popular. She was interested in what was right. She was interested in what God wanted, not what the world told her to do.

The road shifted and turned, and she said a silent prayer as her car followed the road down into the tunnel.

She was going to be fine. Everything was going to be fine. Lifting her sunglasses up so she could see better, she tried to focus on holding her hands steady and keeping her car between the lines. This tunnel didn't last forever. In fact, it wasn't that long at all, and she was going to be just fine.

Her heart pounded, and her lungs wanted to pant, but she wouldn't allow them to. She focused on keeping her breath even and steady, slow and deep.

After what felt like forever, the road shifted again, and she gradually rose up into the sunlight.

The hardest part of the trip was behind her, other than signing the papers.

She hated asking off after she'd just started, but she felt like she needed to get this done before the busy season started, and it would be a true inconvenience for her to take off.

Derek had insisted that she come the entire way, and while she didn't feel like he deserved to have her comply, that was pride on her part. Thankfully, Pastor Biddle had talked about pride a good bit, enough to convince her that not only was she being prideful and contentious by refusing to capitulate to what her husband wanted, but she was also being prideful and stubborn by not agreeing to drive the whole way there.

Of course, it made more sense for them to compromise and meet in the middle. And of course it seemed like that was just common sense. But for her to stand and insist that her way was right was still prideful, no matter how right it actually was. It wasn't a biblical point. On those, Pastor Biddle said, a Christian was to be uncompromising. The problem was, Christians often refused to compromise on things that might be right, but not necessarily biblical. Like meeting in the middle, rather than making the wife that you're leaving high and dry drive the entire way back from your parents' house where she was living to take care of them, so she could sign the papers that you wanted her to sign, while you committed adultery and trashed your marriage.

Look at Jesus. Look at His face. Look at His nail-pierced hands. Look at the beauty He left in heaven so that He could come here and die for you.

She told herself that over and over again as she continued to drive down the road. If she kept thinking about how much her husband did not deserve her coming to meet him, she was going to be in an exceptionally bad mood when she got out of the car, and she'd probably end up yelling at him or something stupid like that. She wanted to be calm. She wanted to be collected. She wanted to be kind. If he was going to do wrong, he wasn't going to force her into becoming someone that she hated, and doing things that she said were wrong, things a Christian shouldn't do.

Otherwise, he'd be right, wouldn't he? Right in leaving her. Right in not becoming a Christian, because obviously being a Christian didn't help her be kind. And right for making fun of her and her faith.

She supposed that was a prideful way of looking at it, but it helped her remember that she was going to be kind, no matter how much she felt like not. It reminded her of that verse in Proverbs: "Commit thy works unto the Lord, and thy thoughts shall be established."

She might not feel like being kind, but her works needed to be kind, and hopefully her feelings would follow her thoughts.

She arrived at the park where they were supposed to meet around three in the afternoon.

She had left early, hoping to drive a good bit of the way back after they talked so she would be able to work the next day. She didn't want to leave Beulah any longer than what she had to, now that she knew what her circumstances were.

She pulled into the park, seeing several vehicles, but having no idea what her husband was driving. The convertible wasn't there and she didn't recognize any of the parked cars.

It was a beautiful, early spring day, and tulips were blooming, giving pretty pink, purple, and red colors against the bright green spring grass.

Several children played at the playground while a group of moms stood along the side chatting.

It didn't seem that long ago when that was her, watching her children play as she chatted with moms from the church.

It seemed like another lifetime ago at the same time. Was that really her life? When she was happily married with beautiful children and great friends?

What had happened?

No, she wasn't going to go down that road. Not now. Taking a deep breath, pushing her shoulders back, and planting a smile on her face, she turned and looked. A couple walked toward her.

The man carried a folder, and they held hands.

Really? He seriously was bringing his girlfriend to sign the papers when they weren't even divorced yet?

She wanted to turn around and get in her car, slamming the door as hard as she could, and drive as fast as she could away from here. That man did not deserve to have her capitulate so easily. He deserved to have someone fighting him.

But she didn't want to fight. She didn't want to be contentious. If this was what he wanted, she would give him this, even though it was wrong, and she felt like he was making a major mistake. Maybe not by ditching her, although she couldn't see how Candy would be a better wife to him than she had been, but by ditching his marriage. God was the ultimate judge, and He abhorred divorce. Derek would have to explain himself to God, and she could just stand back and allow him to do that. To let God take over, take control, and deal with the situation. God could do it, if He wanted to. She just had to let Him. If she stepped in and decided to handle it on her own, God wouldn't. And then, maybe Derek wouldn't get what God really wanted him to have. Whatever that was.

She tried not to hope that it was something really terrible, but she wasn't entirely successful.

"Quincy. It took you long enough. I thought I was going to have to have the sheriff serve you."

Quincy didn't even know if that was a thing.

"Hello, Derek." Her eyes went to Candy, and she tried hard to keep a pleasant expression on her face. "Candy."

"Quincy, it's so nice to see you again. Derek was telling me that he thought you might be at his parents' house. That's along the beach, isn't it? I hope we get to visit soon. We're definitely coming to visit sometime this summer. I need a beach vacation. The real estate market is just booming." She rolled her eyes and talked like Quincy was a confidant and friend, rather than the wife of the man she was holding hands with.

"Here. I just need your signature in a couple of places. This is a separation agreement, and then in six months, our divorce can be final, and it'll be as easy as that."

Easy? He thought divorce was easy?

She wanted to lecture him, tell him that it was not easy to separate two people who were supposed to be one. To pull apart a family that was supposed to be together.

"Did you tell the children?" she asked, looking up into the eyes of the man she had lived with for the last twenty years.

"I figured you could do that. You're really good at breaking things like this to them, you know, saying it gently, explaining how we've grown apart and making it all sound very nice and sweet and wonderful."

Her brows had gone up until she felt like they were probably popping off the top of her head.

"You want me to tell them?" she asked, barely able to get the words out. It seemed so insane.

"Yeah. Make it sound good." He waved his hand in the air. "Could you hurry up, please? We have reservations."

"Reservations?" She couldn't help but ask. She couldn't think of a time when she and her husband had ever eaten at a place that took reservations.

"I just completed a big sale, and we're celebrating," Candy interjected.

Quincy looked down at the papers. Should she just sign without reading them? No. She definitely needed to read them. She wanted to get along, but she didn't want to be stupid either.

After about three sentences, she was glad that she hadn't signed without reading. He wanted everything. He wanted her to just sign it all away.

"I'm sorry, I'm going to have to take this home with me."

"What?" The word exploded out of Derek. Even Candy looked upset.

"I thought maybe we would split things fifty-fifty. This basically says that you get everything."

"That's because I was the one that worked for it all!" Derek roared. "You sat at home on your butt doing nothing while I went to work every day. And I don't get everything. You get the car that you're driving, and the stuff that we put in storage. There are a lot of valuable things in there."

"Not as valuable as the house. And our savings, and your pension, and this is—" Quincy closed her mouth. She'd said she wasn't going to fight. She'd felt peaceful about it yesterday in church. She was confident that God was going to work things out for her good and His glory. And she was going to sit back and let Him.

But sign this agreement that was so blatantly wrong? She couldn't do it without thinking about it.

"I'll mail them to you. You can text me whatever address you want them to go to."

"Sign the papers," Derek commanded, in a voice that Quincy wasn't sure she'd ever heard. It made her want to pick up the pen and sign immediately.

She wasn't sure how it happened, but she felt calm as she said, "No. I'll mail them to you. Text me the address."

She turned, not quickly, but in a calm and controlled manner, and started walking back to her car.

"If you don't sign them, I'm going to sue you for everything you've got."

She almost laughed. She had nothing. And if it was up to Derek, she would never have anything.

> If we split the sale of the house fifty-fifty, I
> won't fight you on the divorce.

QUINCY STARED AT HER PHONE, a sense of peace stealing over her. She wasn't fighting for more than what she deserved. She wasn't fighting her husband at all. But she wasn't allowing him to take advantage of her. That seemed fair.

With a sense of peace, she hit send, and then closed her phone.

Maybe he wouldn't agree to it, but if he came back with anything remotely close, she was going to agree with it, because she didn't want to fight. Sure, he might get a little bit more than what she did, and she might not get exactly what she deserved, but life wasn't about her getting everything that she deserved. And it wasn't fair either.

The stress of fighting him would not be worth the extra money that she would get if she continued to battle back and forth.

She felt like a weight had been taken off of her shoulders, because no matter how he came back, she was content with whatever she ended up with.

Checking to make sure she had put everything she needed in her bag, she grabbed it and went downstairs.

She and Beulah had an uneasy relationship and had settled into a routine of sorts.

It had been a week since she had left to go meet her husband, and every day since then, she and Beulah had worked in the cleaning business, figuring out a schedule that kept both of them busy.

To her surprise, Quincy actually enjoyed the work. Maybe it would get old after a while, but wandering around those big, multi-million-dollar houses, seeing the ocean views, and enjoying the beauty of the ocean made her look forward to going to work every day.

Of course the work was hard, and she was tired by the time she got home, but she truly could see herself doing this for the rest of her life, however long that was.

Taking a stroll out on the beach, she watched the changing sky, feeling like she would never get tired of that either.

On her way home, she saw the same woman she'd seen almost every day, standing on her porch.

She threw her hand up in a wave when she thought the lady was looking. They'd exchanged waves for the last few days after the woman had stopped running inside as soon as she came in view.

The woman's wave was still just a stick-her-hand-up-and-wiggle-her-fingers kind of wave, almost like she was afraid to wave big and didn't want to draw attention to herself. Like she was shrinking in on herself.

Maybe there was something in her past that kept her from wanting people to see her. Or maybe she was here to get away from something. Or perhaps it was almost a fear thing, like the woman was scared.

No sooner had she waved than she patted her leg to get her dog's attention, and then hurried into the house, closing the door behind her dog, without looking at Quincy again.

Odd, but... at least they shared a little bit of a greeting. Maybe tomorrow the woman wouldn't be quite so reclusive.

She could hear Sonny yelling as she turned to go up the path to Beulah and Sonny's house.

"I don't want any of this food. It's all crap! Everything in here has been crap since the day I came!"

She could hear Beulah's voice murmuring something low and soothing, but she couldn't hear exactly what it was.

And then there was a crash, along with some more shouting from Sonny that she couldn't understand.

She ran the last three steps to the door and yanked it open as quickly as she could.

Jackie had requested the day off, and Beulah and Quincy had to arrange things so that Beulah was staying home with Sonny.

"It's okay. You don't have to get upset. No one's going to make you eat that," Beulah said in a calm and soothing voice from her position on the floor, where she bent down to pick up the shattered pieces of a bowl.

"That's what you always say. And then I always have to eat it!" Sonny whirled on his foot and shuffled angrily, stomping his feet as hard as his old legs would allow him to, toward the recliner in the living room.

"Good morning," Quincy said, unsure how Sonny was going to respond to her.

"You're the nice lady. I had the mean lady back there. She was trying to make me eat a bunch of crap. I don't want to." Sonny sounded like a petulant child as he parked his walker, grabbed the remote for the TV, and lowered himself in the chair, crossing his arms over his chest without even turning the TV on.

"Would it be okay if I talk to her?" Quincy said, unsure if that was going to work or not.

"You could try, but I've been talking to her for eighty years, and it hasn't done any good."

It was on the tip of Quincy's tongue to ask him if he knew what her name was, but she didn't. She was pretty sure Sonny was not in his right mind.

"Sorry," she whispered as she walked to the table and bent down to help Beulah pick the mess up off the floor.

Beulah lifted her head, and to her surprise, there were tears on the older woman's face.

"I don't know how much longer I can do this."

"Oh my goodness. It's hard," Quincy said, reaching a hand out to touch her shoulder.

Beulah didn't exactly fall into her embrace, but she lifted one of her own hands up and grasped Quincy's, squeezing it.

"I'm so scared. I'm scared of losing Sonny. We've been together for so long. But then I think I've already lost him." She waved a hand in Sonny's general direction. "He doesn't even know who I am. But I'm scared of losing my business, my independence, of getting old like this too. It's just so overwhelming, and then when he has a day like this, where he doesn't recognize me, and he's violent and mean, I don't think I can keep doing it."

More tears slipped out, and she wiped her cheek with the back of one hand, pieces of glass still clasped in her fingers.

"I don't blame you. It's so much. And so hard. And I've wondered from the time I came how you've been doing it all. Running the business, keeping the houses clean, and the employees in line. And... I know this isn't the same, but when Derek left, that took away my security blanket too. I didn't realize how much I depended on him. But I'm scared to death to start over at my age. I was so glad that you guys were here. Even though I know that things were hard for you, it was a little bit of a soft landing." She paused for just a moment, unsure how Beulah would take her next words. "I guess we can be the soft landing for each other, because as long as I'm here, I'll be working to help you. With Sonny, with the business, with your own health, with everything. But you're not the only one who's scared."

Beulah stared at her, and their eyes met across the mess on the floor between them, across the glass and the wisp of hostility that still floated there too, as Beulah's eyes softened.

"Thank you. It makes me feel so much better to know that I'm not in this by myself. I guess that's the thing. When Sonny starts acting like this, I don't feel like I'm part of a couple anymore. I feel like I'm all alone."

"That makes two of us. And if there's two of us, then neither one of us are alone. Right?" She gave a little smile, and Beulah nodded and smiled just a little back.

"You know, Sonny always said that God's plan was bigger than our understanding. And that all we had to do was just have faith. It always seemed so simple and trite, but... sometimes that's literally all you can do." Beulah's whispered words resonated deep in Quincy's soul. Maybe she'd heard those exact same words before at some point, or many points maybe, but it wasn't until she was in this particular predicament—no husband, no safety net, because she'd just signed away her right to his pension. She could've fought for it. That's what she had been planning on using in their retirement. They'd talked about it together. Beulah didn't need to know that. But Quincy had been more scared than she wanted to admit. But Beulah was right. God's plan was bigger, and sometimes all she had to do, or all she could do, was have faith.

"I think Sonny was a wise man. You were blessed to have him for so long."

Those were the exact right words to say, it seemed like, since Beulah smiled, almost in a dreamy way, and it seemed like all the tension had drained out of her. "You're absolutely right. I was blessed." Then her brows drew down a little, and she nodded her head. "I still am. I have you."

She felt like there was a tenuous bond between them. Not that they were fast friends, not that they were all of a sudden best buds, but something shifted, and Quincy felt like Beulah might eventually be a friend.

Before either one of them could say anything else, Beulah's phone rang.

She let go of where she was still holding onto Quincy's hand and pulled her phone out of her pocket.

Her brows drew down as she looked at the number, but she didn't say anything as she slid the button open with her thumb, still holding glass in her other hand, and put the phone to her ear.

"Hello?"

She was close enough that Quincy could hear, and Quincy didn't know whether to stand up and move away or stay where she was. Beulah didn't indicate what she should do, and she didn't want to do anything to destroy the tremulous band of trust that seemed to have developed between them.

"Mary! It's so good to hear from you."

Mary. That was Beulah and Sonny's daughter. Derek's sister. She had never liked Quincy.

"Mom, I'm coming to visit. I'll be there in an hour."

Beulah's face said this was not good news.

seventeen

BEULAH SLID the phone off and allowed her hand to drop slowly to her side.

Mary was coming.

Her relationship with Mary was fraught with tension and arguments. Nothing Beulah ever did was good enough. She criticized everything and normally left in a huff.

This was not a good time.

"Mary is coming," she said, looking at Quincy.

Quincy had surprised her. She'd always kind of liked her, although she'd felt a little unsettled when Derek and Quincy first started dating, like her place in Derek's life was being usurped by this new interloper, and that seemed to set the tone for their relationship, unfortunately.

They'd never been close, and Beulah admitted that it was as much her fault as anyone's, since she had been consumed with her business, but that was because she had been scared to death that if it wasn't a success, she wouldn't have anything to fall back on. Once Sonny sold his boat and went all in with her business, the pressure was on.

She wished she could go back and do things over. Because she could see, definitely and for sure, things that she could've done better.

Still, she couldn't spend time thinking about that now. She needed to get things ready for Mary. And the first thing she needed to do was to clean up this mess.

"I can take care of this, if you have things that you need to do? To prepare for her coming?" Quincy indicated the mess on the floor and the broken dishes.

At some point, Sonny had turned the TV on, and who knew what kind of shape his brain was in, whether he'd recognize them now or not.

"Would you mind?" she asked, feeling relief like a weight off of her chest. "I need to get the room I'm keeping all of the spare things in ready. And... Mary is rather exacting."

"Does she usually stay in the room I'm in?" Quincy asked with perception.

Beulah nodded. "But don't worry about it. I'm not going to kick you out." She could hardly do that. She felt like she and Quincy might finally be starting to see things eye to eye, and she didn't want to do anything to jeopardize their relationship, even if it would make things easier when Mary came.

"It's fine. I can move out. I can grab my things and it would take me less than ten minutes. I need to get my clothes out of the drawer and take them over to the other room."

"I couldn't ask you to do that."

"You didn't ask me. I offered. And I don't want Mary and me to just start off on the wrong foot because of me being in the room that she's usually staying in. I think it would be better all around."

"You're a real blessing, you know that?" Beulah said with sincerity.

"I guess I've done some growing up in the last month."

"Hardships have a way of doing that to you, don't they?"

"Growing us, or breaking us," Quincy said with a shoulder shrug.

Then she turned to start cleaning things up. They didn't have a whole lot of time.

"I'll grab some extra things. I have an air mattress that will fit in that room."

"That's perfect. I don't need anything fancy."

"If Mary is going to stay for any length of time, we'll get a bed put in there and figure things out. I've put off renting a storage container because it's so handy to have everything in the house, but maybe it's about time we do that."

"There's probably room to put a shed on the property too," Quincy said with a raised brow and questions in her eyes.

"Actually, we could do that. Maybe I'll look into that. I guess... I've been overwhelmed lately."

Quincy's hand came out and rested on her arm in a comforting way. For the second time that day, Beulah was tempted to throw her arms around her daughter-in-law and pull her close. But they'd never really had that kind of relationship, and she wasn't sure how that would be received, so she resisted the urge.

"You've been dealing with a lot, and you've done really, really well. Don't beat yourself up about it."

"Once upon a time, that's the kind of thing that Sonny would've done. Looked up sheds, figured out what the best one to get would be, and then figured out the best price for it."

"That's the kind of thing Derek would do too. But Derek's not here, and Sonny probably can't, and you and I can. We just never have before, so we'll do it now and maybe make mistakes and get better at these kinds of things." Quincy nodded with a deliberate nod, and Beulah imitated the gesture.

"You're right. We're catching on, and we're gonna get good."

They grinned at each other, and then Beulah hurried upstairs. While she was still in the spare room, she heard Quincy quickly gathering her things in the other room. Before Beulah had gotten finished, Quincy was already over with the few things that she had.

"One more load will do it. There's not much."

"I really appreciate you doing this. It's going to avoid a confrontation and hopefully get us started out on the right foot."

"Absolutely. I'm not here to cause trouble. I appreciate the place to land, like we were saying earlier, and I don't want to be someone who causes problems rather than helps."

"You've definitely been helping," Beulah said.

She had clean sheets to put on the bed Quincy had been using, and she almost had it made when she heard a car outside.

A glance out the window showed a car she was unfamiliar with stopping next to the house.

Mary typically drove in on a rental, and it seemed like she got a different car every time.

"I think she's here," she said as Quincy stood in the doorway.

"Do you want me to finish up there?"

"Yes, please," she said. "Just this pillowcase and the blanket."

"Perfect. I've got it."

She hurried downstairs and made it to the door just as Mary rapped sharply on it before twisting the knob and walking in.

"Hello, darling," she said. Mary gave her a disdainful look and a perfunctory hug with no warmth.

"Mother." Her eyes swept the room as the door clicked closed. "When was the last time anyone cleaned here?" Her eyes narrowed. "Mother, you can't have Dad in a place like this. If someone comes to inspect your house, they're going to take him from you and put him in a home!" Her lips pressed together, before she glanced over at her father. "Daddy, how are you?" she said, leaning over Sonny and giving him a hug.

Of course, Sonny looked at her and recognized her.

"Hey there, girlie," he said, using the nickname he'd always used with Mary.

"What did you have for breakfast?" Mary asked, picking something off of his face.

"Nothing. They didn't give me nothing for breakfast."

Beulah's mouth dropped open. She wanted to deny it and defend herself, but she also didn't want to make Mary's father look bad by saying that he had thrown the food she had offered him on the floor, breaking plates, making a mess, and throwing a fit, even though she was serving his favorite—sunny-side-up eggs and oatmeal. It was an odd combination, but he'd always loved it.

"Mom? What's the matter with you? You can't not feed him! And he can't cook for himself."

"Sweetheart, it's a little more complicated than that."

Mary opened her mouth to respond, but as she was lifting her head, her eyes seemed to get caught on something beyond Beulah's shoulder. Her eyes widened and then narrowed as she straightened, putting her hands on her hips.

"You." Her voice held contempt. "What are you doing here?"

The words didn't exactly sound evil, but close.

"Mary. What a pleasant surprise. I have been staying for a while and am working to help your mom with her cleaning company. I've been helping with your dad a little bit too."

"Why aren't you with Derek? Where is he?"

She looked around as though he were standing in a corner somewhere, just waiting for her to say his name.

Beulah figured that Quincy probably didn't want to tell Mary her whole life story, especially since Mary seemed to have come looking for a fight. She was normally unable to be satisfied and critical, but not usually this bad.

"Mary, darling. I'm sure you're tired after your long trip. Let me help you get your luggage upstairs."

"Did something happen to Derek?"

"Derek's fine," Quincy said, grabbing her shoulder bag from against the wall where she'd leaned it earlier. "I'm going to go ahead and head out. I'm going to do the Williams rental first, and then I'm going to stop by the sea cottage and do that one next. It'll be late when I get back. I'll probably grab lunch at the marina with Sharon."

"All right. I won't expect you then."

"Mother, this is really strange. What's going on?" Mary said, as Beulah tried to gently lead her away.

"We can catch up here in a minute. Let's get you inside and settled first. Did you have breakfast? Would you like me to make you something to eat?"

"You need to make Dad something. I can't believe you didn't feed him. Mom, what are you thinking?"

She met Quincy's eyes for a brief moment, and Quincy smiled, a smile that said that she was sorry to be leaving Beulah in the lurch, but she knew that she had to go. Someone had to clean.

Beulah wanted to tell her not to worry about it. It was funny—she wouldn't have guessed that Quincy would become a confidant, but she felt like she could trust her, and she already had with various aspects of the business. Perhaps she could trust her with more.

The door closed behind her, and Beulah let out a sigh of relief. At least Mary wouldn't have Quincy to pick on anymore. Somehow, she felt like Quincy was in a vulnerable place, with her husband having left her, and the different things that she had confessed to Beulah that morning. She didn't figure that Quincy was in the right frame of mind to be dealing with Mary's barbs, which could be rather sharp and pointed. Okay, and downright mean.

"Mother, you've got to tell me what's going on. What is Quincy doing here? Working, no less?"

"She and Derek have been planning for at least six months to move in with us after they sold their house. They were planning on helping with the business all along."

"But Derek's not here."

"No." Then, because she figured that Mary was going to find out sooner or later, and maybe it would be easier for her to find out when Quincy wasn't around, Beulah said, "He cheated on Quincy and left her for the realtor. Quincy found out the day they closed on their house. She decided to come here anyway, and she's been a godsend the last few weeks. I don't know what I did without her."

"Did it ever occur to you that Quincy is lying? That maybe she cheated on Derek? Why are you so quick to believe the worst about your son?"

Mary's eyes were huge and her hands fisted on her hips as though expecting a fist fight.

Beulah sighed. She didn't have the time or energy to get into this right now.

"Quincy showed up when I was expecting them and Derek didn't." She supposed she really didn't know if Quincy was telling the truth. Derek hadn't spoken to her at all. But in all the years she'd known Quincy, she'd never known her to lie. "I've been busy with your father and the business, and I am simply grateful someone is here to help."

"I thought you hired someone to take care of Daddy?"

"Jackie." Beulah tried not to allow her relief at the subject change to show. "But she can't always make it, and when she can't, someone has to stay here and take care of him, and thankfully, Quincy's been able to keep up with the cleaning, and she's helped me organize the schedule. She's really done a good job."

"Mother, I could do that. Why didn't you tell me?"

She put a hand on Mary's forearm. "Why are you here?"

"I wanted to visit you and Daddy. To see how things were going."

"Things are going fine," she said.

Then, as she started to turn toward the kitchen, her eye caught on the date circled on the calendar, and the words "Home health assessor, ten o'clock" written in red.

There was still some grease on the floor. Quincy had picked up the glass and food but not scrubbed. And her husband still hadn't had breakfast this morning.

She tried to shove down the rising panic in her chest. "Mary, I hate to put you off, but I have the home health assessor coming in just a few minutes, and I need to get your daddy some food. It's a long story about what happened this morning, but trust me, breakfast was made. He just didn't eat it."

"I've never seen Daddy not eat," Mary said, looking at Beulah like it was somehow her fault that he didn't.

"There are probably a lot of things happening around here that you haven't seen."

eighteen

"I DON'T KNOW what trade school he went to, but I can't believe I know more tricks of the trade than he does. Or at least, that one trick."

Sharon sat across the table from Quincy, her chin in her hands, her elbows on the edge. They had just ordered and were enjoying the gentle breeze from the water, the muted sound of hustle and bustle of the docks as boats, out since early that morning, long before daylight, returned from their fishing expeditions.

"What?" Quincy asked, when Sharon didn't say anything.

"I'm just not convinced the guy is a handyman. Or a contractor. Or whatever he says he is."

Quincy straightened, pulling back a little, since the thought had never occurred to her.

"What makes you say that?" she asked, her brows drawing down. "Do you think he's some kind of serial killer hiding out here waiting for his next victim?" She was only partially joking. After all, she was by herself with that man for hours as she cleaned his home.

"No. Nothing like that. He just—I don't know. There's just something weird about him. I can't really put my finger on it, but it's not in a bad way. He just isn't who he says he is. Or he doesn't seem like it."

"Well, I asked him if he would ask the owner if we could use the new pavilion to meet. I was feeling kind of bold. Or maybe like I don't care. After the way Mary acted this morning, I guess I just feel like I don't have anything to lose, you know?"

"The worst he can do is say no. It's a pretty bold ask, but why not? It would be perfect for us."

"It would be beyond perfect. It would be the thing dreams are made of. It's so pretty up there."

"It's beautiful everywhere here," Sharon said, looking out over the marina, which, typical for marinas, had been weathered by the salt and spray and years of exposure to the elements. It looked rundown, but serviceable.

"Absolutely. That reminds me, every morning when I walk, I see a woman in a house that you can't see from the road. On the bay side. She has a little dog."

"A woman with a little dog in a house you can't see." Sharon pretended to scratch her head, thinking hard.

"I'm sorry. That's not much of a description, but she has long, honey-blonde hair. And she looks like she'd be gorgeous if I saw her up close, which I never have."

"Well, that's a little better. A gorgeous woman who lives in a house you can't see." Sharon grinned, and Quincy laughed.

"You know exactly who I'm talking about!"

"I think so. Her name is Vivian, although that's really all I know about her other than she's been here for about a year and comes to the diner for lunch on Monday afternoons when it's really slow. Shiloh might be able to tell you more. I've never seen anyone who can get information out of someone the way Shiloh can."

"I know exactly what you mean. I'd barely met her, and I was spilling out my entire life story."

"She really cares about people though. That's the thing about Shiloh."

"She's a great person. And a good friend," Quincy agreed. She blew out a breath. "So you didn't really answer my question. If I'm able to get permission to use the pavilion on the property that Enoch is renovating will you come?"

Sharon pressed her lips together, lifting her shoulder slightly and looking out over the bay. Quincy let her think. That was one thing she'd learned about Sharon: she had a tendency to think things over deeply and thoroughly before she made a decision.

"Your sister-in-law sounds like a real pill. And I wouldn't be able to take off work. Especially not in the busy season. I need the money."

Quincy nodded. She wasn't used to having to work, but she needed the money, too. "I guess that was a perk of being married. I pretty much ran my own schedule and didn't absolutely have to do anything. I loved that freedom, even though I didn't appreciate it as much as I should have."

"I don't think it's possible to appreciate a lot of things until you've lost them. I think that's how we get wiser as we age."

"I can't argue with that. I definitely feel like I know a lot more now than I knew even five years ago, and mostly it's because I've lost things that I didn't appreciate at the time."

Was Derek one of those things? Did she not appreciate him the way she should have?

She'd like to think she took care of him as well as a wife could be expected to. That she treated him well and didn't take advantage of him, but she supposed as she looked back, there were areas where she could've improved. There was a part of her that wanted to say there were a lot of areas where he could've improved too, but thinking like that didn't get anyone anywhere.

"That look on your face says you know I'm right," Sharon said.

Quincy didn't need to answer because the waiter brought their food at that moment. They didn't say anything for a while as she set their sandwiches and salads down and asked if they wanted their drinks refilled.

"So what are your children thinking about their dad?" Sharon asked casually after the waitress left, and they had each taken a bite of their sandwich.

Quincy stopped chewing. Then she swallowed awkwardly.

"They don't know."

"You're kidding. It's been weeks. Almost two months."

"Right. They have no idea, as far as I know. The last time I talked to Derek, he told me it was my job to tell them. And I guess I just feel like it's not."

"Aren't they asking to talk to him when you call them?"

"My daughter just started a new job, and she's working toward a promotion. She's been taking as much overtime as she can. She's focused on that. I've been talking to her, but not as much as we used to and I've been able to avoid any mention of her father. My son, on the other hand, is on a backpacking trip. He's been planning it for years, and he won't be back until this fall."

"Oh wow."

"Yeah. I talk to him too. He has cell phone service, and he has a solar charger. But our conversations are sporadic."

"So it hasn't been too hard for you to hide it."

"I'm not hiding anything. I just haven't told them. And honestly, I don't know how. Although, the longer it goes, the more I think I can just blurt it out. But I don't think they would appreciate that."

"No. You know how shocked you were to begin with. That's how they're gonna feel."

"And so that part of me kind of wishes that I would've told them right away, that way I don't have to try to re-create any feeling so I'm considerate of theirs. If that makes sense."

"It does. I guess… I don't want to tell you what to do, but I would definitely be trying to tell them. And soon. They're going to be upset, knowing that you knew for almost two months and didn't tell them."

"You don't think they'll give me a pass because it's their dad's information to tell? Plus, he's got a pregnancy that they don't know about. They're going to have a half-sibling."

It was so weird to think about her children in that regard. She had wanted to have more babies, and it gave her a pang. After all, if it had been up to her, there would've been a lot of siblings in their family.

It was probably best that they hadn't had anymore, though. After all, she hadn't wanted to raise any of her children in a broken home.

"I'm going to tell them if Derek doesn't. I just... I guess there's still a part of me that still hopes it's just a bad dream, you know?"

Sharon huffed out a breath and snorted. "I know exactly what you mean. I still wake up and hope that my life is just a bad dream."

"No reconciliation with your son?"

"No. I'm blocked on all social media, but occasionally a friend of mine will take a screenshot and send it to me."

"That's so hard."

"Yeah. Tell me about it. But it's life." Sharon's words were gruff and matter-of-fact, but it was obvious the rift with her son caused deep pain.

"Maybe that's what the mystery woman, Vivian, is doing. Maybe she can't stand the pain of what her children have done to her, so she's hiding out, hoping that she'll wake up and it'll all be a bad dream."

"Maybe. She does seem like someone who's carrying around heartache." Quincy thought back to seeing the woman on her porch, how skittish she had been at first. There did seem to be hurt and pain there, but also fear. She didn't say that to Sharon, though, because it was pure speculation just based on her body language and the way she had acted, grabbing her dog and running inside the first few times she'd seen Quincy.

"Are you gonna be ready to head back home and face the wicked stepsister?"

"My sister-in-law." Quincy laughed. "Honestly, I don't think I'll ever be ready to face her. She has a caustic way about her that makes me doubt myself. Even when I was happily married, with two children and a perfect life, she made me feel like I wasn't good enough."

"I think people who do that usually feel that way about themselves."

"I can't argue with that. You're probably right. But that's not the way it seems from my end. I think when you're on the receiving end of someone treating you like that, you don't usually stop to think about why they might be doing it."

"Maybe we should." Sharon's words were simple, but profound. Quincy held her sandwich in front of her and realized that Sharon was exactly right. Maybe they should take the time to try to think about why people acted the way they did, and realize that there might be hurt and disappointment and disillusionment behind it.

"Thanks for the reminder."

"Of course. Isn't that what friends are for?"

"Iron sharpens iron," she said, quoting part of the famous Bible verse.

"I'm your iron," Sharon said, wrinkling her nose.

"I know. It doesn't sound like a compliment, but trust me, it is. Sometimes being sharpened hurts a little, but it makes us better."

"It really does. It's not often that you find a friend who makes you better."

"No. You've got to hold onto those kinds tight."

"You sure do."

"And... that's why you need to join us wherever we find to meet."

"That was pretty sneaky the way you did that," Sharon said, laughing before she put the last of her sandwich in her mouth.

She chewed and swallowed before she said, "All right. You talked me into it. Whoever's there, I'll be there too. Maybe I'll find some more iron."

Quincy laughed, but it was true. Maybe there would be more iron, and they should always be on the lookout for friends like that.

"I want to be a friend like that. Not just have friends like that."

"Yeah. Although, are we talking about friends, or are we talking about sisters?" Sharon asked, and there was a little bit of a dreamy quality to her voice.

"Do you have siblings?"

"Two brothers, who really don't know I'm alive."

"I have one brother. And yeah, I always wanted a sister."

"Your sister-in-law didn't quite fit the bill?"

"Well, maybe she does act like a sibling, but not the kind of sister I always dreamed of having."

"Friends, sisters, I think they're the same thing, especially once you get out of childhood. Unless... unless you don't have a good relationship."

Sharon's voice trailed off, and Quincy wished there was something she could do to help her. She knew she was thinking about her son again, and how they didn't have a good relationship. Maybe she'd always wanted a daughter, too, and her hopes in that area had been dashed as well.

But Sharon seemed to shake off her sadness as they talked about work and leaky pipes, before they finished their lunch. Sharon teased her before she left about Enoch and maybe giving him some more plumbing lessons.

"I'll give him as many lessons as he wants, if he can talk the owner into letting us use the pavilion."

She said it lightly, but as she spoke, she remembered what Sharon had said about not thinking that Enoch was actually a handyman or contractor.

She knew why that bothered her so much. Because it felt true.

nineteen

QUINCY WALKED UP THE PATH, her head full of questions. She'd seen lights on in Beulah's and Sonny's house when she had returned from work, and rather than going in, she had decided to take a walk up along the bay side of the island. It was beautiful, just as beautiful in the evening as it was in the morning. A soft breeze blew gently across the still water, while the brilliant orange of the sun faded out of sight and a canopy of stars stretched across the sky, their twinkling lights promising that she was not alone in the world.

Late afternoon and evening had a tendency to bring out the melancholy in her, and she was grateful to have work. Even when she was watching Sonny, sometimes it seemed like both of them got depressed in the late afternoon. She felt alone, adrift, unsure of what her life was going to look like, after having everything she'd built ripped out from underneath her. During the day, sometimes she even forgot about it, and it didn't really bother her anymore. But in the late afternoon, she often felt helpless and like crying.

She'd seen the woman, Vivian, as Sharon had said her name was, standing on her porch again, and had been really tempted to go over and talk to her.

Maybe Quincy wasn't the only one who was feeling a little lost and alone this time of evening. Plus, it would delay her getting back to the house, and perhaps Mary would be in bed. She really didn't feel up to a confrontation there. Or even up to handling Mary's not-so-subtle barbs.

She just felt vulnerable.

Even though her visit with Enoch had been a confidence booster. It had felt good to be able to figure out a problem that someone else couldn't solve. Someone capable and strong.

She'd never really thought of herself as the kind of woman who absolutely needed a man, and she didn't like the idea of being dependent. After all, if she was dependent, her whole world could come crashing down.

But didn't that teach her to depend on God? Didn't that show her that God would take care of her? Wasn't that an experience that God could use to teach her and help grow her? If she didn't allow herself to be vulnerable, to be part of a team that built something together, didn't that very action say that she didn't trust God to take care of her if anything happened? And hadn't He taken care of her exceptionally well so far?

Sure, she had all of the feelings of dejection and desertion, all of the heartbreak, all of the feeling like she wasn't good enough, but God had given her a soft landing. And... maybe He was even working something out between Beulah and herself, fixing that relationship that she had allowed to crumble over the years, instead of dealing with it like she probably should have. God had opened doors that she had never considered even touching.

Wasn't that worth the heartache and the fact that she had allowed herself to become vulnerable by depending on someone else?

She hadn't gotten that question answered when she saw Vivian standing on the porch.

So tempted to go over and say something to her, she refrained, instead throwing her hand up in a wave, which Vivian returned, if not enthusiastically, at least in a friendly way.

She even thought there might've been a smile on her face, although it was hard to tell in the dusky twilight.

She walked a bit more before she turned around, and on her way back, Vivian was gone. Or maybe the shadows were so dark that she couldn't see her sitting on one of the rocking chairs she knew graced the front porch. Maybe someday she'd sit in one of those rocking chairs beside Vivian and they'd talk, and she'd find out what the mystery woman was doing in Whispering Hope Harbor. Maybe she'd find a friend. A good friend, one of those friends that stuck around for the rest of one's life. Iron.

She wanted those kinds of friends, but she couldn't have them if she walled herself off and didn't allow herself to work through the problems that relationships brought. The problems that she and Beulah had, and... yes, even the problems between her and Mary.

Lord, sometimes there's nothing a person can do to fix a relationship. It takes two people to have a relationship.

There was no answer, and she thought about Derek and her. If it were up to her, there would still be a relationship, but Derek didn't want one.

Was that true? Or did he just not want the kind of relationship that Quincy wanted? To be married, depending on each other, loving each other, and spending the rest of one's lives together. And if she couldn't have what she wanted, she didn't want anything?

But that was reasonable. It was reasonable for a wife to expect her husband to want to spend the rest of his life with her.

But if she didn't get that, could she swallow her pride and take a lesser relationship?

Funny that she'd never thought about things like that, not until her marriage had blown up in her face. Was that what God was trying to teach her? To look at things from a different perspective, a perspective she wouldn't even have considered if she was still married?

Lord, help me to learn the lessons You're trying to teach me. Help me to see the lessons You're trying to teach me. I want to be more like Jesus, and I know that it's not going to be easy.

She thought about the crucifixion, and all of the pain and suffering that Jesus had gone through. She couldn't expect to become more like Jesus if she didn't suffer some. And sure, she didn't like suffering. What was that verse? That verse about suffering for the present time. She searched around in her mind until she was able to quote it to herself:

> **For I reckon that the sufferings of this present time**
> **are not worthy to be compared with the glory**
> **which shall be revealed in us.**

Yeah, the suffering she was feeling was nothing compared to the work God was doing in her. It was a small consolation.

By the time she stepped up on the porch, she was determined to do what God wanted her to do.

She should've known that immediately, she would have a test.

Mary stood on the porch, her arms crossed, her eyes narrowed.

The porch light was dim, but it was on. Usually when Quincy sat on the porch, she kept all the lights off, enjoying the darkness and the soothing balm it brought to her soul.

Mary didn't seem to know anything about soothing balms, or enjoying the darkness. Rather, she looked like she was ready for a fight. All she needed were boxing gloves. And a little suit that gave her a wedgie.

Quincy bit back a laugh.

"Good evening, Mary."

"You can stop smirking anytime," Mary said, showing that indeed, she was not going to be an easy person to get along with. She was not out there to make pleasant and polite conversation.

"You can act all goody-goody if you want to, but I have no idea why I was not informed about the condition of my father. And I'm willing to bet it was because you were telling my mother not to tell me."

Where in the world did she come up with that?

"I'm sorry you think that," she began, trying to figure out what she could say that would not make Beulah look bad, but would also exonerate herself. After all, if she were Beulah, knowing that Mary was going to react like this, she would hesitate to tell her anything either.

"Stop with the bull crap. I have every right to know what's going on with my parents, and just because you and Derek are having problems, which anyone could have foreseen the moment you guys started dating—"

"I'm sorry. I guess I'm confused about what we're talking about."

She shouldn't have interrupted, but she didn't want to talk about Derek with Mary. She didn't know if she could do it without saying some really, really bad things about her husband, and she knew that wasn't the right way to be. No matter how bad he had been to her.

"Oh, you're so self-righteous, aren't you?"

"Mary, I'm sorry for whatever I've done to you. I really am. I'd like to get along. But I don't know how. It seems like everything I do, you construe as having some kind of wicked, evil motivation behind it."

And that was the problem. Mary just assumed the worst about her, no matter what she had done. She could see the pattern over the years, with Mary always thinking that she was being competitive, or taking Derek away, or trying to poison him against his family, even if Derek had come up with the idea that he didn't want to see them as much anymore, or family gatherings were too stressful for him so he went to as few as possible. Somehow, Mary always blamed it on her.

"I wish I could believe that, but your track record tells a completely different story."

"I don't agree with you, but I would appreciate another chance?"

What else could she say? She'd apologized, told Mary that she wanted to get along, and asked for another chance.

Lord? What else?

"How about you just move out. That will solve everything. I'll move in with my mother and dad, and I'll take care of them."

"What about your job?" she asked, before she thought about what she was saying. Mary couldn't just leave her job.

"I'll figure that out."

"All right." She paused for a delicate moment, before suggesting as humbly as she could, "There are two bedrooms upstairs. You have one, I have the other. Do I need to move out in order for you to stay?"

"I don't think this house is big enough for the two of us."

That sounded like a juvenile thing to say, but Quincy kept her mouth shut.

"What really happened between you and Derek? Mom gave me the story about him cheating on you, but I'm not buying it. Do you have a lover on the side?"

There wasn't anything she could do to make herself look better in Mary's eyes. She would always look like the villain.

Don't be so negative. God can change people's hearts.

Before she opened her mouth again, she said a quiet prayer. *Lord, help Mary to see Jesus in me. Help me know what to say so that You can work in her life.*

"I made a commitment to my husband, and I never broke it. And I have no plans on breaking it. Although, he asked for a divorce. I didn't want to give him that. But then I thought, I don't want to fight with him. I really don't know what to do. And if you have advice for me, I'm all ears. But otherwise, Derek is going to divorce me and marry his mistress, who's pregnant with his child. In the meantime, in my opinion, that doesn't make me less family than I was when I got married. I love your mom and your dad, and I'm gonna do every-thing I can to help them. That was my plan, that's what I said I was going to do, and that's what I'm going to keep doing until your mom tells me she doesn't want me here." She took a breath. "I'd really like to get along with you. I think both of us have been through some hard things. And maybe you feel just as betrayed by Derek as I do.

After all, this wasn't what I was expecting from my husband. But regardless, for your mom's sake, I'd really like to get along. Will you help me?"

"Derek was always a jerk," Mary muttered, and then, without answering Quincy's question, she turned on one foot and walked into the house, and although the door didn't slam behind her, she shut it with a firmness that felt cold and unwelcoming to Quincy.

Was she doing the wrong thing by insisting on staying? Should she leave?

There were no answers, but rather than following Mary inside, she sat down on the porch swing and stayed there for a long time, long enough to be sure that Mary was asleep before she slipped in.

twenty

MARY OPENED her door quietly in the predawn darkness. Beulah had told her the evening before that they would be leaving early that morning. Mary clenched her fist at the idea that Quincy was going with her mother to clean that day. How had Quincy come in and wormed her way into the family? She and Derek had always been hours and hours away. Mary was the one that her mother depended on. Mary was the favorite child. At least after Derek left. And now Quincy came in, and all of a sudden Beulah was saying "Quincy this" and "Quincy helped me here" and "Quincy helped me there."

Mary narrowed her eyes. Quincy was a conniving little witch.

She swallowed against the guilt that she felt for being so mean and unkind in the face of Quincy trying to be nice. It only made her hate her more. What was she, perfect?

What if the fault was not Quincy? What if it was her?

She tried to shove that thought aside, but wasn't successful. She knew that being mean to someone who was trying hard to get along was not something a Christian should do. But she'd been out of church for so long, she wasn't even sure if she really believed there was a God anymore. After all, if God loved her, why had all the bad things happened to her? Why had He allowed that? If there was a God, He definitely wasn't loving. He was just sitting there laughing at her. Laughing that she was never good enough, that first it was Derek who was the favorite, now it was Quincy. All Quincy had to do was show up and her mother thought she was a patron saint.

Mary came, and her mother acted like she couldn't get her to leave fast enough.

She stepped into the kitchen, where her mother was already pouring two cups of coffee on the counter.

She turned around with a smile on her face, which faded just a little when she saw that it was Mary standing at the bottom of the stairs. So her mother was expecting Quincy?

"Good morning, Mary," Beulah said before she turned back to the coffee. "Would you like a cup?"

"You have two on the counter. I assume one's for me."

"Of course."

Her mother finished filling the cups, set the coffee down, and then, almost as though she were trying not to bring attention to it, she got a third cup out of the cupboard and filled that up.

So she was pouring a cup for Quincy and wasn't expecting Mary.

It made Mary unreasonably angry.

"Three cups? There's only two of us down here."

"Quincy will be coming down soon. And she and I will be leaving. Remember I told you yesterday that we have a big job to do up in Nags Head, and we will be gone all day." Her mother shifted the curtain and tried to look out the window. "Jackie hasn't shown up yet."

"I told you, I can watch Daddy. You can tell Jackie she doesn't need to come."

"Oh, I hate to do that. She depends on this for her money to help take care of her family."

"Then she should be more dependable," Mary said. She hadn't mentioned what had happened about her job, and she had been exceptionally dependable.

"I suppose if she comes, and you want to tell her that she can go home, you can."

It annoyed her that her mother was taking Jackie's side. Instead of calling her and telling her that she didn't need to come, she was pushing Mary aside.

"Mother. I told you I would watch him."

Plus, she didn't really believe that her dad was that bad. Did he really need to have a full-time caregiver? Her mom acted like it was some kind of major inconvenience to be watching him. She didn't exactly say that it would've been a relief to have the assessor say that he needed to be moved to a care facility, but Mary could read between the lines. That's what her mother really wanted.

"All right. I'll do that. If she shows up."

"Good morning," Quincy said softly from the bottom of the stairs.

Mary didn't turn to look at her, but her mother gave Quincy a big smile and returned her greeting. "There's a cup of coffee here for you. I'd like to leave in the next ten minutes."

"I can put that in my tumbler, and I'll be ready to go."

"I should have poured it in there to begin with. In fact, I think I'll take mine with me too."

Of course, her mom acted like Quincy had the most brilliant idea in the world. Anyone could've thought about putting the coffee in an insulated cup with a lid on it. Of course. That's what the rest of the world always did. Quincy was not some kind of brainiac who had brilliant ideas.

"I ordered lunch for you and Sonny at the diner. Shiloh told me that if she had a slow moment this morning, she would run it over. That way you don't have to worry about cooking."

"You shouldn't have done that. I like to cook."

Mary knew she was being belligerent and exceptionally unkind, but Quincy and her goody-two-shoes attitude was absolutely insufferable. She was just trying to brown-nose her way into her mother's good graces. What was she trying to do, steal Mary's inheritance?

"All right. I guess if you don't want it, I can text her quickly so she doesn't waste her time."

Quincy had her phone out, ready to text, but Mary shook her head.

"Let it be. I'll work on supper."

"Thank you so much, Mary. I'd really appreciate having something to eat when we get home. I'm going to be exhausted, I'm sure." Beulah set the coffee carafe back and proceeded to work on putting the lids on the drinks she had poured.

"I'm gonna be exhausted too. I'm a lot more used to cleaning than I was when I first came, but a day like today is going to be tiring."

"But we'll feel really good once that house looks amazing. It's one of the most beautiful houses we clean. Actually, it's my favorite." Beulah smiled at Quincy, and they seemed to share a look that spoke of a bond between the two of them and shared experiences that made Mary feel left out. There was Quincy again, trying to inject herself into Mary's position.

"You don't have to worry about Daddy. I'll take excellent care of him. He and I always had a special relationship."

"You sure did. He loves you, and he knew who you were immediately yesterday. That really surprised me."

"Mom. Stop making it seem like Daddy is worse than he is. He's old and a little forgetful. It's not that bad."

She didn't want to face the idea that her dad might be failing, and faster than she realized.

But by the end of the day, she had to admit the fact that her mom, far from exaggerating, had probably been underreporting what was actually happening.

Her dad had thrown a fit, thrown his breakfast across the room, breaking all of the glassware on his tray, had yelled at her, called her Tracey, Julie, and Bernice, none of them names she recognized or could put a face to at any point. At one time, he thought he was on a ship and had yelled at her for not keeping the lines where he wanted them, and explained to her in great detail about how the ropes would get tangled. He didn't seem to realize that they were still in their living room.

He had refused to eat anything, then complained that she didn't feed him, accused her of stealing his wallet, his money, his life savings, and, when she wouldn't allow him to use the telephone to order the two-thousand-dollar ring that had been advertised on TV, she thought they were going to get into a real physical wrestling match.

By the time Beulah had come home, the only thing she had for supper was egg salad sandwiches, and that was because there was egg salad already mixed up in the refrigerator. And bread sat on the counter.

"How was your day?" Beulah asked as she walked in, her face flushed, dried sweat making her hair stick back. She walked like her feet hurt and bent forward slightly, as though her back hurt as well.

She felt bad for her mom, but honestly, Mary felt the same way.

"I'm sorry." Mary began, not meaning to greet her mother with an apology, but one was due.

She was faintly aware of Quincy walking in behind Beulah as she continued. "I didn't believe you about Daddy." She glanced at the couch, where her father had finally fallen into a fitful sleep. She talked low, careful not to wake him up.

"You were right. It was awful. Ninety percent of the day he didn't know who I was, argued with everything I said, he broke more glasses and... you were right. I didn't realize how hard it was."

Her mother came over, patted her arm before putting her arms around her and wrapping her in a hug.

"I've stopped feeding him on glassware. That's why I bought the paper plates and the plastic silverware. He doesn't like them, and he'll complain about them, but when he throws his food, he doesn't break anything at least."

"He doesn't break any silverware or glassware, but sometimes he hits something that breaks," Quincy interjected.

Mary hated to do it, but she squeezed her eyes shut tight, then opened them and stepped back from her mother.

"I owe you an apology too. I thought you were here to weasel your way into my parents' good graces, possibly stealing my inheritance from me, but Mom really needs the help." There was no doubt that Quincy looked exhausted as well. She wasn't quite ready to be friends with Quincy, but Quincy had been right. Her mom was overloaded.

"You don't owe me an apology. That's a valid concern, but I guess I wasn't even thinking about inheritances. I feel like I've been knocked off my feet and landed somewhere where I don't even know where I am. I'm just trying to stand up. I don't have any ideas of what I'm gonna do in the future."

Mary's heart hurt a little for Quincy. It was funny how close their scenarios were. Although Quincy had not lost her job. But she'd lost her husband, same as Mary, and was floundering, same as Mary. They probably had more in common than they didn't. And Mary was the reason that they weren't getting along.

Still, she wasn't sure she was ready to completely trust Quincy.

"Thanks for being gracious," she said instead. "I'm sorry. I had planned to make a nice hot meal for supper, but all I have is egg salad sandwiches."

"I understand, and I just appreciate food," her mother said, gracious as always.

"Same. I'm starving."

She wasn't trusting Quincy, but... maybe they had called a truce. And that felt good.

twenty-one

PULLING into the house that Enoch worked on was not exactly like pulling into home, but just like Beulah had her favorite house—the biggest one they did, which sat upon a bit of a hill, with a glorious view of the ocean, stately and majestic, with enough bedrooms to accommodate an entire wedding party as well as some guests—Quincy also had her favorite. It was the sea cottage, and she didn't even know who it belonged to. Enoch was their contact, and he was just the contractor. Not that it mattered. She certainly didn't have enough money to buy a house by the ocean, even if it was exceptionally rundown.

Although, as she looked around, setting her equipment down, she had to admit that over the time that she'd been here, Enoch had not been idle.

The kitchen wasn't finished, but he'd gotten the living room and the dining room completely done, from the walls and ceilings to the tile floor, which looked exceptionally expensive. It was a blue-green color that seemed to change with the mood of the ocean. That was a figment of her romantic imagination, she was sure, but the floor had to be her favorite flooring ever.

It was easy to clean too. Maybe he'd put some kind of clear coating on top of it that got rid of all of the grooves and made the grout silky. She'd heard of such a thing but couldn't remember what it was called.

She had just finished mopping and had given herself a moment to lean on her mop and admire the floor when Enoch's voice interrupted her.

"Do you like it?" he asked.

She startled, glanced at him, as he stood in the doorway. His hair ruffled like he'd just run his hand through it, and wearing a simple white T-shirt with jeans that had been splattered with paint at one point and looked like he'd worn them for a decade or more.

One side of his jean leg caught on his work boot, as his thumb hooked in a belt loop. The other hand leaned against the doorjamb.

A couple of days' worth of beard growth gave him a rugged look that made Quincy's heart skip a beat.

When was the last time it had done that in response to looking at a man?

She shook the idea away. She hadn't heard from her husband in weeks. She'd talked to her lawyer, she'd drawn something up, she'd approved it, and she said she'd sent it out. But so far, either Derek hadn't gotten it, or he wanted to give her a little bit of time to squirm before he called and exploded on her.

"I love it. I was just thinking that it's my favorite floor I've ever seen. There's something about that color. And what did you put on the top of it?"

"That's epoxy. It's supposed to make it easier to clean. But... it wasn't simple to put down." One side of his mouth quirked up, like there was a story there, but he didn't offer any more information.

"I love it. It really is easy to clean. I don't know if that's the purpose or not, but it certainly has made my life easier."

"Well, I'm all about keeping things simple for you."

He didn't sound like he was being sarcastic, but it almost had to be a sarcastic comment, right? After all, what did he care about whether or not her life was simple?

"Speaking of, you have permission to use the pavilion anytime you want. I vouched for your good character, and assumed that there would be no wild parties."

"I might look like a simple cleaning lady, but wild parties are actually my thing."

They shared a smile. She knew, with her gray-streaked hair, the crow's feet around her eyes and mouth, and her somewhat matronly figure, that she did not look like a weekend partier. And her maid's uniform did not add to that image at all.

She looked exactly like what she was: a middle-aged woman who couldn't keep her husband and who had to work in order to earn a living. Nothing more, but hopefully nothing less either.

"I guess I'll have to change my assessment of you."

They laughed again, and then she said, "Thank you so much for asking. I truly would've done it myself, but I don't have the owner's contact info, and you didn't seem to want to give it out. I respect his privacy."

"I appreciate that. I think sometimes people don't."

"I know there are times where I would prefer to not have to ever see anyone again." She paused for a moment and then realized with a start that that wasn't entirely true anymore. "But I think I'm kind of coming out of that stage."

"Something happen?" he asked, and his words did not sound like he was trying to pry. They sounded like he was being a friend.

"Yeah. I guess it's the story of a lot of women. My husband left me for a younger model, she's pregnant, and he wants a divorce."

"And you're giving it to him?" he asked. Again, it was an easy question. Like she had the choice as to whether or not she wanted to answer it, and he would be okay either way.

"I was gonna fight him. I didn't say vows just to break them. And I'm okay trying to work through the hard stuff. After all, a lot of life is hard stuff."

"You can say that again," he said, shifting a bit, leaning his shoulder against the jamb as he crossed his arms over his chest.

"And marriage is even harder sometimes. Although, some people seem to have a marriage that just flows naturally."

"I think there are people like that. But maybe those are people who are the same. You know?"

"Maybe. You mean like opposites attract but similar personalities have less friction?"

"Less spark too. There's always that."

"Yeah. I suppose there is. But my experience is that as you get into the decades, as you start counting the years you've been married in decades, sparks and happiness are choices, along with contentment. And if you don't make that deliberate choice, you have a tendency to not be that way."

"I think that's wise. I didn't know that when I was younger. Did you know that when you got married?"

"I didn't know anything when I got married," she said, laughter in her tone. She shook her head at her naivety.

"I guess that makes two of us."

"You're married?" she asked, and she hoped the words didn't come out too quickly. She didn't know why she had just assumed that he wasn't. Maybe because there had been no wife around? But of course, even if her husband had not cheated on her and left, chances were, he wouldn't have come with her to clean Enoch's house, and Enoch would not have seen her husband. She was such a silly schoolgirl in some ways.

"I was. But I'm not anymore. And... I guess I did the same thing. Didn't fight."

"I don't know about you, but I wanted to," she said, not probing for more. He had shifted again, not leaning against the doorjamb anymore, and had dropped his arms, like he was getting ready to go back to work.

"Do you know how much longer it's going to take you to finish this? Not that I'm trying to push you into getting done. I'm going to miss coming here." She paused. "Unless the owner would like to keep us on after it's finished?"

She hardly dared hope, and found herself holding her breath while waiting for his answer.

"I guess that's another thing I can ask him."

"You don't have to." It didn't matter, really. They had plenty of work to keep them busy. They didn't need this one. "Should I just let you know when we're going to use the pavilion and make sure that the dates are okay?"

He tilted his head to the side as though thinking about that. "Anytime that suits you from now to Thanksgiving should be fine. There won't be anyone using the house until at least then."

"All right. I appreciate that." She kind of wanted to stick around, talk some more. Enoch was an easy person to confide in, or maybe it was just an easy friendship. Despite that little spark of attraction that she had felt earlier. "I better get going. I have two more places I need to do before I'm done for the day."

"I thought Tuesdays were your slow day?" he asked, moving forward to pick up her mop bucket.

She stepped back, allowing him to take it, and smiling her thanks.

"We're getting into the time of year where every day is a busy day. I've heard that July and August are even worse, but it's kind of hard to imagine how I can get more work done than what I'm already doing."

"I'd tell you to take care of yourself, but I do think it slows down. I suppose like the ants, we need to work while it's time to do it, and take off and rest during that season."

"Go to the ant, thou sluggard; consider her ways, and be wise," she began.

He finished the verse. "Which, having no guide, overseer, or ruler, provideth her meat in the summer, and gathereth her food in the harvest."

After he finished, she stared at him for a moment, and it felt like there was a connection, across the distance of the room, across the distance of the unknown in their lives. The little friendship seed that had started to grow maybe blossomed a little more between them.

Later, as she drove away, the thought surprised her that she'd never really had that kind of connection with Derek.

twenty-two

"YOU REALLY NEED TO TELL THEM," Sharon said, as they sat at the marina for their usual Wednesday lunch. The amount of time that Quincy could spend had been evaporating as they got deeper into the summer season and she got busier. But, at the very least, they picked up sandwiches and sat on the picnic bench outside for fifteen or twenty minutes.

Sharon also was busy, although all of her pools were open, and cleaning and maintenance were all she was doing now. Her busy time had started before.

She'd been thinking about hiring a helper, but didn't have quite enough work and was afraid that she wouldn't be able to pay someone a living wage.

But they weren't talking about that. They were talking about Quincy finally telling her children about Derek leaving her. As far as she knew, it had been two full months, and Derek hadn't talked to his kids once. Or at least, not about Candy, the child they had on the way, or the divorce.

"I know. I just hate the fact that if there's a dirty job, he always sticks me with it."

"I know you know about the whole being a servant, washing

others' feet, putting them first." Sharon held her sandwich in front of her and lifted her brows. She wasn't lecturing; she was just gently nudging Quincy.

"Thank you. I appreciate a friend who tries to make me better."

"Iron and iron," Sharon said, and then took a big bite of her sandwich.

That was true. Sharon had been iron for her, and she appreciated it. She had needed that, to keep her from wallowing and falling into bitterness.

"Is Mary still living there?"

"She's still there. She hasn't mentioned anything about leaving, and I'm afraid if I ask her about leaving, she's going to accuse me of wanting her gone. So I haven't said a word. I have asked Beulah several times, but she just shrugs her shoulders. I think she's afraid to ask too."

"Mary is pretty touchy. I've talked to her a couple of times when we've met in the grocery store or on the sidewalk, and it seems like it doesn't take much of anything to offend her."

"It doesn't."

"But she takes such gentle care of her dad. It's obvious that she adores him."

"She does. Sometimes I wonder if maybe she loved her parents but felt like they gave Derek preference over her. I sometimes get those vibes from her."

"It would be interesting to talk to her about it."

"She would never talk to me. Not about that. Not about anything that would make her look vulnerable."

"Don't say never. Remember, God specializes in miracles."

"He sure does." She grinned. "What we're doing tonight is a bit of a miracle."

"It is. Getting permission to use a pavilion with such a beautiful view of the ocean."

"I never dreamed that we would be able to. And I think that Beulah might be coming."

"Really?"

"Yeah. Mary has been taking care of Sonny, so Beulah doesn't feel bad asking her to watch him in the evening. She seems to enjoy it."

"You should ask her to come."

Sharon's comment was so offhand, deliberately studious, and she wasn't meeting Quincy's eyes.

"Oh my goodness. Are you serious?" But she knew immediately that Sharon was, and she was right. She should ask her.

Sharon lifted a shoulder and took another bite of sandwich rather than answering. She'd thrown the suggestion out there, and there was nothing else she needed to do. Just allow Quincy's conscience to work for her. Which it was, overtime.

"All right. Maybe one hard thing at a time. If I'm going to call my children, I'm not sure I can talk to Mary too."

"Is Shiloh coming?"

"She is." She paused, running her finger around the rim of her paper plate. "I've been tempted to walk up to Vivian's house and ask her if she'd like to come too. It seems like that would be less of an intrusion than asking to have a one-on-one conversation with her. I'm not sure why."

"Well, she'd certainly be welcome if she wanted to come, but... I'm not sure that she would. She's deliberately keeping to herself. I don't think I've seen her since you and I last spoke about her."

"I think she seems scared," Quincy said quietly. Not meaning to gossip about the woman, but wanting to bounce the idea off of her friend, to see if maybe she had noticed that and wondered about it too.

"She does? I guess I haven't seen her enough to notice."

"Maybe it's just my imagination. I have a tendency to exaggerate things. Project feelings and drama onto someone's life that isn't there."

"I hadn't noticed that about you. You seem very logical and practical. Pragmatic even."

"I think that's a compliment."

"Yeah. I meant it as a compliment."

"All right." She gathered up her paper plate. "If I'm going to get this next house done in time to call my kids before we're meeting tonight, I better get going."

"Same. I actually have an additional house I need to do, so I might be a little late this evening."

"You could've canceled our lunch date," Quincy said, feeling bad that she had taken up so much of Sharon's time when she had extra work to do.

"And miss talking to you? Not a chance."

Quincy smiled, returning Sharon's hug, before they both took their trash to the garbage can, where they said goodbye and parted, walking different directions.

She might've been a little distracted as she cleaned the next house. Thankfully, it wasn't very dirty at all, and she had a new and great appreciation for people who made sure to tidy up before they left. She hadn't been working that long, but she'd gone into a few houses that looked like people had just thrown their trash wherever they felt like it and not bothered to take care of anything, almost as though they thought the cleaning lady was there to simply be their servant.

Regardless, she was done early and walked to the little lookout above the bay and sat down on the single bench that was there, the wind rifling through her hair as she held her phone in her hands.

It had to be a video call. She would get them both on at once. And then, as gently as she could, she'd break the news. She needed to be kind and not say anything mean about Derek. That was probably going to be the hardest thing. Other than seeing her children hurt and upset. She would be angry at him all over again.

Dialing Stacy's number first, she chatted for a minute or two, asked her if it was a good time, and then got Randall on the phone as well.

"I was just getting ready to tuck into my sleeping bag, Mom.

You're lucky you caught me with service. For the last two weeks I haven't had any."

"I know. I've tried to call you several times, but I didn't leave any messages because I knew that you told me that you would be in and out of service. I try not to worry."

"I sent you a text today to let you know that I was fine."

"I know. That was part of the reason I decided to call tonight. I knew you had service, and... I have something to tell you both."

"You have cancer," Stacy said, her hand going to her throat and her eyes widening.

"No. I'm fine, I'm healthy, I haven't even been to the doctor lately, and your dad is fine as far as I know as well."

"As far as you know?" Stacy asked, picking up on that immediately.

"That's what I need to talk to you about."

"Mom, I'm not liking this," Randall said, his brows drawn down as he held his phone so close to his face she could only see his eyes and nose.

"Listen, let me just put it out there, we'll get the worst over, and then we'll deal with the fallout... Your dad left me."

"You're kidding!" Stacy said immediately, falling back onto the couch, her hand again going to her chest.

"No. He had an affair with our realtor. She's pregnant."

"Oh my goodness. Did he just tell you that?" Stacy asked.

In the meantime, Randall was quiet. It was typical of the twins. Stacy did a lot of the talking, while Randall processed things. Then he would come up with ideas to fix things, while Stacy handled the PR. They were like their own little business, between the two of them. Both of them having strengths and weaknesses that bolstered the other one. Maybe because they had grown up so close, they had learned to function that way, or maybe that was the way God had made them to begin with. Quincy had never been able to figure it out.

"No. He didn't just tell me. I've known for a while."

"And you didn't tell us?" Stacy asked, sounding hurt.

"I'm sorry. I thought he would. I felt like it was his information to share. But I kept talking to you guys, and neither one of you mentioned it, and I knew, and I felt guilty for knowing and not telling you."

"I suppose you're right. You really shouldn't feel guilty, Mom."

Stacy's voice was a lot more subdued.

"I do anyway. I question myself. Was there more I could've done? I had no idea that he was even thinking about cheating, or that he wasn't happy, apparently. But... he told me on the day we closed."

"That's been almost two months," Stacy said, after a short pause while she probably figured out the timeline.

"I know. I think at first I couldn't have told you without crying and being a little hysterical. It was rough."

"It still looks like you're at the Outer Banks with Grandma?"

"I didn't have anywhere else to go. We sold our home, and I did stay in a hotel the first night, because I already had that booked. But... I didn't have anywhere else to go."

"You deserve to be able to buy yourself a house. Dad can't just sell your house and then move in with some floozy—"

"I think we need to be kind. She's carrying a child, and that will be a half-sibling of yours."

She let that sink in as two seagulls flew overhead, squawking at each other. The waves lapped gently at the shore as the sun settled lower in the sky.

She had the pavilion to go to tonight, and she needed to be there in an hour and a half. That was probably plenty of time to talk to her children, and then, hopefully she would have the support of the friends that she'd made on the island as she tried to process the fact that she'd just told them something that she had hoped to never have to say to her kids.

"So how are you doing now?" Randall asked, his eyes a little narrow, like he was trying to see her through the phone and examine every square inch of her.

"I'm doing better. Honestly. I'm busy here with Grandma. She needed help with Grandpa, who you know was dealing with some dementia."

"Still?" Randall asked.

"Yeah. It doesn't get better." She almost said "it only gets worse," but they could talk about that some other time.

"And I've been cleaning with her. For her. And Aunt Mary is here as well."

Stacy wrinkled up her nose. "Aunt Mary was never very nice to us."

"I think she has her own problems," Quincy said, knowing that was true, but silently agreeing with her daughter. Mary never had been very nice to them.

"So are you guys... divorced?" Randall asked.

"No. Originally he basically wanted to keep almost everything for himself. And... I didn't want to fight about stuff. That seems very unimportant when I think about my entire life unraveling, and everything I've built, my marriage, my family, everything that means something to me, unraveling in front of me. But... I also have to live. So when he offered me basically nothing, I went to my lawyer, drew up something that I felt was more fair, and sent it to him. He hasn't been in touch since that happened."

"So you haven't seen him since you left?"

"I drove back once to sign the papers he wanted me to. But, like I said, the agreement wasn't fair, and while I didn't want to fight him, I also didn't want to give him everything that we both worked for. He deserves a share."

"Half. I think half is fair. I mean, not that you're asking me, but, sure Dad worked, but you took care of us."

"I know, Stacy. But life usually isn't fair. Even in my agreement, I didn't ask for half. I just asked for enough that I feel like I can get by while I'm working."

"You shouldn't have to worry about whether or not you're getting by, Mom. You gave up a lucrative nursing job so that you could raise us, and Dad wasn't around hardly at all. Without you, we wouldn't have had a parent."

"Like I said, sometimes life doesn't seem like it's fair, but God isn't going to let anything happen to me that He doesn't want to have happen. And if I get less than half, I know that God's gonna take care of me. I just know He will."

"I wish I had your faith, Mom. You always were confident that God would take care of us, provide, or work things out. I never could believe that."

"I wish you could. He loves us. And sometimes it's hard to see, but just like a parent sometimes has to discipline their child—it doesn't feel like love at the time, but it's because you love them, because you care about them, because you want them to grow to be a productive adult—that's why you do it."

"I know. I guess I just always hoped that as I got older, my faith would grow more like yours."

"I don't think faith grows unless we feed it. And that means trusting God in the little things. Deliberately. Choosing that every day."

"I remember you saying that growing up. That you read your Bible, prayed, and had a relationship with the Lord to have a foundation. You compared it to the foolish man and the wise man who built his house on the sand."

"That little song?" Stacy asked, grinning at her brother.

He nodded. "The wise man built his house upon the rock, the wise man built his house upon the rock, the wise man built his house upon the rock, and the rain came tumbling down. The rain came down and the floods came up, the rain came down, the floods came up, the rain came down, the floods came up, and the wise man's house stood firm."

They ended up both singing it together by the time they were done, and Quincy smiled. Those little songs that the kids learned in Sunday school seemed silly, almost, at times, but they had such good messages in them.

They talked for a little bit longer, with the twins asking a few more questions—questions she really couldn't answer, since she hadn't talked to Derek in weeks. She promised to keep them informed, and Stacy and she made a tentative lunch date, saying that they would figure out what was halfway and meet there so that they could both do it in a day. Quincy warned them that she was getting into the busy season with cleaning, but that she should have plenty of time to get together once the tourist season was over in September.

She hung up, sad, with a gritty feeling in her stomach, but also feeling like a burden lifted off of her shoulders. She had told her children. She had done the hard thing. And she had done it when Derek had been too cowardly to do it himself.

twenty-three

"DID SONNY HAVE A GOOD DAY?" Quincy asked as she stepped onto the porch. Beulah was sitting on the porch swing, obviously waiting on her. A covered casserole dish sat beside her, most likely the Jell-O salad that Quincy had made the night before. A wrapped loaf of freshly baked bread sat on top of it. Beulah had been experimenting with sourdough and had hoped she would get home in time to bake the bread she had set out that morning.

"Jackie said he did okay. Mary looked exhausted though, and didn't do more than grunt when Jackie left."

"Is she still trying to get you to let her take care of Sonny by herself and let Jackie go?" Quincy asked. She had thought Mary would leave by now, but it had been ten days, and as far as she knew, Mary hadn't mentioned going home.

"She actually said something about it yesterday. I kind of brushed her off, and we got into something else. I suppose I'm going to need to have a deep conversation with her." Beulah sighed, looking out over the bay. "I don't want to let Jackie go when she's been such a great employee, especially when Mary has not always been dependable. And about the time I don't have someone to back her up, she's going to leave me high and dry."

"Has she done that before?"

"It was her signature move in high school."

Quincy paused, shoving a hand in her pocket, and then trying to decide whether she should say anything or not.

"I'm not telling you what to do. I just know that I appreciate people not judging me based on what I did in high school."

Beulah's eyes shot to hers before her brows drew down and her lips flattened.

"You're right. I'm in mother mode. I guess everything that my kids did in their childhood kind of overshadows the adults they've become."

"I don't know how dependable she is," Quincy said, glancing at the closed door to make sure that her words weren't going to be overheard. "I don't want to encourage you to do something and then end up with no one to help you take care of Sonny. The last thing we need is for the assessor to come and decide that we're not doing a good enough job."

"I know. We already had a hard time with the last assessment."

"If it's okay with you, I was going to ask Mary if she wanted to come with us tonight."

"I think that would be really nice," Beulah said, her eyes holding admiration and gratefulness.

Quincy wasn't doing it for Beulah's response. There had been a part of her that had been suspecting that Mary had gone through something that she wasn't telling them about. She just seemed... vulnerable, as much as someone who was unkind and snippy could be. Or maybe Quincy was getting the feeling that she was hiding her pain behind that meanness.

It wasn't an easy thing to think, especially when the meanness was directed at her so often, but she felt like it was true.

"Wish me luck," she said, and she turned toward the door. "Then I'm ready to go. I wasn't going to shower before we left. I'll do that when we get home, so I don't hold us up."

"All right. I'm ready. I already said goodbye to Sonny."

They were pushing it time-wise, to ask Mary at the last minute. But Jackie had already said that she was hoping to pick up extra hours, and Quincy was fairly certain she would come keep Sonny in the evening.

As she walked in, Mary looked up from where she was just finishing up the dishes at the sink.

"Hello," Quincy said.

Mary dipped her head, giving her a dismissive glance, before turning around to scan the room. The TV was on, but the sound was muted, and Sonny snored in his chair.

He'd been spending more and more of his time sleeping. Or maybe Quincy just hadn't been home when he was awake. She had to admit she'd been busy and hadn't really been paying attention. Her divorce, talking to her children, and trying to make sure she stayed on top of the cleaning business had been sucking up all of her extra brain power.

"I just wanted to ask if you might be interested in coming with your mother and me. We're going to meet some friends at a beach-side pavilion. Just have some snacks and stuff and chat." It was a simple escape from regular life. There wasn't much happening on the weekends, although there was one bar in town, and it was always full. But Quincy had never been inside of it, and she doubted that Shiloh or Sharon frequented it either. As far as she knew, Beulah hadn't been in the bar since she'd moved down that spring.

Not that that was the only thing happening on the weekends. It was just... the town didn't offer much in the way of entertainment. Other than church on Sunday, if one could call that entertainment.

Since she'd been there, she'd only made it to church twice. Every other time they had houses to clean since Sunday was one of the checkout days. Unfortunately.

"No. You guys go ahead. I'm watching Sonny."

"I think Jackie would come stay here tonight if you wanted to come. I just wanted to offer."

"You did your good Samaritan good deed for the day, so you can feel happy with yourself and pat yourself on the back as you leave. But I'll stay. Don't bother Jackie."

"All right. Can I bring you anything home?" she asked, ignoring Mary's unkind words, loath to leave. For some reason, the feeling that Mary needed someone to talk to just as much as she did was heavy on her heart.

"No. If I need something, I can get it myself."

"Was Sonny difficult today?" she asked.

"If you must know, it was the worst day I've had since I've come. Anything else?"

"No. I guess not. Although... if you need a break, I'd be happy to switch my cleaning job with your caring job if you'd like."

"You can stop trying to be nice to me. It's so fake and I can't stand it."

"I'm sorry you think it's fake."

She couldn't think of anything else to say, so after waiting for a moment, staring at Mary's back, she turned slowly and walked to the door. After letting herself out, she nodded at Beulah. "I'm ready."

Her voice sounded a little shaky, but if Beulah noticed, she didn't say. She simply stood up from the swing, watched as Quincy grabbed the casserole dish and the bread, and then they stepped off the porch together.

"I don't want to pry, and you don't have to tell me if you don't want to, but I have the feeling that something happened to Mary."

Quincy spoke as they walked along the sidewalk. Usually, she and Beulah didn't need to make small talk. They'd gone past that a while ago, and she'd almost say that Beulah was a friend. The awkwardness that defined their relationship to begin with hadn't completely disappeared, but more and more she felt comfortable with Beulah. She definitely wanted the woman's cleaning business to succeed, and to lighten her load as well. Dealing with what Beulah was dealing with with Sonny, on top of her business, would be a load for anyone. Not to mention, Quincy held high regard for the woman, because she didn't shirk from her duty. And she hadn't complained at all, not that Quincy had heard.

"I haven't asked. She seems so prickly. It seems like everything I do just makes her mad. She takes offense at everything, and I basically just walk around on eggshells, hoping that I don't upset her."

"Same," Quincy said, laughing a little. Then she sobered, looking at the pink of the sky and thinking that, despite the fact that her marriage was a mess—what was left of it—she felt content. Maybe that had to do with finally talking to her children and knowing that that hard part was behind her. She was sure there would be more pain and tears, maybe even drama, but she'd already faced the most difficult parts. Everything else should be easy in comparison.

"I feel bad for Mary. I wish I could do something to help her. But she just thinks I'm being fake, or trying to get something, either her inheritance or to somehow become the favorite child or something. It seems no matter what I do, she sees it as something evil. I don't know how to change that."

"I don't think you can. I think it's going to be up to her too. After all, we have a tendency to see what we want to see, and make our reality what we already think it is."

Quincy walked along, thinking about that. Did she do that? She thought she tried to look at things objectively and give people credit where it was due. Maybe she gave them more credit than they deserved. Maybe her reality was the opposite of what Mary's was, who always looked for the bad and assigned that to each person.

While she looked for the good and gave people the benefit of the doubt, erring on the other side. Maybe the reality of everything was somewhere in the middle. Maybe that was why opposites attracted. Because they had a tendency to balance each other out, and between the two of them, come up with a view of the world that was more accurate than either one of them separately.

"I just appreciate you caring. I know you do. Obviously, I don't know your heart, but I've seen the way you work, I've seen that you're willing to sacrifice, and you truly care about Sonny, and I believe you care about me too."

Quincy nodded, and she supposed that Beulah was talking about the two weeks they'd had where there hadn't been quite enough money to cover payroll, and Quincy had told Beulah not to pay her.

Beulah had caught up the next week both times, but still, there had been no guarantee that she would ever see that pay, and yet she'd continued to work.

Beulah didn't say that specifically, but as she thought about it, Quincy realized that maybe that was when their relationship had started to thaw.

"Thank you for including me tonight. I'm looking forward to actually getting out and talking to other ladies. Do you realize how long it's been since I've done that?"

"That's a bad thing about our schedule. It's too bad they don't have a church service on Monday, which is our slow day. Although, I'm starting to think that in summer, there's no such thing as a slow day."

"You just about have the gist of it. And that's right. Even in the winter, we usually have something that keeps us out of church on Sunday. I... miss it. A lot. And not just because of the social aspect. There's nothing like a pastor preaching from God's word that keeps you on the straight and narrow."

"You can't earn your way into heaven, though. Being good isn't as important as love."

To her surprise, Beulah stopped. Quincy took two more steps before she realized that Beulah wasn't going anywhere. She turned, looking at the older woman. "What?"

"I disagree. Absolutely. And I think I have Bible to back that up."

"Okay," Quincy said cautiously, cognizant of the fact that this was obviously a subject that Beulah felt strongly about.

"The Bible does say that we are to love, and I don't argue about that point. But it also says that we are to be holy because God is holy. So we can't earn our salvation. I think we agree on that."

"We do."

"But if we love Jesus, He said to follow His commands. And so many of those commands had to do with being good. It does matter what we do. It matters a lot."

"All right. As you were talking, I was thinking about different verses in my head that tell us to be kind and to love and to be patient, avoid fornication and adultery, and of course there's the Ten Commandments."

"Yeah. All of those things are extremely important. But I suppose the modern Christian just focuses on love, and if we truly love the way the Bible tells us to, maybe we wouldn't have to think about anything else."

"Where Jesus says that all the law and the prophets hinge on those first two commands to love God and to love others?"

"Exactly. That keeps us being good, because we don't commit adultery, don't lie or cheat, because we wouldn't want that done to us. And if we love people, we won't hurt them anymore than we would hurt ourselves."

Quincy was quiet for a moment, thinking that Derek hadn't really loved her. If he had he wouldn't have cheated on her. Because he hurt her. Deeply.

Almost as though the thought brought him up, Beulah's phone rang, and after glancing at it, she said, "Derek."

"Should I hurry ahead so you have some privacy?" Quincy asked.

Beulah shook her head, swiping on her phone before putting it to her ear and saying, "Hello?"

Beulah didn't seem to be upset or care whether Quincy listened, so she did so unabashedly. As far as she knew, Derek hadn't called his mother in almost a month.

"Mother. I suppose Quincy has told you by now that she's left me."

Wow. He didn't even try to do any small talk. Quincy's fingers drew into a fist, and she had to deliberately untense her hands and make sure she didn't drop the casserole.

"That's not what I heard," Beulah said cautiously.

"I'm sure Quincy doesn't want to face the music. Regardless, I have a girlfriend, and she and I would like to come see you for a little bit. Will that be a problem?"

"I would love it," Beulah said softly, and while her words were not enthusiastic, Quincy believed they came from her heart. Of course Beulah loved Derek and wanted to see him.

Quincy was lost in throught and to her surprise, she looked over to see that Beulah was no longer on the phone.

"Did he say when he was coming?" she asked, annoyed that her voice sounded breathless. Thankfully, they were almost to the pavilion. She could see the twinkle lights glowing in the distance. And several figures moving around. Sharon was probably already there, unless she had run late from working. And definitely Shiloh.

"Yes. He's coming tomorrow. He said he would stay for a week. Weren't you listening?"

"I heard the beginning of it, but then I kind of zoned out. It made me mad that he lied. But I don't expect you to believe me any more than you believe him. And he's your son. You've gotta love him no matter what he does."

"You're absolutely right. I'm going to love him no matter what he does, and I'm going to love you the same way."

"Thank you." That was all she could ask. "I can make myself scarce for the next week. In fact, Sharon might even let me stay—"

"No. You're part of this family. Whether he wants to stay married to you or not, as long as you want to be here, you are welcome, and I will not allow either one of my children to treat you any differently. You've helped me these last several months, and I really needed it. It would be pretty bad of me to repay your kindness by kicking you out of my house."

"It wouldn't be kicking me out. I just don't want my presence to make things awkward."

"I'm not even sure he knows you're here."

"I can't remember whether I told him or not."

"Regardless, you're welcome, and you don't have to stay away. He's just going to have to be okay with it. He made the choices. He's going to have to live with them."

"Thank you."

Seeing Derek and Candy together after what happened was going to be difficult. She really appreciated Beulah making it as easy as possible. The woman was a saint. She didn't know why she hadn't realized that years ago.

twenty-four

QUINCY SAT IN THE DARK, the last rays of the sun fading from the sky. Sharon sat beside her, telling a story about something that had happened at one of the rentals where she cleaned the pool. It was a funny story, and Beulah and Shiloh sat listening, little smiles on their faces. Beulah sat on the other side of Quincy, close enough that Quincy could just move her pinky finger from where it sat on her lap and touch Beulah's leg if she wanted to. Shiloh sat on the other side of Beulah. Even though Beulah and Shiloh had lived in the same town, Whispering Hope Harbor, for years, their friendship hadn't really blossomed. But tonight, it seemed like they had developed something new and hit it off in a way they hadn't up until that point.

Maybe Beulah would tell her about it later. Maybe she wouldn't. But it didn't matter. Despite the fact that her estranged husband was coming with his girlfriend the next day, Quincy felt a contentment that she hadn't felt in a long time. Plus a peace to go along with it that made her soul want to sing. It made her feel safe.

Thank you, Lord, for the friends that You've given me.

As she said that in her head, she thought that if she hadn't gone through what she went through with her husband, she might not have made these friends. If they had moved here together, maybe she would be like Beulah, never really noticing that Shiloh was at the diner and was a beautiful soul, just waiting for someone to offer a deep and abiding friendship to her, which she would return.

"So what are you going to do while your ex visits?" Sharon asked, and Quincy wondered if maybe she'd missed a little of the conversation.

"I told Beulah that I would leave if she wanted me to," she started.

Beulah cut in. "But I told her that she was just as much family as Derek was, and she had been there helping for the last two months, and I certainly was not going to ask or expect or even want her to leave."

"That might make things awkward," Shiloh said, her eyes deep and knowing.

There were secrets there, things that Quincy knew Shiloh kept hidden. She doubted it was a matter of trust, and more a matter of some things just weren't things that a person could talk about. She understood that now more than she ever had before.

"I guess we'll see how it goes. If things get too awkward, I'll probably try to keep to myself. But, with as much work as we have, I won't be around much anyway."

"Please don't feel like you can't be around. Honestly, after the way Derek has acted, he doesn't deserve to be the one who gets to stay while you leave."

"Thank you for that. I do appreciate it." She smiled at her mother-in-law. And, to her surprise, Beulah reached over, wrapped her hand around Quincy's, and squeezed.

Quincy squeezed back, and they left their hands like that. Just a warm, tender touch that said that they were there for each other.

She never expected to have that kind of relationship with Beulah, but that seemed to be the direction they were headed. And Quincy was grateful.

"I hope everything works out," Sharon said. And Quincy remembered that she was estranged from her son. She knew better than any of them the pain of not getting along with family.

"God's given me some trials this year that I was not anticipating and did not want. But I feel peace. Just a contentment, knowing that whatever God wants is what is going to happen, and He's not going to allow anything that He doesn't approve. That is so comforting."

"I bet it is." Sharon looked a little envious, almost as though she didn't know what that was like.

Their situations were different, painfully so, but Quincy wished that she could share some of God's peace with her friend.

The topic changed to other things, and the four of them had an easy camaraderie, along with food and tea that Shiloh had brought from the diner. It was delicious, and Quincy wasn't sure which was the most healing—the food, the companionship, or the sound of the ocean crashing against the shore and the feeling of the night around them. The breeze, the knowledge that the sun was coming up in the morning, as it had for thousands of years every day.

That made her feel grounded in a way she couldn't explain.

And even the thought of her estranged husband coming the next day couldn't shake the contentment she felt.

So her marriage might never be put back together again. She might be divorced. Her children would have to split their time between homes. All of those things that had upset her so much still hurt, still gave her twinges of sadness, but a calm reliance on God's plan seemed to override all of those other feelings and make her feel that no matter what, she would go through the trials and come out stronger, with a stronger faith in God, stronger trust in Him, and a better view of the world, more capable of helping others. And wasn't that what life was all about?

twenty-five

QUINCY LEFT the next morning early, cleaning the Williams house again before she went to Enoch's place.

The kitchen still wasn't done, but he'd hung flowers on the porch, and the old boards had been replaced with new ones, sanded to perfection and finished so they glowed. Two cozy rocking chairs sat swaying softly in the breeze, with a stand between them, and it wasn't hard to imagine an ice-cold pitcher of lemonade or iced tea sitting there on the stand, with the scent of flowers in the air and a friend beside her in the rocking chair. It was such a beautiful picture, she paused for a moment before stepping inside the house.

Enoch was working on the stairs, and he lifted his head as she walked in.

"Good morning," he said, and then he looked around. "It's still morning, isn't it?"

She laughed. "I think it still is, technically. But it's pretty close to noon."

"I've been working since before daylight, and time got away from me a little bit."

"It has a tendency to do that when we're doing something we love."

"That's true," he said simply.

She didn't know whether it was a micro expression or just a feeling she got, but she suddenly got the strong feeling that being a handyman wasn't something that Enoch typically did. It was on the tip of her tongue to ask, but she closed her mouth around the question. They were friends, she thought, anyway, but not that kind of friends. Maybe someday.

"Before you get started, do you want to take a break? I have some iced tea, and I finished my front porch in case you didn't notice."

"I did notice. And it's gorgeous. I can imagine a pitcher of iced tea sitting on that stand, and two friends sharing a beautiful day and some deep conversation."

"That's exactly what I had planned," he said, as though she had described what he wanted to do with her.

That couldn't be right. She'd said deep conversation, and either he'd missed that, or... maybe they were better friends than what she was allowing herself to think.

"I hope you don't mind. I put the southern amount of sugar in this tea."

"I could use the southern amount of sugar. I've got another place to clean after your place, and then I have some administrative stuff to do after that. I probably should see if you could double the sugar."

"I don't know about that. I don't want you to have a diabetes attack on my front porch. That would be a bad way to christen it."

"I think you're cutting me off of the sugar."

"I think the southern amount of sugar is enough to give anybody a diabetes attack. Doubling it would probably prove fatal."

They laughed together as she set her mop bucket down and then accepted the glass of tea he handed her, before he opened the door, holding it for her to walk through.

She settled into the far chair while he sat down beside her.

"I probably shouldn't be doing this. I'm so busy. But maybe that's why I decided to go ahead. Because times like this are precious."

"And here I thought it was because I did such a good job on the porch."

She glanced over at him, smiling. She wanted him to see that she was sincere. "You did an awesome job on the porch. I can see why you do this for a living." She paused, and then taking a breath, she added, "There are times where I've gotten the impression that you're not actually a contractor. But after seeing this porch, there's no way I could doubt it."

He snorted a bit, took a sip of his tea, and then set his cup down on the stand between them. He leaned forward, steepling his fingers as he put his forearms on his knees.

"Your impression that I was not a contractor is correct."

"Really?" she asked, almost choking on her tea. "I was actually kind of joking."

"Well, I feel a little bit bad because you had some misconceptions, and instead of correcting them, I allowed you to keep them."

"It's okay. You don't have to tell me anything you don't want to."

"It's not really that I didn't want to tell you. It's just... I came here to get away from some things, and I wasn't ready to talk about them."

"I understand what you mean about not being ready," she said. She supposed she was more ready than she had been to see her husband with another woman and to be in the same house as she, but she had to admit, she appreciated the time that had elapsed to allow her to prepare for the moment.

"I owned a successful business on the mainland. Had a wife and family. But I was so determined to make one million dollars, and then ten million, and then I set my sights on one billion."

"Wow. That's more money than I can even dream about."

She would've been happy with six figures from her divorce. Although she would still have to work in order to not depend on someone else to pay for her living.

"I grew up poor. I guess I had somehow determined that I would never be poor again."

"Very Gone with the Wind of you."

He gave her an odd look, almost as though he didn't understand the reference, and then grinned a little.

"So did you make it to one billion?" she asked, sipping on her tea and leaning her head back against the rocking chair, wondering what it would be like to be rich—as in millions of dollars, never have to worry about money again, kind of rich. She couldn't even imagine it. What did a person do when they weren't trying to survive?

"I was not quite halfway there when I lost my wife and family."

"I'm so sorry. Car crash?" she asked, thinking about how devastating it would be to lose not just her husband, but her children too. How hard.

"No. My wife got tired of being alone, and I don't blame her. Looking back, I was never home. Always chasing the next business deal, sinking all of my time and effort, and my heart, into my business."

"Oh. I'm so sorry."

"The kids resented me. Saw me as an ATM. I had no relationship with them. Been trying to fix that, but... yeah. I burned out in the business, realized that I was focusing on all the wrong things, and it was too late."

"Did you talk to her about it? If there wasn't another man involved, or even if there was, I guess, she might be convinced to come back. I know... I know I didn't want to see my family broken." She couldn't imagine that his wife wouldn't feel the same.

"No. She had another man. I suppose she was cheating, but I have a hard time even saying that. Because I never put her first the way a husband should. It was always my business. My fault. She was tired of being alone." He looked at his hands. "A woman doesn't get married thinking she's going to be by herself all the time."

"No. She doesn't." She supposed Derek had done that to her. She was alone a good bit, but she had been faithful. She hated to point that out to Enoch though—that his wife could be alone and still be faithful. He was giving her grace, and that was probably a good thing.

"What about you? Now you know I'm the actual owner and I'm not a contractor."

"You could be. This porch is as nice as any porch I've ever been on or seen. Although, you could've told me that I was talking to the owner whenever I asked to use the pavilion."

"I know. I'm sorry. I saw you were there last night with your friends. I hope you enjoyed it."

"We did. Such a beautiful spot."

"Yeah. I had actually started to fix that up when my wife left me. I guess I had in mind that once I hit one billion, we'd come here and spend time as a family. I don't know."

He looked at his hands a bit more before deliberately sitting up and leaning back in his chair, rocking just a bit.

He lifted his brows, reminding her that he had asked a question. She'd forgotten.

"My husband left me for another woman. She's pregnant. He wants a divorce, and I suppose I'm gonna give it to him, although he doesn't want to give me anything and I'm going to argue about that a little." She looked at his shoulder. "He and his pregnant girlfriend are going to be at the house today when I get home. I'm living with my mother-in-law."

"That's kind of a convoluted situation," he said, irony in his voice.

"Isn't it? It's funny—my mother-in-law and I had a not-great relationship for the entirety of my marriage. But after my husband left, I came here because it was what my husband and I had planned to do. To help her with her business and to help her take care of her husband who is dealing with dementia."

"I see," he said.

"Anyway, I have a better relationship with her now than I ever did during our marriage. Funny the way these things work, isn't it?"

"Funny the way God puts trials in our life to shape us into the people He wants us to be. Even if those trials aren't what we wanted. Like the dissolution of a marriage."

"Yeah. I suppose. Hard lessons, but you're right. God works it out perfectly."

She wouldn't have thought when she first met Enoch that she would ever be sitting on his front porch, talking about God with him, but it felt natural and right.

His shoulders shifted underneath the T-shirt he wore, and she felt that little stirring in her stomach again.

But she was still married, and so she looked away. Tonight she would see her husband. Maybe he would have papers. Maybe he would've signed them. She wasn't quite sure exactly how it worked, although her lawyer had told her. She supposed she hadn't been paying attention the way she should've. Probably because she didn't want to have to hear. She didn't want to have to know how to pick a marriage apart and separate the pieces.

"I'm sorry if I shared too much. It's been weighing on me for a little while that I wasn't completely honest with you. Or at the very least, allowing you to believe things that weren't true." Something twitched in his jaw, and then he turned his eyes to her. "And I like you."

His words hung in the air. Even the breeze seemed to still, refusing to take them away.

Finally, she decided to just be honest. "I like you too. But I'm still married. And I don't know when that's gonna change. I'm pretty sure it's going to, or I'm going to have a lot of things to work through, including a child my husband fathered that's not mine."

She swallowed. "I would've thought by now I would be excited about the possibility of grandchildren, not looking to raise another myself."

"You think that there's a possibility that he'll break up with his girlfriend and come back to you?"

His words were soft. They didn't seem like they held any kind of disbelief, or like he cared either way.

"I suppose there's still a big part of me, bigger than I like to admit, that still hates the idea of seeing my family broken and my marriage dissolved. But no. I don't really think there's much chance of that at all. They were in a big rush for us to get divorced so he could marry her. And in my eyes, once we sign those divorce papers, and especially once he says 'I do' to someone else, there's no going back."

He nodded. "When my wife got married to her lover, I guess I kind of felt the same way. I can't fix the past. But I can learn from it. And I can build something new." He looked around the porch. The new wood, the beautifully sanded railing, the rocking chairs and the coziness, and the flowers that trailed softly in the breeze. "I guess that's what I'm doing here. Building something new."

She nodded, understanding what he meant. But she didn't think she was there yet. "I think I'm still clearing the rubble away. Trying to figure out if there's anything in it that I can salvage."

He nodded, rubbing a hand over his chin before he looked back out over the railing. "I can respect that."

twenty-six

QUINCY GOT DONE EARLIER than she thought she would, unfortunately. There were so many days where she would've loved to have gone home early, spend a little time with Sonny, maybe help cook supper, but had ended up being late. Figures the day that she didn't want to be home at all, she would be early.

Rather than going into the house, she decided to take a walk along the shore. The evening was beautiful, and the water called to her.

She lifted her face to the breeze, avoiding the back of the house and heading down the path through the small scrub brush. She had recognized that little red convertible that was parked along the road, and part of her felt cowardly for skipping out. Maybe she should go and say hi before she took a walk.

But her feet had already taken her down to the edge of the water, where she turned and headed north. Why was she so nervous? It wasn't like she cared what they thought of her. And it wasn't like it mattered. He had already decided he didn't want her. She supposed she just didn't want the confrontation. Or maybe she was afraid he was bringing divorce papers with him, and... she didn't want to face him.

Maybe she just wanted a few more moments without the knowledge that her marriage was ending. Although, that much had been obvious for months now.

She hadn't gotten anything sorted out in her mind before Vivian's house came into view.

This time, seeing Vivian on the porch, instead of just waving, she turned and started walking toward the path that led to Vivian's house.

She kept her eyes on the woman, only taking them off when she needed to see where she was placing her feet.

Vivian stood with her arms wrapped around her stomach, the breeze whipping her long skirt, her hair blowing back as well. But she didn't turn and walk into her house.

Why had she fled from one confrontation only to face another?

Or maybe she had chosen the easier route—the potential for another friend versus dealing with her soon-to-be ex and his pregnant girlfriend.

Regardless, she made it to the bottom of the porch and put her hand on the railing. But did not go up.

"Hi," she said, a little breathless. More from nervousness than from her exertion.

"Hi," the woman said. Her voice sounded cultured, but not aloof.

"I've seen you so often, I... I wanted to come say hi for a while, but tonight, my soon-to-be ex-husband is at my mother-in-law's house with his pregnant girlfriend. I suppose I would rather come here and meet a total stranger, perhaps be snubbed, than go home and face the things I know I need to face."

"Wow. That's rough," Vivian said. "Why don't you come on up and sit a while. You're welcome to stay here until you're ready to go home. Even if that means it's not until tomorrow morning."

Quincy smiled. She had a feeling that Vivian was going to be a kindred spirit, and she had been right.

"I thought you and I were going to be friends," she said as she got to the top of the steps and held out her hand. "I'm Quincy."

"I thought we might be friends too. About the third time I saw you. I'm Vivian."

"I confess I already know your first name. I asked about you in town."

"And someone knew my name?" Vivian said. Rather than sounding pleased, she sounded scared.

"Not in a creepy way. Just the owner of the diner. She said that she thought you didn't want a whole lot of people to know that you were here. I don't think she shares your name with just anyone."

"Then she's a friend of yours?" Vivian asked, and although the fear seemed to be gone from the surface, there was still an undercurrent there.

"Yes. We're friends. We actually got together last night and hung out with my mother-in-law, which I know sounds a little crazy, but she's really a great woman. And also another friend." She paused for a moment, thinking it was probably too soon, but she added, "There's always room for one more in our group."

"I don't know that I'm ready for a group yet. Just having one friend seems to be a bit of a stretch for me."

"I see. Is there some danger?" She asked that question on a hunch.

"Why don't you sit down for a while." Vivian pointed to one of the two chairs that were on the porch. They weren't rocking chairs, but the porch looked almost as cozy as Enoch's had earlier that day.

Just thinking about Enoch gave her an odd sensation in the pit of her stomach. But she shrugged it off. Maybe she was just hungry. She hadn't had supper, skipping it in favor of her walk.

"Thank you." She chose the far chair, so Vivian could have the one closer to the door. Whether that made a difference or not, she wasn't sure, but she hoped she was being considerate.

"So do you live with your mother-in-law?"

Maybe because Vivian seemed so guarded, Quincy gave information freely.

"I just moved in. My husband and I were supposed to move in

and help her with her cleaning business and with taking care of her husband who is dealing with dementia, but my husband announced on the day that we closed on our house that he and our realtor were together and expecting a baby. He wanted a divorce. So I came here without him."

"Good for you," Vivian said, her eyes squinting as she grinned.

She casually pushed her hair away from her face. Her fingers, slender and delicate, long. Every move she made seemed to be classy and graceful.

"What about you? You don't have to tell me if you don't want to."

"I think I can trust you. I've been watching you, thinking about how nice it would be to have a friend, but... I'm a little afraid."

"Well, I'm not gonna hurt you, if that's what you're concerned about."

"I guess I'm more concerned that you might be an undercover cop, or a private investigator."

At the idea, Quincy laughed. "I'm sorry. But if you knew me, you'd know how absolutely absurd that is. I could never be a cop. For one, I could barely get my kids to listen to me. I'm certainly not going to have enough authority to boss any people around, or enforce rules. I'm definitely a follower, not a leader."

"I think sometimes we find out that there's more to us than what we think there is, once our husbands are no longer in the picture."

"I guess my husband isn't completely out of the picture, but I definitely agree with you. Since I've moved here, I've figured out that a lot of times I depended on my husband to take care of me, when I was capable all along. Still am. And God has helped me to become stronger than what I thought. Not because of me, but because of Him."

Vivian's brows lifted, and her eyes widened, and then she nodded slowly before she looked back out over the bay, where the moon had risen and shone on the water, soft ripples breaking the reflection into hundreds of thousands of tiny pieces, which waved and swayed gently with the movement of the water. The soft sound of the small waves hitting the shore drifted across the night air.

"I've had trouble trusting God. It feels like He's let me down."

"I can't speak to your situation. I can only tell you what He's done for me. And what He says in the Bible too, I suppose. But I know that every time it felt like God was allowing me to go through something that was too hard, I reminded myself that God doesn't allow me to go through anything that hasn't gone through His approval first. And everything that I've gone through has been with a desire for me to learn about Him, mostly, but also about myself. How weak I am, and how I need Him."

"I don't need a reminder about how weak I am."

"I guess I didn't say that very well. It's just that suffering doesn't necessarily mean a lack of love. It just might mean that it was an experience that I needed to have in order to become more like Jesus."

"How do you become more like Jesus when you're hurting?"

"Didn't He hurt at the crucifixion? Didn't He go through a lot of suffering? But yet He never questioned whether or not God loved Him. He never questioned whether or not God cared. I think for a little bit, He did doubt whether He was able to go through it. Or whether God would really make Him. He said, 'If it be Your will, let this cup be taken from Me.' But He never said, 'I can tell that You don't love me because You're making me suffer.' He knew He had to."

"But that was to save us. That wasn't necessarily to make Him a better person."

"No, maybe we suffer for different reasons, but the idea is the same. No one goes through life without pain and suffering. It's how we grow. You can't become stronger by having everything handed to you, right?"

"I suppose not. But some suffering... seems too heavy to bear."

That made Quincy wonder exactly what had happened in Vivian's past, but she didn't pry. After a few beats, she said, "I think because of sin, because the world isn't perfect, because man didn't obey, there's a lot more suffering than there would've been had the world stayed in the perfect place where God created it. But I still believe with my whole heart that God doesn't allow anything into our lives that He hasn't approved, and He promises to walk with us through it all, no matter how hard it gets for us."

"Sometimes it feels like He's not there."

Quincy was silent. She couldn't convince Vivian that God was there if she couldn't or wouldn't believe that He was. It reminded her of what she had thought about different perceptions of reality. Maybe that was why it was so important to use the Bible as a foundation. So that the perception of reality didn't interfere with what was actually true.

"Do you know the verse that says...

> *we glory in tribulations also: knowing that tribulation worketh patience; And patience, experience; and experience, hope; And hope maketh not ashamed; because the love of God is shed abroad in our hearts by the Holy Ghost which is given unto us."*

"It's been years since I heard that verse. I kind of forgot it existed," Vivian sounded thoughtful, and Quincy decided to let the matter rest. She didn't have to convince Vivian of anything. Vivian was allowed to not believe God was good if that was what she really wanted to believe.

Quincy couldn't imagine what would be in her life that would cause her to think that God had abandoned her. But she knew it was a feeling that was shared by a multitude of people. Someone who had been abused, or who had lost parents or loved ones might feel like God didn't care about them. And Quincy, while she believed with her whole heart that that was not the slightest bit true, couldn't really think of words that would convince someone that their suffering could be used to glorify God, and that was more important than not suffering at all. In fact, the older she got, the more she felt like a life with no suffering was not going to be a life worth living. Not that she enjoyed suffering. She absolutely didn't. Which was the whole reason she was here on Vivian's porch, instead of enduring the suffering of facing her ex and his pregnant girlfriend.

"This is a beautiful spot. You have such a pretty view from your porch. And those sunsets—my goodness."

Quincy attempted a subject change and was gratified when Vivian went along with it.

"It feels like it's healing my soul every time I see them. And, to your point earlier, it makes me feel like God really is there. Maybe He does love me sometimes. After all, the way those sunsets make me feel, it's just peaceful."

"Yeah. Peaceful. And awed."

"That is a good word."

They chatted a bit more about the weather, and Quincy learned that Vivian had been there for about a year, which was what Sharon had said. Sharon was pretty good with her information. They'd been chatting for an hour when she decided it was probably a good idea for her to get up and go.

"We decided we'd meet every Monday night. Weekends are busy for all of us because those are the turnover days for the vacationers."

"Oh, they are?"

"Yeah. Friday through Sunday. Not all houses, but a lot. We're busy throughout the week over the summer too."

"You all work in hospitality?"

"I guess. Sharon has a pool servicing business, and of course you know Shiloh. And my mother-in-law and I clean houses." She paused for a moment. "Did you have a job?"

"Keeping my husband happy. And according to him, I wasn't any good at it."

There was definitely pain in her voice, but she was obviously trying to cover it with a forced cheerfulness.

"I would say that he probably was a jerk. But that's not very nice, and I don't know him at all, so forgive me if I'm overstepping." She pushed to her feet. "I'd say the same thing about my husband, but I've been trying to keep my mouth shut unless I can say something nice."

"If you don't have something nice to say, don't say anything at all?" Vivian asked with a little laugh.

"How many times did I say that to my children, and it's me that needs to be reminded of it."

"Yeah. I need to be reminded of that sometimes too." She placed a hand on the back of her chair, standing still, although the breeze still blew her skirt around her ankles. "Thanks for stopping in. I haven't struggled to say kind things because I haven't had too many people to talk to. But I've struggled to think kind things, and it's good to have a friend."

"You're welcome to come up to my house anytime. Although, my mother-in-law and father-in-law will both be there, and right now my husband and his girlfriend are there as well. So... your house is a little nicer."

Vivian laughed. "You're welcome here anytime. I don't go many places."

"All right. I'll remember that. You know I'm often walking in the morning. I might stop in."

"Please do."

As she left, she heard a little barking from inside and remembered the dog that she typically saw on the walk. She had forgotten all about it.

But she didn't think that mattered, because she was pretty sure she was going to be seeing more of Vivian again, and soon.

twenty-seven

BEULAH AND SONNY'S house was glowing as she came down the beach. The moon was almost full, and even if it hadn't been, she had walked the beach so many times she wouldn't have been afraid of the dark, but seeing the house all lit up made her feel cold, although she wasn't sure why. Maybe because she knew what was waiting inside. She could hear raised voices, but couldn't make out the words, as she got closer, and she was tempted to turn around.

But avoiding her problems wasn't going to get her through them, and that was what she needed to do—get through them.

So she mentally girded up her loins, smiling at the familiar Bible phrase, and then walked up the walk, as the voices became more clear.

"I can't believe you're siding with her! I'm your own son!"

It was Derek, his voice raised in anger.

"Quincy, come here and give me a hug. You've been so standoffish." That was Sonny. He must be talking to Candy. Did he call her Quincy?

Quincy bit back a smile. She bet that made steam come out of Derek's ears.

"Dad, how many times do I have to tell you her name is Candy."

"But you're married to Quincy. Isn't this your wife? Looks like she's gonna have a baby soon. I'm gonna be a grandpa. That's awesome."

Quincy bit her lip. He had already been a grandfather. And a good one.

"Dad, not Quincy. Candy."

"Quincy, Candy, same deal," Sonny said. Quincy had made it to the door, where she could look in and see him, waving his hand in the air like it wasn't that big of a deal. Oh, if he were in his right mind, he would know how big of a difference there was between those two names.

Regardless, she put her hand on the knob, and just as she went to twist it, her eyes met Beulah's, who had obviously seen her or maybe heard her.

She gave a little nod, as if giving Quincy permission to come in, although she had already told her that she was welcome anytime, just as welcome as her son.

Twisting the knob, she opened the door and stepped in, feeling like she knew a little bit of how Daniel must've felt when he stepped into the lions' den.

She closed the door behind her to absolute quiet in the room.

"Quincy, I'm so glad you made it. Did you have a nice walk?" Beulah asked, solicitous as usual.

"I did, thank you," she said, and now that she was in the room, she could see Mary seated over on the other side of Sonny, quiet for once.

Maybe she could see that everything that Quincy had been saying was true.

"Quincy! I'm so happy to see you!" Candy rushed to her like they were old friends or something.

Maybe they were, in a manner of speaking, because she would've said that Candy was a casual friend back when she was her realtor, before she knew that she was sleeping with her husband. But as

Candy came to her, she opened her arms, allowing the younger woman to give her a hug.

As she tried to return it, she looked over Candy's shoulder and saw Mary staring at her. She couldn't read the expression on her face.

"I'm so happy to see you. You were so sweet to me the last time we met."

"Yes. I know what it's like to be pregnant. How are you feeling?"

"Oh my goodness, my ankles are swollen, I feel like a buffalo, and I still have two more months!"

Quincy nodded, listening as Candy went over her list of grievances. Two more months. That meant that she had been five months pregnant when Derek had told Quincy that he was leaving her.

They had been sleeping together for five months before that?

That revelation rocked Quincy's world and threw her off-kilter.

"I need to talk to Quincy alone." Derek interrupted Candy as she was just going on about the heartburn she experienced at night and how she was dealing with that.

Quincy could've talked to her for a while about it, because with the twins, she had heartburn for the first time in her life. But she looked at her husband as Candy stepped back, a little bit of fire flaring in her eyes before she covered it with a sweet smile.

"Of course, dear," she said, her voice holding a southern helping of syrup.

"Out on the porch," Derek said to Quincy.

"Wait a second. I'm confused. That's Quincy. Who are you?" Sonny pointed at Candy. "Quincy is Derek's wife. They've been married forever. I remember back in high school—"

"Candy is going to be my wife, Dad." Derek snapped at his father, obviously fed up.

"Derek. Your father can't help what he's going through. Some patience, please." Quincy's voice was low but firm.

Derek had the grace to look slightly bad before anger flared in his eyes and he lifted his chin. "Out on the porch."

She had a good mind to tell him where he could take his porch and shove it, but she didn't want to fight, and while she didn't feel like he had the right to order her around anymore, he was still, technically, her husband, and she turned, after a glance at Beulah, and opened the door that she had just come through.

Derek didn't say anything until the door was closed firmly behind him.

"Why are you dragging your feet about this? You told me you were going to send a counter offer from your lawyer. It's been six weeks, and we've heard nothing. The baby's going to be here and I won't be married to Candy."

"I guess I don't understand why that matters," Quincy said, and then she wished she would've bit her tongue.

"Of course you wouldn't understand," Derek said, his voice low but absolutely dripping with venom. And anger. She couldn't recall ever feeling such loathing from a person in her life before.

"I sent you the papers. My lawyer and I discussed it over the phone, she sent me a rough draft, I approved it, she gave me something to sign, and told me she would be mailing it to you. That's what happened. I don't know why you haven't gotten the papers."

She did not add that if he would've had a settlement that was fair to begin with, she wouldn't have had to do these extra steps, and the thing would've been signed whenever she drove to meet him six weeks ago.

"You're lying."

She stepped back, as though he'd slapped her. Maybe he had. It felt like it.

"I have never lied to you. Not once."

That was the truth.

"I've never lied to you either," he snapped back.

Her brows went up. He was lying at that moment, because he had told her that he would be faithful to her until death parted them.

"Oh, I'm sorry. Did one of us die?"

"What are you talking about?"

"You told me you would be faithful to me until death do us part. If you've never lied to me, then one of us must be dead."

"Don't be stupid," he snapped again.

She took a deep breath. He was calling her names, insulting her, snapping at her, and being generally unkind, but that was just because he was upset. Angry. Maybe under a lot of pressure from Candy to have a wedding. Perhaps he was unsure about getting married to her, having second thoughts. Whatever he was experiencing, it was causing him to act out. Although he was an adult, and she really thought that he ought to have better control of his emotions.

"I can call my lawyer in the morning. Find out what's going on."

"Are you gonna do that, or are you just gonna say you're going to?"

"I don't believe that there is a time in our marriage where I ever said that I was going to do something and I didn't follow through. I've never lied to you. I've never cheated on you, and you have no reason to doubt my word. I'm sorry that you're doing so now, but you're doing it without a shred of evidence."

"Just get me the freaking papers so that I can sign them and rid myself of you."

"I told you. I'll call my lawyer in the morning."

"See that you do."

She turned to the door, since she was closer, and put her hand on the knob. But she couldn't resist turning back to her husband, saying, "I'm not sure what the problem is, or what it was, but Derek, I really hope you find what you're looking for. Truly, I do."

She turned the knob and walked inside.

twenty-eight

THE NEXT MORNING, Quincy was up early, getting her walk along the beach in before work. For some reason, instead of walking along the bay, which was so much closer, she crossed the road and walked over the dunes to the ocean side of the island. Watching the sun come up over the ocean, hearing the roar of the waves against the seashore, and thinking about how big and wide it was, and how far it stretched, and how small she felt in comparison to it.

She turned and started walking north, as she normally did in the morning, thinking about her confrontation with Derek the night before and how she had tossed and turned in her small bed, barely sleeping that night.

She hadn't said anything to Mary or Sonny, and had only said good night to Beulah before climbing the stairs, but she wouldn't have expected them to talk about it anyway. Not with Derek and Candy still there.

With the glare of the sun, or maybe because she was so distracted, she didn't realize that someone was walking toward her until he was almost upon her.

Enoch.

He looked as surprised to see her as she was to see him.

"Good morning."

She thought about their time on the front porch the day before, and how he'd said point-blank that he liked her. She wasn't sure exactly what he meant by that, but she didn't think he probably went around telling women that he liked them just for kicks and giggles. She also knew that he had shared things with her that he didn't normally talk about with people, and that made her feel special.

But it was like she'd told him. She was still married. She tried to remember that as she smiled and stopped, shielding her face with her hand.

"Good morning. It's beautiful out this morning."

"Every day is a beautiful day. Every day I have health, and I'm alive to see the sunrise."

She nodded. "I should be more grateful for the little things, instead of complaining about the things I don't have that I want. Good reminder."

"I'm sorry. I wasn't trying to remind you of anything. Just spouting my philosophy. Some days I have to say it to myself in order to remind myself to stop complaining and whining."

"I wake up like that sometimes. Actually, this morning I did."

"Really? Something I can help with?"

"No. My ex—my husband, soon to be ex, I suppose—is here with his girlfriend. He doesn't think I'm moving fast enough with the divorce, and told me about it last night." She looked off at the ocean, continuing to shield her face from the sun. "I suppose he's right in a way."

"I don't blame you. Divorce is a big step. Just as big as marriage, I guess. Harder in some ways, and definitely more painful."

"Sorry about your experience," she said.

"If I hadn't had that experience, I wouldn't have been able to tell you about it."

"Yeah. You're right."

"I can also tell you that sometimes you don't appreciate what you have until it's gone."

"Thank you. I don't know if he'll ever appreciate what he had, if that's what you're insinuating. But it's a nice thought."

"He will. I could guarantee it. I also think that sometimes God has to close the door behind you before a better one opens."

"I think that's a good philosophy. Always look for something better to happen, especially when you're sitting in what feels like the pit of despair."

"It does make the pit of despair seem not so bad, or maybe it just makes it easier to stand up in the slime."

"I do feel like I'm in slime, so you're right about that much," she said.

"I'm praying for you. It's not easy."

"Thanks." He looked at her for a moment more before he raised his hand in farewell and walked away. She waited a little bit more before she started walking. He was praying for her. That meant more than almost anything he could've said. It also told her a lot about the kind of man he was. It was the kind of man she wanted. Someone who prayed without her asking him to, who had his own relationship with the Lord and wasn't depending on her to connect him with the Almighty. The way Derek had. Because obviously, Derek didn't have the values and morals that he claimed to, or maybe something else happened.

Regardless, by the time she was finished with her walk, she realized she had spent more time thinking about Enoch than she had about Derek, and she considered that a good thing.

twenty-nine

BEULAH PUT two pieces of toast in the toaster and pressed down on the lever.

Last night had been awkward. But Derek and Candy had gotten there late enough that everyone was tired, and they hadn't spent a whole lot of time talking. Derek had been upset about the shape his father was in, and Beulah had had to bite her tongue because she wanted to tell him if he visited more, he would know, and it wouldn't have been such a surprise.

Derek acted like everything was okay, like it was perfectly normal for him to be there with a woman who was big with his child, and that they were all supposed to just act like it was just fine.

"Thanks so much for letting us sleep in your bed last night," Candy said as she walked into the kitchen, one hand on her protruding belly, dark circles around her eyes. She looked like she hadn't slept at all. Just as much as Beulah hadn't.

"Of course. Like I said, Sonny often falls asleep in front of the TV anyway. Quincy would've gladly given you her room, but her bed is a single, and it would've been difficult for the two of you to share."

"Quincy doesn't need a bed, but it's a nice thought." Derek

199

walked in, still not seeming to be in a better mood than he was the night before.

The ideal solution would've been for Mary to give up her room. She at least had a double bed. But she had been strangely quiet the night before. No caustic one-liners, no biting remarks either. She'd just been watching. Beulah wasn't sure what to make of that. Perhaps Mary was going to hit her with both barrels after Derek left.

"We decided we're leaving today, Mom." Derek went over and put an arm around Candy, indicating that he was talking about the two of them.

Candy looked up at him, total admiration in her eyes, but he wasn't paying attention to her. He was looking at Beulah. "I don't know why you didn't tell me that Quincy was here. Didn't you know how awkward it was going to be for us to have to deal with her?"

Beulah's mouth opened, and her jaw felt like it was hitting the floor.

"I didn't know you didn't know where she was," she finally managed to sputter. What she really wanted to say was that if Derek had talked to her at all, maybe he would've known, but he hadn't even told her that he was leaving his wife, hadn't told her that he had a girlfriend or that she was pregnant, not until he showed up. And if he thought it was hard for them, how hard did he think it was for Quincy?

"You should've known," he muttered, annoyed.

Beulah felt very much like she had the night before. Instead of being happy that her child was visiting and enjoying his company, she wanted to run away down to the beach and sit there alone until they left. How was she supposed to navigate dealing with her son and his girlfriend and his ex? And on top of that, Sonny had been confused almost constantly, and then she'd barely even given her business any thought. At least Quincy was taking care of that. That was such a load off her shoulders.

She'd barely thought about that when Derek yelled, "Dad!" And then almost immediately he said, "Mom! Aren't you watching him?"

Beulah had spun around at the sound of his voice, and she was already hurrying forward. Sonny stood at the counter, a fork in one hand, getting ready to poke it into the toaster, his brows down.

"Honey, you can't do that when the toaster is plugged in." She yanked the cord from the wall, just as he stuck the fork down one of the slots.

"Don't tell me what I can and can't do. I don't know why this stupid thing isn't working. I want to heat my coffee up."

Beulah, used to his confusion by now, knowing that this was the way he got sometimes, barely twitched an eyebrow, but behind her Derek exploded.

"Dad, what's wrong with you? That's a toaster. You don't put coffee in your toaster."

"Don't tell me what I can't do, son," Sonny said, and then before she could stop him, he took the coffee that was sitting on the other side of the toaster that she hadn't seen and dumped the entire thing into the toaster covering the bread that was in there and making her thankful that she had immediately unplugged it.

"Dad! That's the stupidest thing I've ever seen. You just poured your coffee in the toaster. What is wrong with you?" He shook his head and looked at his mom. "You need to do something with him. He's a danger to everyone in this house. If you hadn't been standing there, he could've burned the whole thing down, or electrocuted himself, or both." He bumped Candy's shoulder with his hand. "Come on. We need to get out of here. It's dangerous for us to stay."

Despite how he had treated her while he was here, Beulah's heart sank. She barely saw him, and she wanted to spend more time with him. Time that wasn't wasted in fighting and harsh words.

"Don't expect to see a whole lot of us. Especially if Quincy is going to be here. You know that we can't stay here with her."

"Why not? You're married to her. You should be spending time with her. I don't know why you haven't been around lately." Sonny's voice was gruff and sounded like it had growing up, a few times that he had gotten really upset with Derek and dressed him down.

"And we don't want our child around someone as dangerous as that. You need to get him sedated, get him into a home with people who know how to take care of him so he won't act like that anymore."

Beulah reeled back, feeling like he'd just slapped her.

"It has nothing to do with how he's being taken care of, and everything to do with how dementia affects a patient. And if you had any concern for your parents at all, you could look into it and see that for yourself." Quincy's voice came from the bottom of the stairs.

Beulah appreciated her butting in. She wanted to use stronger words with her son, but he was already angry with her. She could hardly correct his misconceptions without causing him to be even more upset.

"You're the whole reason we're leaving. I wanted to spend time with my mother, let her get to know Candy. Candy deserves to know her family, but you ruined it all. Like you always do. I hope you're happy."

Derek's eyes shot daggers at Quincy. She looked rather angry herself. But she didn't say anything else. She simply looked at Beulah and said, "I'm going to go out for a walk. Call me if you need me."

Beulah nodded, knowing that Quincy had already gone for a walk, but was heading out again to try to ease the tension in the room, since her presence ramped it up rather than fixing anything. Even though her words to Derek were absolutely true.

The door closed behind Quincy, and everything in the room was quiet for a moment. Then, without saying anything, Candy ran to the door, opened it, and hurried out.

Derek took two steps to follow her, but Mary's voice came from the top of the stairs.

"Why don't you leave them alone. Seems to me like you've done nothing but mess things up."

"Quincy might hurt Candy."

"You mean she might tell Candy some of the truth. About the jerk that you've been, about the lack of attention you paid her, or the way you ignored your children?"

"You stay out of this. It's none of your business. Plus, your own life is such a mess that you have absolutely no right to be trying to fix mine."

Mary looked regal as she continued down the steps, and if she was surprised at Derek's words, she didn't let on. "I doubt you know anything about my life. And regardless, sometimes the people who make the biggest mistakes have learned the hardest lessons, and it's easier to listen to their advice than repeat their mistakes. But I don't suppose you would know that."

"I don't want to hear it. I'm not gonna stand here and listen to any lectures from you. It looks to me like you're living here, and that's pretty sad for a forty-year-old woman who's such a spectacular failure at life that she has to move back in with her parents. Don't you even have a job?"

"Have you not noticed that our parents could use some help?"

"Dad needs to go to a home, and Mom needs to learn how to take care of him properly, so he doesn't do any more crazy stupid stuff like he just did. Did you see that he poured his coffee down the toaster? After he tried to get the toast out with a fork. I don't know what's wrong in this house. It's probably Quincy. She jinxes everything."

"I don't think that anything is going to be resolved until you are able to look at yourself and take responsibility for the actions that you have done, rather than blaming everyone else." Mary didn't give him a chance to respond before she looked at Beulah. "I'm going back upstairs. If you need me to watch Dad, you're gonna have to do something else with him." She nodded at Derek, then turned around and walked back up the stairs.

How had her family come to this? She'd only had two children and thought for sure that they would love each other forever. They'd been so cute growing up, defending each other, protecting each other, and while they hadn't taken lavish vacations or even done a whole lot of traveling, who needed to when one lived by the ocean? Every day was a vacation.

She'd realized eventually that that wasn't true. Living by the ocean was like living anywhere else. It became regular life. But still, every day was a beautiful view, and it really was more about a person's attitude. Maybe she hadn't taught her children that well enough.

"I think you and I need to get away. I'm pretty sure I forgot our anniversary. When is it anyway?" Sonny asked, coming over and putting his arm around her.

She leaned into him, even though his words didn't really make any sense at all. It just felt good to lean into someone strong, even if just for a few moments. To take the burden off of her. She felt like she was drowning. Just taking care of Sonny would be enough for anyone, but to try to deal with Derek—whatever midlife crisis thing he was going through—and to constantly remind herself that he was being defensive, maybe because Quincy was here and he was angry, and then to add Mary into the mix, who seemed to have a chip on her shoulder against Quincy. And Quincy being the only person who had actually reached out to her and tried as hard as she could to help in every way. She had been kind, taking care of Beulah the way no one had for a really long time. And taking the burden of the business off of her shoulders, being completely trustworthy.

It all felt like so much.

Lord, I need Your strength, because this is way too much for me to do on my own.

thirty

QUINCY RUSHED OUT of the door, wishing she had taken a longer walk rather than going back to the house.

She had tossed and turned the night before, with images of Enoch overshadowing images of Derek and Candy's laughing face, with Mary's scolding in the background.

She couldn't get those images out of her head, and sleep had been elusive.

Beulah had deliberately scheduled today to be a late day for everyone, since she knew Derek and Candy were going to be there. So Quincy figured she could take a nice long walk on the beach. She had one foot on the top step when the door opened and Candy's voice called out, "Wait! Quincy, please wait."

Quincy didn't turn around, but she stopped, then closed her eyes and drew a deep breath of the salty ocean air. She could be nice to this woman. This woman who knew that she was with a married man, who knew that man had a wife and children and a family and plans for the future, and she chose to sleep with him anyway, and didn't care about all of the repercussions that were going to be reverberating throughout multiple people's lives. Not just Quincy, but their children, their in-laws, their friends—so much pain and heartache from one woman's decision to start a relationship with a man she shouldn't have even looked twice at.

But she couldn't put all the blame on Candy. Derek was there too, and Derek knew he was married. Derek shouldn't have allowed anything to happen.

"Quincy?" Candy's hand came down lightly on her shoulder.

Quincy took another breath, and then turned, praying that Derek wasn't standing beside her.

To her relief, it was just Candy on the porch with her.

"Candy. Looks like you didn't sleep very well." She hoped that didn't come out as an insult, but there were deep black circles around Candy's eyes, and she looked exhausted.

"I didn't. Derek tossed and turned most of the night. He wasn't happy to find you here."

"I don't know why he would be surprised I was here. This is where we were planning on coming."

"I know. But I guess he just assumed that you wouldn't be hanging out with his parents without him."

"Beulah needed help. Sonny's in really bad shape, getting worse. She wanted to try to keep him home as long as possible. She thought it would be best for him. But he needs a full-time caregiver, and I am helping her with him as well as with her cleaning business."

"And she is trying to run that business."

"Exactly."

"Well, Mary is here. She could help."

"I'm not sure what's going on with Mary."

That was all she was going to say about Mary. She wasn't going to get in trouble for talking behind Mary's back. And she definitely did not trust Candy.

"I know you hate me." Candy looked deep into Quincy's eyes. Quincy maintained eye contact, as much as she wanted to turn away. This woman was a human too, and she'd made mistakes. Big ones. Broken up a family. But God would deal with her. Quincy's command was to love her.

Lord, how do I love someone who hurt my family the way this woman has?

Even as she asked, she knew that Candy wouldn't have had any power to hurt her family if Derek hadn't allowed it.

They've done so much harm to me, caused so much harm to my children as well. God, You can't really want me to forgive them, can You?

Candy wasn't asking for forgiveness, but in order to be kind, in order to say the right thing here, she needed to overlook what Candy had done, to pay for that with her pain and suffering, and allow Candy to get off free.

Although, Quincy didn't think that God would let Candy off free. Quincy just had to pry her fingers up, and not want to punish Candy herself, but allow God to deal with her.

"I don't hate you. I guess I'm still dealing with pain, and trying to figure out what my family is going to look like going forward. Because it's not the way I thought it was going to be. But I don't hate you."

There. She was trying to be as honest as she could be.

"I love him. I don't expect you to understand. But it's true. I love him."

Quincy bit back the words she wanted to say. She had loved Derek too. She had loved Derek for decades. She had been with him through his ups and his downs, through his lack of success, and every failure until he finally succeeded in his business. But Candy was too young to understand that, and she wouldn't care anyway.

"I'll pray you have a happy life together."

She could say that much. And it would be true. She didn't necessarily want God to punish them, or want anything bad to happen to them. She wasn't sure if she could say that she wanted good things to happen to them, but she didn't really want to see either one of them suffer.

Wasn't it just a couple of days ago that she was thinking that God had to close the door before He could open one to something better?

"I just know it'll make everything a lot easier if we can get along."

"I think we can. I'm not sure Derek wants to get along, but I can't leave Beulah right now. She needs more help than I can give her."

"Mary's here."

"Yeah. I don't know if she's staying."

"Derek wants to leave."

"I heard that."

"Thanks for not being mean," Candy finally said.

"I hope things work out for you," Quincy replied. Candy leaned forward to hug her, and Quincy swallowed the resentment in her throat and hugged the young girl back. She needed to let go of resentment, let go of the bitterness, and move on with her life. This part of it was gone. The part that she built with Derek, the family she'd had, the things they'd done. It was over.

"Maybe you could mail those papers?" Candy said as she stepped back.

It made Quincy wonder if that was the whole reason Candy was trying to be friends with her. Not that it mattered.

"What I said to Derek yesterday is the truth. I talked to my lawyer, she wrote up something, I approved it, and she said she was going to send it. I will call her at nine o'clock and see what happened. That's the best I can do."

"Thanks," Candy said.

The door burst open, and Candy and Quincy both jumped back in order to keep from being hit with it.

"You ready?" Derek snapped, looking at Candy, before his eyes slid to Quincy. "You'll be hearing from my lawyer."

"I'm going to be calling mine just as soon as she's in the office. I'm sure she won't be in before nine."

"Something better happen."

"As long as it's fair, I'll move as fast as you want to. I'm sure you and Candy would like to get married before the baby comes."

"And I'm sure that you're trying to do everything in your power to make sure that doesn't happen," her husband snapped.

Quincy bit down on her lips to keep from answering. She'd already explained her position. She'd told the truth. If he didn't want to believe it, rational argument was not going to convince him. He was going to believe what he wanted to believe, no matter how hard the truth stared him in the face.

He held their suitcase in his hand and marched down the steps, leaving Candy to make her way down after him.

He did not look back as he got in the car and started it. Candy lifted her hand in a small wave before she got in the car. They were gone a few moments later.

"I know I raised him. But I'm not proud of who he's become." Beulah slipped her arm around Quincy's waist, and Quincy leaned her head against Beulah.

"You could only do your best, and then you can just hope that the people around you make good decisions." Boy, did she know how true that was. Unfortunately. But she supposed that if she hadn't gone through what she had, she wouldn't be able to relate to Beulah so well right now. After all, she didn't blame Beulah for the way Derek was acting. Just like she didn't blame herself for the fact that her marriage had imploded. It was Derek making bad decisions and hurting the people around him.

"Thanks for being kind. I don't know if we'll ever have a family that's together again, but I appreciate your kindness. It... means more to me than I can say."

Quincy lifted her head and smiled at Beulah. "It's how I would want my kids to act. I'd like to be able to have both of them in the same room with their spouses, and... I guess ex-spouses if it ever comes to that, without people wanting to rip each other's throats out."

"Speaking of, may I have a word with you?" Mary stood in the doorway, looking at Quincy.

thirty-one

"I'M GOING to head back inside," Beulah said, looking first at Quincy and then at Mary. It was obvious to Quincy that Beulah hoped Mary was reaching out to reconcile, but regardless, there was no doubt Beulah wanted Quincy to be kind.

There was a part of her that had a flash thought that she was sick of being kind to everyone, and she wanted people to just be kind to her for once. Why couldn't someone apologize to her? Take the first step to reconcile with her? Why was it always her that had to try to be kind to people, to overlook things, to forgive and forgive and forgive some more?

Why, Lord? Why are You always putting the burden on me?

He gives burdens to people who can handle them. Whatever trials you face make you stronger.

> **Count it all joy when ye fall into divers temptations;**
> **Knowing this, that the trying of your faith**
> **worketh patience. But let patience have her**
> **perfect work, that ye may be perfect and entire,**
> **wanting nothing.**

Right. God was shaping her, trying to make her be more like Jesus. Apparently, she was a tough case, and He needed to use some heavy hitters on her.

"I'd love to talk to you, Mary," Quincy said, as Beulah disappeared inside.

"Don't you usually take a walk in the morning? Would you like to head up the beach for a little bit?"

She couldn't tell from Mary's tone whether Mary was trying to reconcile, or whether she was just trying to get her out of sight so she could yell at her, or maybe she wanted to take her somewhere where it would be easier to bury the body.

She rolled her eyes at herself. Mary wasn't violent. At least she didn't think so.

They walked for a little bit in silence. Quincy didn't figure that it was up to her to break it, since she wasn't the one who asked to talk. Mary had something on her mind, and maybe she was just trying to figure out how to discuss it with Quincy.

So Quincy let her think. Meanwhile, she tried to enjoy the beautiful morning. It was a little foggy and cloudy, but warm enough that the ocean breeze didn't feel chilly. The bay was choppier than usual, and gray, but there was a beauty there that still awed Quincy. She wondered if she lived there for decades if it would ever get old.

"I have a new appreciation for the ocean, and even the bay, than I had when I grew up here," Mary began. That probably wasn't what she had wanted to talk about, but Quincy could make small talk.

"Every morning it's like a new personality. I never get tired of watching it. And it always makes me feel... settled. Not safe exactly, but settled."

"Never safe. The ocean is so unpredictable. But there is a wild and rugged beauty that I didn't appreciate as much when I was younger."

"Maybe you have to go through a few things before you learn to appreciate what you have, or appreciate the beauty in something else."

"Or maybe you learn to appreciate things that seem like they're normal, and then you move away and you realize they're not."

"Or you lose it and realize it's not." She thought it was normal to have a solid marriage, where she trusted her husband and didn't think that there was anything wrong. That it was normal to have someone else to depend on. It was normal to assume that she would be spending the rest of her life with the person who had vowed his life to her.

"I guess sometimes our first impressions, or the impression that we're living with, isn't the right one."

Mary seemed a little uncomfortable, so Quincy nodded and said, "I see what you're saying. We make assumptions that aren't necessarily true. And then it keeps us from seeing other things."

"Yeah. I have spent my life assuming that your motivations were nefarious in some way. But over the last few weeks of watching you with Mom and Dad, and then seeing how you handled Derek... he was a jerk."

"Thanks. I don't wanna talk bad about him, but it's nice to hear someone else confirm my impression. He was not nice."

"No. He wasn't the slightest bit nice, and you were. You were the one that was wronged, you were the one who was cheated on, you were the one he left, you were the one that Candy stole her husband from and broke up her family, and yet you were the one who was kind." Mary took a breath. "I stood there watching you and wondered if I could have been as kind as you were. And I'm pretty sure I know what the answer is."

Quincy didn't say anything. Not for a while anyway, as they walked slowly along the beach, the water lapping on their left, scrub brush and the occasional house on the right.

"I'd like to take credit for that," she finally spoke. "But I can't. If there was anything good in me, it's only because of God. I, in my flesh, wanted to rip their throats out, or drown them in the ocean. Or some other kind of murderous thing. I definitely did not want to be nice."

There. That was the truth. She wasn't really a violent person either. She couldn't remember the last time she committed an act of violence on someone, but her thoughts toward her husband and his girlfriend were not benign.

"Well, that's a relief. There were times where I wondered if you were even human. I've never seen anyone treat their ex, who had been so unkind to them, so nicely. I've seen a lot of women trash them, and I've seen a lot of major fights that last for decades, but your way is different."

"It's not my way. It's God's way, and I'm just doing my best to try. I have not succeeded all the time."

"Well, you succeeded yesterday, and today as well. Derek deserved that dressing down. You were defending Dad, who doesn't know any better." Mary's voice cracked a little, and it reminded Quincy that the whole thing with her dad had to be really hard on her. After all, it couldn't be easy to see her parent slip away.

"I'm sorry. Sonny was such a great guy. I wish I had known him better."

"He was an awesome dad. Mom was great too, but she was a little standoffish, you know?"

"I bet she had a lot on her mind, especially after your dad lost his boat."

"If their personalities had been reversed, I don't think Dad would've lost his boat, and Mom would've been a stay-at-home mom. But Dad was a lot more easygoing, where Mom was the one who was more of a drill sergeant and could make things happen. I guess it would be natural for a kid to gravitate toward the parent who seemed less strict."

"I believe that makes sense. But I think your mom has mellowed some."

"I've never seen her as mellow as she is with you."

"Maybe that's because she's realized that she's at the end of her rope trying to take care of your dad. Or maybe she's scared about the future. I bet that she is probably exactly what you and I were talking about—she never thought that she'd be looking at a future without her husband. Or even if she knew it in some abstract way, the reality is staring her in the face that she's losing him, and I bet that's scary."

"It's a lot of pressure. Especially with her trying to keep the business afloat too."

Mary stopped and turned to face Quincy. "I'll just level with you. I didn't trust you. I'm still not sure whether I trust you completely or not. I felt like you were trying to get in to steal my inheritance. And..."

Mary left the sentence hanging there, as though she wanted Quincy to respond.

"I can't tell you that I'm independently wealthy and don't need money. I do. Although, your mom has opened her home and not mentioned a word about rent or groceries, and so right now I really don't need anything. But I have no retirement, because I was counting on Derek's pension and his Social Security. Mine isn't worth anything. Because I quit my job and stayed at home to watch his children. I couldn't earn anything while I was doing that." She paused, looking out over the bay, before looking back at Mary.

"I can't say that that's not what I wanted. I was so grateful to be able to stay home with my kids. I loved being Mom. I loved everything about it. And I did not want to work outside the home. But at the same time, Derek was able to do so much more because I was at home, taking care of everything. We saved money on childcare when the kids were younger, and he didn't want for anything."

"He always talked about what a good wife you were."

"I never heard that."

"I hated it. Maybe he did it just because he knew it annoyed me, but it felt like you were 'Quincy the perfect,' and I avoided him just so I wouldn't have to listen to him."

"I'm sorry. It's funny—you hated hearing it, and I would've loved to have heard even just a compliment."

"Regardless, I was hoping that... if we can't be friends, could we at least call a truce?"

Mary looked scared, almost, like she had no idea what Quincy was going to say.

"I'd really like to be friends. I understand that it might take you a little while to truly believe that I am what I am, but I'm not here for your inheritance, I'm not here for the money. Although, I'm not gonna turn a paycheck down, because like I said, I don't know how I'm going to support myself in the future, when I'm too old to work. And cleaning is not an easy job."

"I understand. Didn't Derek leave you anything?"

"He wants to keep it all pretty much. I had really considered letting him have it. But then I had my lawyer draft something that I considered more fair. He claims to have not gotten it, and I need to call my lawyer when I get back."

"Well, don't let him take everything. You deserve half. Probably more, because he has built a career that he can capitalize on, while you are starting from nothing."

"That's what my lawyer said basically, but I'm not trying to impoverish him or take everything that he's built. But he's the one who chose to dismantle the things that we had put into place and to go out with someone else. So I don't know. I hate that it even has to be done." She truly did. She really hated the thought of taking stuff from Derek, because she felt he deserved it. But at the same time, she deserved to be taken care of as well. It wasn't her choice to split everything.

"If you need help, I've got a good lawyer."

Quincy's eyes widened. She wanted to ask exactly why Mary had needed a lawyer. And what was going on there. But... this new relationship, if she could call it that, felt so tenuous that she didn't.

"Come on. I didn't mean to stop. We can keep walking. I just wanted to fix the mess I've made..." She huffed out a breath. "I didn't apologize. I meant to do that. I'm sorry. I have been unkind. Downright mean, I guess." She shoved her hands in her pockets and looked away. "I felt like I was justified, but unkindness like I showed you was never justified. You didn't do anything to deserve it. As much as I wanted to look back over our lives and pin all the blame on everything that was wrong with our relationship on you, if I'm being honest, I'm really the one at fault."

"I'm sure I could've done better. I know I could've. I didn't always have to respond to everything that you did that was unkind. But when I was younger, I was a lot dumber. Although dumbness isn't really an excuse."

"I could lean a lot on my stupidity. Why don't we just do that." Mary laughed, and Quincy joined her.

Looking up, she realized that they were by Vivian's house, and she stood on the porch. Before she could lift her hand and wave, Mary did, waving her hand and shouting, "Hey there, Vivian!"

Vivian returned their wave with a smile bigger than Quincy had ever seen on her.

She waved as well, although she didn't yell out, and Vivian didn't say anything either.

Her little dog yapped at her feet as they made their way past the front of the house.

There was no chance of Vivian hearing, but Quincy waited for a few steps before she said, "How do you know Vivian?"

She had just barely gotten to know Vivian, and felt like she had been doing a huge thing to actually sit on her porch and talk to her. But there was Mary, who hadn't been there as long as Quincy had, who was acting like she was a long-lost friend. Had she grown up in Whispering Hope Harbor?

"Oh, it's funny. One of the first days I watched Dad I had taken him down to the bay. I felt like being along the water would help him. Like I was really judging Mom because I just felt like Dad was not doing well because he wasn't out enough, and she wasn't doing things right." She shook her head, laughing humorlessly at herself. "I was being a brat, I guess. I didn't realize how difficult it was. But anyway, I got him down there, and he was fine. He knew me and everything was going well. But then, you know how he gets. One second he's okay, the next second he's doing something nuts that you don't even understand what he's doing. He accused me of kidnapping him, told me he didn't know who I was, said I had taken all of his money, and he saw Vivian at the beach and started power walking toward her. I didn't even know he had that kind of ability left, since all he really does is walk around in a hobble."

"Yeah. I've not seen him do anything even close to a power walk since I came."

"Well, he was walking, and I was trying to keep up with him. When he stretches those legs out, he can cover about twice the ground that I can when I'm walking."

"He is tall."

"Yeah. So anyway, he's shouting, I'm begging him to stop, and Vivian—I think she would've run the other way, but her dog came running toward us. She started running after Tootsie, that's her dog's name, and Tootsie was running to Dad, and anyway, we all met up and Dad petted the dog, but he insisted to Vivian that I had kidnapped him." She laughed. "Once I convinced Vivian that I was not his kidnapper, but his daughter, she was able to talk Dad down off the ledge, so to speak, and he really liked her. He told her how pretty she was, and how much she reminded him of his wife, which I don't know whether that was true or not. I've seen some pictures of Mom when she was younger, and she was gorgeous."

"Really? I'd love to see them sometime," Quincy said before she even thought about it.

But she was glad she said it when she saw Mary's eyes light up. "I'd love to show them to you. Mom never gets them out. It's almost like she's embarrassed about it or something. But if I looked that good, I'd be having those babies blown up and put on the wall where everybody can see them."

"Your mom is pretty modest. And also, like we said before, practical."

"Yeah. There's no point in sitting around thinking about the past and how you used to look. Just dealing with what you've got, I suppose."

"That's true. Although, I don't think it hurts to appreciate past effort and achievement. Although looks aren't really an achievement, you know? We can't really do anything about them."

"We can improve what we've got," Mary said with a grin.

"I suppose. Although, I always wonder what exactly we think we're improving. After all, my natural face is the face God gave me. Do I think He didn't do a good job? Do I think I need to paint it up to make it look better?"

Mary laughed and shook her head, and maybe she rolled her eyes a bit. "I've never thought of anything like that. I just slap makeup on and try to make myself look as close to Hollywood standard as possible. I guess Hollywood standard is not necessarily the standard that I should be comparing myself to, but who thinks of that?"

"Yeah. It doesn't really matter. I don't think it's something that God's going to talk to us about one way or the other."

"No. Anyway, that's kind of how Vivian and I met, and then we've seen each other occasionally on the beach since. She has a rather troubled past and has some major decisions to make for her future." Mary lifted a shoulder and held out her hand. "I can't say anymore."

"Goodness."

Wow. Quincy wasn't sure what to say. Vivian had confided more to Mary than she had to Quincy. The way Mary had treated her had obviously colored her opinion of her. Since Vivian thought she was someone who was trustworthy. It was funny how a person saw what they wanted to see.

Just like Derek saw her as someone who was wicked and...evil? She wasn't sure exactly, but he saw her as bad for sure.

"You got quiet all of a sudden," Mary said.

"I guess I was just thinking that we can look at things differently. Like Derek leaving me, cheating, having Candy. I have been looking at that as the worst thing that ever happened to me. But what if I'm looking at it wrong? What if I look at it like the best thing that ever happened to me, because it freed me from all of the ties that I had, everything that was holding me down, and I can do anything I want to. My life is mine to control. I can make any decision I wanna make, and I don't have to check with Derek, I don't have to think about how this is going to affect all the plans that we've made. I can do anything." She laughed and shook her head. "It totally changes, reframes, everything I was thinking. And turns my divorce into something really good."

"I think you can take anything and turn it into something good. The best thing that ever happened."

"If I just think about this day as the best that it could possibly be—the very best day of my life—and everything that happens to me is going to contribute to making it that way, it totally changes my attitude about the day."

"My problem is continuing to think that way. I slip back into negative thinking so easily."

"Maybe we can help each other. I can remind you, and you can remind me, and maybe that way, we'll remember."

"I'd love that."

It wasn't long after that that they turned around, but the whole time they walked back, Quincy was thinking about what she had been talking about with Sharon—iron sharpening iron. That seemed to be a theme in her life, that, and starting over. God doing a new thing. It started with that idea, and rose from there. Maybe, just maybe, she should be thanking her husband and Candy.

thirty-two

"HEY, HAVE A MINUTE?" Quincy walked into the diner, seeing Shiloh wrapping silverware at the counter.

"I sure do." She looked around the diner. "You came at my slow time."

Her soft, Southern accent held a hint of a smile, but her voice, warm like honey, made Quincy feel like she'd stepped into her grandmother's house, even though Shiloh and she were about the same age.

"Let me help you wrap silverware."

"Sure. We can do it at the booth back there in the corner."

She walked over, picking up the unwrapped spoons and forks, while Shiloh grabbed the napkins and knives.

They'd done this multiple times together, and Shiloh had assured Quincy that if things didn't work out between Beulah and her, Shiloh would always have a job for her at the diner.

Quincy appreciated the fact that she had a backup plan, even though she was going to do everything in her power not to need it.

"You seem different," Shiloh said as they settled into their opposite benches.

"I feel different. We had originally planned to keep our light workday, so Beulah would have time to spend with Derek."

"That's your ex, right?" Shiloh said, although Quincy knew very well that Shiloh knew exactly who Derek was. Her brows had raised, like she wasn't sure she was understanding correctly.

"Yes, you're right. He didn't give us very much notice that he was coming for a visit, and I didn't have time to talk to you about it."

"It's okay. We all know that summer is a busy season, and we're there."

"I know. But like I said, we had planned to have a light day, but he left."

"Did he bring his girlfriend?"

"Yes. Candy was with him." Quincy gave her a short version of what had happened.

"But I guess I don't understand exactly how that made you feel better. I wasn't getting the feeling that you felt like you needed to make up with Candy in order to come full circle. And things don't seem like they're any better between Derek and you." She paused for a moment with a fork in one hand, twisting and studying it as though it were infinitely interesting. "I was getting the idea that you were still hoping to reconcile."

"I guess the idea of not having my family together is really hard for me, still. But I had a revelation. I know we've talked about God doing a new thing. And I realized that it depends on how you look at things. I can look at it like it's the worst thing in the world, or I can look at it like today is gonna be even better than yesterday and tomorrow is something to look forward to. Whereas, initially during our breakup, I dreaded tomorrow. And I felt today was pretty awful too. And I felt like all of my best days were in the past."

"That doesn't give you a whole lot to look forward to. And a person can't live on memories."

"No. I guess that's why God gives us heaven to look forward to. He even tells us in the Bible to comfort ourselves with the idea that there will be a rapture, and He makes promises about what's going to happen in the future—promises of heaven, promises of being with Him, promises of being reunited with our loved ones. Why would I think for one second that the best days were in the past? Everything that's worth anything is in the future!"

Shiloh laughed a little. "You're really excited about this."

"Well, yeah. I don't know why I didn't see it like that before. But I didn't even tell you the best part."

"Okay?"

"Mary wanted to talk to me after Candy and I were done. She and I took a walk and she apologized."

"No." Shiloh dropped her hands to the table, and her jaw was almost there as well.

"Yes. I'm serious. She said she saw the way I was treating Candy and realized that I really was the person that I claimed to be, and that I wasn't what she thought. That she had had the wrong perception. That's really where I was getting the idea about how we form our own reality. Her perception of me was so wrong, but when she looked at it a different way, when she was forced to see me in a different light, she realized that everything she thought was absolutely upside down. And I got to thinking, maybe our reality is based on what we think. And the Bible tells us to think on things that are true and lovely and of good report, and if we're in a bad spot, we can flip our reality to be completely different. It's just a matter of what we think!"

Shiloh laughed. "I love it. I absolutely love it. I think the next time we get together at the pavilion, we need to talk about it."

"I really want to share with everyone. Although I honestly think that maybe Mary will come next time. She... she's got some things that are bothering her. She hasn't talked about them, but I'm pretty sure there's a past there."

"I wouldn't be surprised if there is. Seems like all of us have some kind of problem that we're fighting. Issues, pain, hurt."

Quincy nodded, thinking that not everything in Shiloh's life was perfect either.

"Speaking of, I have a friend, my best friend actually. We've been separated by distance for a really long time. She got married and has been living in North Dakota for three decades. Because of some really bad things, she recently decided to leave her husband, but God wouldn't allow her. Anyway, I don't want to give her story out without her telling it. I think she'll do a much better job. But suffice it to say that her name is June, and I'd like for everyone to meet her when she comes. I think she's got some wisdom that will help us. And she's so grounded in the Bible that we could all learn something from her."

"Maybe she'd start a Bible study. And we need to give ourselves a name too while we're at it. We keep saying 'the next time we meet at the pavilion.' We need a club or something."

"Maybe we can bring it up for a vote when we're there."

"Yes. I can make a group text and warn everyone that they need to think of their best ideas and bring them for a vote."

"That's a good idea. I'd like a group text."

"I think I have everyone's number. Except for June. Is she gonna be a part of it?"

"Are we accepting new members?"

"I don't want it to be exclusive. I want anyone to feel welcome anytime."

"Well, we probably won't attract younger girls or happily married women."

"Maybe they need to have a club of their own. But if they want to, they could come. After all, don't you think we have some things we could teach them?"

"I wish I had an older lady who was willing to teach me things when I was younger and just making decisions. I wish someone would've guided me a little better. But... I don't know if I would've listened."

"Same. So much the same. I thought I knew everything, and now... I feel like I know less than I did when I started."

"I think the more you know, the more you realize you don't know."

"That sounds very sage."

They grinned at each other, and then Shiloh grew serious again.

"How are things going with that mystery guy?"

Quincy knew exactly who Shiloh was talking about. They'd talked about Enoch more than once.

"He admitted that he's not a contractor. He had a business. And said he was more interested in making money than he was in his family, until it was too late. He lost them, while on his way to making one billion dollars."

"One billion dollars?" Shiloh put a hand up. "Wait a second. You mean he's rich?"

Quincy paused for a moment, and then a laugh escaped her. "I guess I didn't even catch that part. I mean... I heard it. But he just doesn't seem rich. He doesn't seem pretentious at all. And I totally wasn't even paying attention. I just felt bad for him for losing his family."

"Well, if he was on the way to one billion, that's a little crazy. He must be a millionaire."

"I don't know how much he's worth now, but he did say that he made his first six figures and then he made seven figures and then he was working on eight figures, and once he hit eight figures he wanted to go for one billion. I think he said he was halfway there. But... maybe he lost everything when he lost his business. I don't know."

"So... you said he said he liked you, correct?"

"Yeah. But I guess I just kind of got the idea that it was the way a friend likes someone."

"But friends don't go around saying 'I like you.' You know I like you—you don't need me to say that in order to know that we're friends."

"True."

"And that's even more true for male-female relationships."

"I don't know." She sighed, looking at the silverware that was partially wrapped in her hands. "I haven't thought about male-female relationships for so long, other than hoping and praying that my children find good mates who love the Lord and want to serve Him and will treat them well."

"I'm here to tell you that a guy doesn't tell you that he likes you if he's not interested in you as more than a friend."

"Maybe Enoch is the one exception to that rule."

"He's rich, Quincy. Have you been missing this?"

"He might've lost everything. I really don't know."

"Does it look like he lost everything? I mean, what he's doing with his cottage—does it look like a guy who lost everything in business? Or is he doing the high-end stuff?"

"He's doing the high-end stuff. You're right." She paused, thinking. He didn't seem like a rich person. And she didn't want that to color the way she thought about him.

"I think it's better if I don't think about that. Because if I think that he's rich, it's gonna intimidate me, and I'm gonna be awkward around him." She set the wrapped silverware down. "But I think it's too late. I hadn't thought about it the way you pointed it out, and now that I have, I think you're right. I think he's a millionaire at least, and I think he's got a ton of money. And I think that's going to make me feel weird."

"Why would money make you feel weird? It should make you feel excited! Weren't you just saying that everything was going to turn out even better?"

"But does money make things better? I mean, enough to pay your bills, enough to buy a few nice things, maybe go out to eat once in a while to give yourself a break from cooking if that's what you want, but... I don't want a ton of money. There are too many complications to go along with that."

"I guess you're right. I mean, I always feel like I could use more. If I had money, I'd fix up my diner, expand, put more seating in, hire more help, expand the menu. But would that make me happier?"

"Exactly. We think it will. We think that more equals better, but I'm not convinced that it does. I actually think maybe... less equals more happiness. Which is a contradiction, but I don't know. Maybe June will know."

"I don't know about that. Her experience is mostly in relationships. She has a really great testimony, and I know she'll be a blessing to everyone. But she's never been rich, so I don't know that she can tell us about that."

"But the Bible can. It says it's easier for a rich man to go through the eye of a needle than for him to enter into the kingdom of heaven, and isn't that where we want to be? So... we don't want to have something that's going to make it harder for us to get to heaven, do we?"

"No. That's a good point. You're right."

They were almost finished wrapping the silverware, and it was a good thing, because several customers came in.

"I'd probably better get going. I said it was a light workday, but not that we didn't have anything to do."

"I'm glad for your good news. And I can't wait to see everyone on Monday. I think it's going to be the best meeting yet."

"I think so too. The best, of many more best to come."

It sounded crazy, but Quincy felt in her heart that it was true.

thirty-three

"I'M SO glad you all could make it. And I'm really excited that we have three new ladies with us today. Before we do anything else, because I know you guys all have ideas for a name that we can call ourselves, I just wanted to thank you all." Quincy looked around the group of ladies sitting at the pavilion, the waves crashing in the distance, the cotton candy sky serene and beautiful above them, stretching out into the horizon. So much beauty, so much love. How could she have ever doubted that God was good? Or that He loved her? He'd shown it over and over again through this trial. And these ladies were a big part of that.

"I find it really amazing that God brings the right people into your life at just the right time. When my husband left me, cheated, and said he was having a baby, it was so much at once, and I didn't know how I was going to go on. I didn't even feel like I could. I didn't want to kill myself, but I just didn't have any hope. And then I came here, and Beulah, you opened up your home to me. Even though your son wasn't with me. You gave me a chance."

"You've been a bigger blessing to me than I've been to you, that's for sure. And I don't expect that to change." Beulah, her eyes crinkling, her face kind, looked up at Quincy, and Quincy felt a burst of love for this woman who had raised her husband and yet loved Quincy like a daughter.

"Shiloh, you welcomed me the moment I stepped in here and have given me friendship, a true friendship that I don't think I've ever had in my life before. Thank you."

"I think you're giving me too much credit, and I have to say that your friendship has been just as much of a blessing to me."

"You're kind to everyone, and your diner is a welcoming place for all of us. And Sharon, we kind of are sisters in crime. Our jobs are not exactly the same, but we both cater to tourists in slightly different ways. We have so much in common, and I love you."

Sharon waved her hand, obviously embarrassed, but Quincy wanted the ladies to know what they meant to her. Sometimes she realized she had gone through life and the people who had been close to her didn't realize how much they mattered.

"And Mary. Wow. We started off crazy, and you really challenged me. Thank you for helping me grow, thank you for showing me that I was looking at everything all wrong."

"I was looking at it far more wrong than what you were."

"And Vivian and June, I'm looking forward to getting to know the two of you. To being able to share your burdens, and hopefully help you the way these other ladies have helped me. But most of all, it makes me feel grounded and secure to have such great friendships."

She looked around at each of the ladies who had helped her through this difficult time in her life, each in a different way, each with different personalities, each using what they had to be a blessing. She couldn't have asked for a better group.

But, they had business to attend to.

"All right. We can do this several different ways. Everybody can write their name suggestion on a piece of paper, we could put it in a hat and pull out the name and that's gonna be it, or we can put them all on a list and we can all vote on them."

"I think I'd like to hear them all. Because while I like mine, I might like someone else's better." Shiloh waved a piece of paper around, and Quincy assumed it had her suggestion on it.

"Yeah. I think that's a good idea," Sharon echoed.

"All right then, if everyone's okay with it, write down your name if you haven't already, and then just hand it to me. It won't matter who it came from, because I don't think we will vote based on who suggested it. At least I'm not going to."

"I'm not going to either. I'm excited about it. We're going to have a name for our group. That's super neat." Shiloh seemed to bubble.

Quincy gathered up all the names and then read them off one by one.

"The Girls. We Glow. The Happy Tribe. We Overcome. The Seaside Sisterhood. Woman Warriors. The Ladies That Love Jesus."

"All right, does anyone have a favorite?" She grinned. "I know I do."

Somehow "The Seaside Sisterhood" hit her as the perfect name. Mostly because the ladies sitting here were more than friends - they were sisters of her heart.

"I think we should all write down our choice. That way we're not influenced in our votes in any way."

"Sounds good to me." Quincy made sure that everyone had a piece of paper and a pen, as people wrote down their choices. She read the suggestions twice more so that everyone had a good idea in their head of what they were and didn't forget anyone. She didn't want anyone to think that she wasn't giving their name choice equal billing with everyone else.

Even though she had a clear favorite. And it wasn't even her suggestion.

Regardless of what they chose as their name, she didn't think she had ever felt this happy and content before. She felt safe here. Not that she thought that safe places were the way to go. She actually thought it was best to spend most of one's life in places where you don't necessarily feel safe. How else was a person to grow and learn to become strong if all they did was pamper themselves and make sure that they never faced any kind of serious hardship?

But when a person needed succor, when they needed a listening ear, helping hands, someone's shoulder to cry on, or someone to cheer with, or to celebrate with, it was nice to be in a safe place, surrounded by people who loved you and wanted the best for you.

"All right, I have them all together now, and I'll read them all one by one."

In the end, it turned out that it was unanimous. Everyone loved The Seaside Sisterhood.

"There's just something about it, isn't there?"

"I feel like I'm with sisters, even though none of you are actually related to me," Sharon said. "I feel like I can talk to you guys and share things. And I grew up with brothers. I've always wanted sisters. So that appealed to me too."

"All right then, ladies, we meet on Mondays, and until Enoch stops allowing us to meet here, this is where we'll be. Anyone is welcome. Although, I don't know if we're the right group for every-one, because we're all a little bit odd."

"I've felt very welcome, and right at home. Thank you for allowing me to come," June said.

"I guess I didn't introduce June, but we were all talking earlier. She's been my best friend for thirty years, and I'm excited that she's finally moving to the shore with her husband. Which she'll talk about at some point." Shiloh lifted her brows and looked around the group. "I know we've talked a little bit about doing a Bible study, and I was thinking that June would be the perfect person to lead it. We don't have to do that if no one wants to, but... I'd like to."

"I'd love to do it. But I can't commit to definitely being there until this fall when things slow down," Beulah said, looking around the group and shrugging her shoulders. Everyone there knew how busy things got in the summer for everyone.

"I think that's a really great idea. Let's do it this fall," Vivian spoke for the first time. She was getting comfortable with the group, but she still hung back a little, and every once in a while, Quincy would notice a flash of fear flow across her face. Hopefully they could figure out what the problem was and fix it. Although, she wasn't so naïve as to think that they could fix anything. That just wasn't possible.

"All right then, unless someone has a problem, we'll start the Bible study with June leading the first Monday in October. If there are any supplies or anything you need us to get, you can let us know, okay?" Quincy looked at June.

She nodded, and then said, "Someone had mentioned a group text. I thought that was a good idea. That way if I do decide to use any materials, which I wasn't thinking of doing, I can let everyone know, maybe even send a link."

Everyone called out their number as June added it to her phone, and then sent a text to everyone. In her phone, Quincy dubbed the group "The Seaside Sisterhood." It felt perfect. And the future, with her sister-friends at her side, looked bright.

thirty-four

"SO WHAT DO YOU THINK?" Enoch looked around the room and then back at Quincy, his brows raised. "Not too bad for a CEO turned contractor?"

She looked at the beautiful blues and teals of the room. Her favorite floor ever, perfectly balanced by the white and cream on the walls, with accents that brought out the sea colors.

"It's gorgeous. Definitely the most gorgeous house that I get to clean."

"Are you just saying that because the owner is standing in front of you?"

"Well, it's true that I don't usually get to see the owner, but no. It's the honest truth. You did an amazing job, and whenever I think about how the house looked when I first came six months ago, I'm even more impressed."

"Thank you. I feel like I've done a little bit of growing since then. It's been therapeutic."

"I kind of thought that that might be what it was. You had talked about building something new, and that got me thinking. Probably that was the spark that turned my thinking from viewing my husband cheating and the divorce that he wanted from the worst

232

thing that ever happened to me, to... the best." As she said it, she realized it was true. The last six months had been difficult, no doubt, especially the first few, but once she realized she needed to shift her thinking, to focus on the good, to see that reality often reflected what a person thought about it, things started changing.

Although, she had put her name to the separation agreement, and the divorce was imminent.

"Is it final yet?" Enoch asked, as they both stood in front of the floor-to-ceiling windows that looked out at the beautiful Atlantic Ocean. It was October, but the sky was still a deep, rich blue, and the ocean was calm, putting on a placid face for the day.

"Not quite. I've signed the separation agreement, and the divorce will be final soon. In a way, I feel lighter. Like... a burden has been lifted. I didn't realize I was thinking about it as much as I was."

"I can't relate. When my divorce was final, I went for two weeks without showering or eating. I don't really have too much of a memory about any of that."

"Ouch."

"Yeah. Looking back, I think it was a type of mourning. But it seems like you've shifted your thinking far earlier than I did."

"But it wasn't really my fault. And I'm not saying that your divorce was your fault—"

"It was. What led to my wife leaving was my fault."

"I wouldn't say that completely. Honestly, I appreciate you taking the blame, but regardless of how absent your spouse is, the right thing to do is to stay with them."

"Thanks for defending me. But I guess you're right. You're just proving your point. I do blame myself, so I suppose in a way the divorce becoming final was my failure."

"You can reframe that," Quincy said with a grin. She had become something of an expert at that. Not that she wanted to reframe things to make them less aligned with reality. That wasn't what she wanted to do at all. But she did want to make sure that she was looking at things in a way that was positive, but still real. She didn't always get it right.

"Are you and your friends gonna keep meeting at the pavilion all through winter? What are you gonna do when it gets cold?"

"I don't know. I guess we haven't gotten that far. But we've started a Bible study, and June is amazing. The depth of her knowledge of the Bible is just fabulous. She has gone through a really difficult time, and I feel like she did what God wanted her to. Which was not the easy thing."

"I don't think that what God wants us to do is usually the easy thing."

"Sometimes I think that God gives us easy stuff. Maybe a rest from our labors. But then we have to get back in it, you know?"

"I know. And I agree. Maybe a little rest, but then you pick up the standard and keep going."

He shifted on his feet, and then he turned toward her.

"A few months ago, I told you I liked you."

"I remember," she said. In the intervening months, they'd talked often as she'd come to clean, and she wouldn't say that he was a really great friend, not like her Seaside Sisterhood sisters, but she definitely considered him a friend. And felt comfortable with him.

"That hasn't changed." He said it simply, while staring at her.

"I kind of hoped it hadn't. But... my divorce isn't final yet, and I don't usually hear good things about rebound relationships." She paused for a moment and then met his steady gaze. "But I don't intend to have relationships. If I do move on with someone else, I don't want to move from person to person to person. I want to be very serious and intentional about my next relationship. I want it to be my last."

"I understand." His gaze turned thoughtful, and then he shoved a hand in his pocket. "I suppose, when you're ready, I'd like to somehow figure out if the possibility is there for you and me to have that forever, last relationship for both of us. Will you consider that?"

His words were a little hesitant, like it was important to him, but he wasn't sure how she would take it.

"I will. You're on the top of my list. And it's a short list. Containing one name."

"That's good to hear. I guess that's what I wanted. You can take as long as you want, as long as I know that's the truth."

"I wouldn't know how to lie about it, to be honest."

"Thank you. I wouldn't want you to lie to me."

"It wouldn't feel fair to either one of us."

He nodded, and then they turned and looked back out over the ocean. The same ocean that had been crashing against the shore as June had led them in their first devotion. It had been powerful and had bonded them in a way that just getting together and talking hadn't. She looked forward to the fall and winter of studying the Bible together, growing in the Lord, and encouraging each other to do right.

She didn't know exactly where it would take them, but maybe Vivian would trust them enough to tell them what she was afraid of. Maybe June would share about the relationship that almost dissolved and how she saved it. Maybe they would be able to help Beulah as Sonny continued to decline. And perhaps they would even figure out a way to help Sharon reconcile with her estranged son.

As she fixed her beet salad to take to their gathering the next day, she was thinking about all the things that they could talk about, when a message came across the group text.

I'm not going to make it tonight. The police have come to arrest me.

thirty-five

JUNE

LORD, *please give me the words to say, to point these ladies to You.*

June looked over the group, all of them together, minus one. Who would've thought that Shiloh would be arrested? And yet, God knew. God knew why, God knew what He wanted each one of them to learn from that.

At least, with all the things that June had experienced in her life, being arrested was not one of them.

"I feel like it's unfair. I don't think Shiloh did what they're accusing her of."

"Or if she did, she didn't mean to," Mary said. Like that made it okay.

"I spoke with the chief of police before we came. The case against her is pretty compelling, and what they're accusing her of is not good." The ladies were not going to believe it when she told them.

"What is it?" Quincy asked, her brows coming down. She would probably be the most affected, since her friendship with Shiloh had only deepened over the summer. Shiloh had befriended Quincy when she had most needed it, and when she had been vulnerable and in need of someone to walk alongside her.

The news was going to be the most devastating to her, but June couldn't sugarcoat it.

"The police chief says that she's going to be convicted of murdering her husband."

There were gasps around the table, and June didn't say anything. Lost in thought. After all, it could've been her. Only through the grace of God, because she had thought more than once how much better off she would be without the man who constantly belittled her and put her down and told her how incompetent and awful she was. She had been tempted more than once to leave him, and almost had at one point.

But God.

So much of her life hinged on those two words. But God.

Maybe she, more than any other woman in this group, could relate to Shiloh. But she didn't think there was anything that any of them could do. Other than to support her the best they could.

But how?

June looked around the circle. She thought she knew the answer, but it was going to be up to the ladies as to whether or not they wanted to commit. All she could do was ask.

<u>Join Jessie's list and be the first to know about new releases and sales on her books!</u>

Read *The Pebble Beach Diaries*, the next book in The Seaside Sisterhood series in which we catch up with a familiar friend after a long wait. Will June get her happy ending after all?

The Complete Sweet Water, North Dakota Reading Order:

Series One: Sweet Water Ranch Western Cowboy Romance (11 book series)

Series Two: Coming Home to North Dakota (12 book series)

Series Three: Flyboys of Sweet Briar Ranch in North Dakota (13 book series)

Series Four: Sweet View Ranch Western Cowboy Romance (10 book series)

Spinoffs and More! Additional Series You'll Love:

Jessie's First Series: Sweet Haven Farm (4 book series)

Small-Town Romance: The Baxter Boys (5 book series)

Bad-Boy Sweet Romance: Richmond Rebels Sweet Romance (3 book series)

Sweet Water Spinoff: Cowboy Crossing (9 book series)

Small Town Romantic Comedy: Good Grief, Idaho (5 book series)

True Stories from Jessie's Farm: Stories from Jessie Gussman's Newsletter (3 book series)

Reader-Favorite! Sweet Beach Romance: Blueberry Beach (8 book series)

Blueberry Beach Spinoff: Strawberry Sands (10 book series)

From Strawberry Sands to: Raspberry Ridge (12 book series)

Swoonfully Jolly Holiday Stories:

Holiday Romance: Cowboy Mountain Christmas (6 book series)

Cowboy Mountain Christmas Spinoff: A Heartland Cowboy Christmas (9 book series)

New and Much Loved: Mistletoe Meadows (4 books and counting!)

Laughing Through the Snow: Christmas Tree, PA Sweet Romcoms (6 short reads)